STRANDED AT CUPID'S HIDEAWAY
Connie Lane

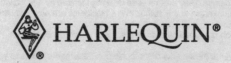

HARLEQUIN®

TORONTO • NEW YORK • LONDON
AMSTERDAM • PARIS • SYDNEY • HAMBURG
STOCKHOLM • ATHENS • TOKYO • MILAN • MADRID
PRAGUE • WARSAW • BUDAPEST • AUCKLAND

Thanks to Mary Morrish, my medical advisor, and to Ken Kabb of North Coast Sailing School, captain of the real *Jade Moon*. The weather was perfect and she's a beautiful boat—too bad I'm not a better sailor!

ISBN 0-373-16932-9

STRANDED AT CUPID'S HIDEAWAY

Chapter One

Laurel Burton thought she knew everything there was to know about Cupid's Hideaway. Though the bed-and-breakfast inn on Lake Erie's South Bass Island was her grandmother's brainchild and retirement project, Laurel spent enough time in the rambling old house to know every inch of the place and of the business.

She knew how many bottles of champagne it took to fill the ornate tabletop fountains in each of the inn's four distinctive—and distinctively named—guest rooms and how many cases of bubble bath were used in the heart-shaped bathtubs and which of the regular guests preferred what kind of scented candles. She knew that the plants in the Almost Paradise room needed to be turned and watered on Mondays and Thursdays, that the martini bar in Smooth Operator had to be restocked at least once a month, that the red velvet drapes in Close to the Heart were a bitch to clean and that there had to be a pair of blue suede shoes under the bed in Love Me Tender. Always.

And even though she didn't know it for sure, because when it came to profit and loss there was some information Maisie liked to keep to herself, Laurel could guess the kind of killing her grandmother made in the gift shop just off the lobby. There was a big markup on scanty lingerie. Almost as much as there was on massage oil, discreet sex toys and teas that were—or so Maisie swore—guaranteed aphrodisiacs.

Laurel knew Cupid's Hideaway, all right. Basement to attic. Wraparound front porch to backyard garden. Front to back and side to side.

But she never knew the place was haunted.

At the bottom of the winding stairway that led to the guest rooms, Laurel's legs froze at the same time her stomach caught fire. Noah Cunningham couldn't be standing at the main desk chatting with her grandmother. It wasn't possible. It had to be a ghost.

"Deep breaths, Laurel," she whispered to herself. "Deep breaths, just like you tell your patients in labor and delivery. In and out. Slowly. Slowly." She steadied herself and closed her eyes, sure that when she opened them again, the hallucination would be gone.

She was wrong.

Eyes closed. Eyes opened. He was still there.

Live and in living color.

Not the ghost of anything but her own past.

Laurel was carrying an armful of newly laundered, flowery smelling towels and she pressed them close in hopes of keeping her heart from banging its way right out of her ribs. Good thing neither Noah nor Maisie had seen her yet. Noah was leaning against the front desk, and his attention was on Maisie. She was too busy flittering around and giggling at everything Noah said to pay any attention to anything but him.

Laurel had the advantage. At least for the moment. She could see without being seen and she used the opportunity to regroup and collect her thoughts and her wits. It didn't hurt that she also had a chance to size up the man she had tried not to think about for the last four years.

Noah was still as handsome as hell and twice as tempting as sin. Just like in the old days. Still the same chestnut brown hair, cut closer at the sides and shorter on top than he used to wear it back in the days when it always looked as tousled as it did when he just got out of bed. The cut wouldn't have worked on most guys, at least not most guys of Noah's age and professional reputation. It was a little too young, a little too cocky, a little too nonconformist. But then, she supposed that made it a classic case of truth in advertising. The haircut suited Noah's personality, and if what she'd heard from colleagues was true—things they insisted on telling her even though she insisted she didn't want to hear them—Noah's way of wearing his hair had spawned a trend of sorts with the medical students he regularly lectured. Wasn't that just like Noah? An innovator when it came to everything, even hair.

Laurel ignored the tiny thread of resentment that threatened what was left of her composure. Instead of regretting the past, she concentrated on the present. And on the man standing not twenty feet away. The one she'd walked out on four years before and swore she'd never see again.

His profile was the same, of course. Firm chin. Nose that was a little crooked from his days playing college rugby. He was a shade under six feet tall, and one look was all it took to tell Laurel he was still running a few miles every day. His exquisitely tailored navy cashmere suit made the most of a body that was long and lean. It did great things for his nice, tight behind, too.

Caught off guard both by the thought and by the memories it conjured, Laurel sucked in a sharp breath and warned herself to get a grip. Noah's rear was none of her business, not anymore, and just so she wouldn't forget, she forced her gaze up and away from it. His jaw was long enough and square enough that it should have warned people he could be stubborn beyond reason. No one ever guessed. Not until it was too late. Or in Laurel's case, not until it was way too late.

She knew why, of course. She'd known it all along. It was because of his smile. The one that lit up a room and invited confidences and made everyone he honored with it feel as if Noah was singling them out for special treatment.

For a couple of incredible months, that smile was the first thing she saw in the morning and the last thing she saw at night. It was still the thing she remembered most about him. That, and how much it hurt when she found out his smile wasn't any more sincere than he was.

Funny how old, healed wounds could slice open so quickly. Laurel blinked back tears and thought about the irony of it all. Judging from the blush in Maisie's cheeks, she wasn't troubled by any of the old stories. But then, Noah and Maisie had always gotten along famously. Looked like his smile was still working its magic, and Laurel supposed she should be grateful it was. While Noah and her grandmother were busy acting like old buddies, she could compose herself. She could collect herself. This might be her only chance. Unless…

She glanced to her right, gauging the distance between herself and the ornate front door that led out to the porch and the lawn that sloped down to the lake.

She could make a break for it, and if she was quick and quiet, no one would ever know she'd been there. The coward's way out? There was no denying that. But then again, maybe it was better to be a coward than it

was to be a stammering idiot. And if Noah turned
around, if he saw her, if he talked to her, something told
her that acting like a stammering idiot would be the
least of her problems.

Her mind made up, Laurel had already made a move
toward the front of the house when she heard Maisie
call out. "There she is! It's Laurel. Laurel, come here,
sweetie, and see who stopped to visit!"

Laurel gritted her teeth. Her breath tight in her throat,
her palms damp against the stack of towels, she pasted
a half surprised, half I-really-don't-have-time-to-stop-
and-chat smile on her face and crossed the lobby toward
the man who four years earlier had broken her heart
into a million tiny pieces that still hadn't found their
way back together.

The closer she got, the more Laurel saw that she
wasn't the only one who was surprised by this unexpected encounter. As if it was happening in slow mo-
tion, she saw Noah's mouth drop open and his disbe-
lieving glance go from Maisie to Laurel and back again
to Maisie.

"But…" He spluttered. "But you said—"

"I said Laurel was cruising. Yes, I know." Maisie
smiled and nodded, and her perfectly styled, perfectly
white curls bobbed along with her. Reaching across the
desk, she patted Noah's hand. "She was cruising. She
was—"

"I was out on the lake on my sailboat," Laurel in-
tervened. There was no use letting Maisie try to explain.
Something told her there was no easy explanation. Not
for this. "Out on the lake," she said with a glance over
her shoulder toward one of the windows that looked at
the water. "For three full hours. You calling that cruising, Grandma?"

Not one to let something as simple as the truth get in her way, Maisie twinkled. "Well," her grandmother said, "technically…"

"Technically, nothing." Laurel plunked the pile of towels on the desk. Though she wasn't sure what was going to fall out of her mouth, she turned to greet Noah. She couldn't quite force herself to offer her hand just like she couldn't quite look him in the eye. She started out by staring at his lips, but that didn't work, either. Too many old memories there. Instead, she concentrated on the splashes of red and yellow on his two-hundred-dollar Italian silk tie.

"Hello, Noah," she said. "What brings you to Cupid's Hideaway?"

As soon as the question was out of her mouth, Laurel had the feeling she might not like the answer. She darted a look around the lobby. There was no sign that Noah was there with a significant other, and she let go a long, shaky breath. It was bad enough seeing him so unexpectedly. She wasn't sure how she would have handled it if she knew Noah and some woman were checking in for a little hanky-panky in the land of heart-shaped tubs and massage oils with names like Love Nibbles.

"He's here to visit, of course." It was Maisie who answered, Maisie who hurried around to the front of the desk and grabbed Noah's arm and tugged him toward the parlor where, this time of the evening even when there were no guests, she kept a fire blazing in the fireplace, and tea and cookies on the old rosewood buffet in the corner. "And isn't it a nice surprise?"

It wasn't, and Laurel congratulated herself. At least she had the presence of mind not to point that out.

"We'll get some tea," Maisie said, "and I'll call

Meg. I know she's home tonight. She probably wouldn't mind at all if I asked her to stop by and cook you up a nice dinner.''

"Maisie!"

The name came in unison from both Noah and Laurel, and they looked each other square in the eye for the first time, as if deciding who should go first. Noah won. Of course. Noah always won.

"I'm afraid I don't have time for dinner," he said and the familiar voice caused a tingle to sparkle up Laurel's spine.

She warned herself that tingling was not in her own best interests and, turning, gave her grandmother the kind of look that was known to quell noisy preschool patients and whiny senior citizens who more often than not gave her a hard time about getting their flu shots. "He doesn't have time for dinner," she said, and before she could convince herself this was a perfectly ordinary conversation in perfectly normal circumstances, she turned to Noah. "Why don't you have time for dinner? What are you doing here, anyway?"

"I just need to get the—" Realizing he was explaining to the wrong person, Noah swung his gaze from Laurel to Maisie. "If you could just get it for me," he said. "I'll get out of here. I have a meeting in Chicago tomorrow and a flight out of Cleveland tonight."

"Tonight? Oh." Maisie's smile wilted around the edges. "Oh, dear," she whispered. "Oh, dear." Her eyes wide, she looked to Laurel for help.

With a sigh, Laurel surrendered. "What Maisie means," she told Noah, "is that it's seven forty-five. The last ferry for the mainland left forty-five minutes ago."

Noah pinned Maisie with a look. "Are you telling me—"

Maisie turned to Laurel.

Feeling like an interpreter caught in the middle of two people who weren't going to speak the same language, even if one of them knew what the other was saying, Laurel rolled her eyes. "What that means is you can't leave. Not tonight." Another thought occurred to her and she brightened. "Unless you charter a plane over at the airport and—"

"Oh, I don't think so, dear." Maisie's grin was as sheepish as her smile was mischievous. "Frank at the airfield has a granddaughter, you know. And today's her birthday. He left for Toledo this morning, so he could celebrate with the family. I hear he's not coming back until tomorrow."

"So…" There was only one conclusion, but apparently Noah didn't quite have the nerve to put it into words. Whatever he was doing there, it was obvious he was getting more than he bargained for.

"So you'll stay the night!" Maisie's mind was made up, and she brushed her hands together as if she could get rid of the problem that easily.

But, though Maisie knew Noah, she didn't know him nearly as well as Laurel did. And Laurel knew he wasn't about to get railroaded. Getting railroaded wasn't his style. Especially when getting railroaded meant staying on the island.

It was the second time in as many minutes that Laurel's memories threatened to overwhelm her. She didn't give a damn if Maisie noticed. She intended on reading her grandmother the riot act later for cavorting with the enemy. But come hell or high water, there was no way she was going to let Noah know how much seeing him again had thrown her for a loop.

Desperate for some time alone to process everything that was happening, Laurel grabbed the stack of towels and went to the linen room on the far side of the lobby. She pushed the door open and set the towels on an empty shelf, and when she saw that they weren't stacked just right, she pulled them out and piled them up again. She wasn't stalling. At least that's what she told herself. Right after she told herself that the one and only reason her hands were shaking, and her knees were weak, and her heart was flopping around like a Lake Erie walleye was that there was a touch of flu going around the island and she'd probably picked up the bug at the clinic.

The strategy worked. For exactly fifteen seconds. Fifteen seconds of peace and quiet. Fifteen seconds of deluding herself. Fifteen seconds, and she knew there was only so long she could hide.

Smoothing a hand over her green-and-blue sweater, Laurel forced herself to the front desk. She was just in time to see Maisie shaking her head.

"No room at the hotel over near the marina," she was telling Noah. "Booked solid. Fishermen. I know that for a fact because I saw them check in this morning when I stopped in to say hello."

"Then there's got to be another bed-and-breakfast," Noah ventured. He must have realized how tacky he sounded because he amended the statement instantly. "Not that this doesn't look like a terrific place. It does. Maisie, you've done wonders with it. But it doesn't look like there's anyone else staying here tonight, and I wouldn't want you to go to any trouble just because of me, and—"

"No trouble at all!" Maisie grinned like the Cheshire cat. "And you're right. There are no other guests. You'll have your pick of the rooms. Won't that be nice? Now let's see. What do you need?" Her snowy eyebrows raised, Maisie looked around as if she expected to find Noah's luggage. Of course, he didn't have any. When he walked into Cupid's Hideaway, he had no intention of staying.

"Toothbrush? Toothpaste? Comb? Mouthwash?" Maisie ticked off the list on her fingers. "We have it all in the gift shop, but of course we wouldn't expect an old friend to pay."

"He's not an old friend," Laurel said.

"I'm not an old friend," Noah concluded at the same time.

Maisie laughed, the sound of it brushing softly against the lacy curtains and the pink lightbulbs and the gold cherubs painted on the ceiling, which featured a perfect blue sky studded with fluffy white clouds. "Of course you are," she said, firmly ignoring Laurel. She turned a smile on Noah that was every bit as persuasive as his own and blushed as pink as the angora sweater she was wearing. "You're my old friend. I hope you haven't forgotten that. And I would never ask an old friend to be anything but a guest in my establishment. No more arguments," she said when Noah opened his mouth to speak. "It's my fault you missed the ferry. I should have warned you the schedule has changed now that it's fall and the tourist season is over. The least I can do is offer you a place to stay for the night and a nice, hot breakfast in the morning. Be a sweetie, will you, Laurel? Help Noah pick out what he needs from the gift shop and then get him settled in a room."

Gift shop? Room?

For a couple minutes, Laurel had been lulled into thinking she had some semblance of control. She'd spoken to Noah, she'd stood within three feet of him and she hadn't lost her cool or the self-respect it had taken her four long years to rebuild. But now Maisie was asking the impossible. The gift shop? Laurel looked that way. Because it was late and there were no guests, the lights in the shop were off but she knew what was waiting in the darkness beyond the closed door. Edible underwear. Furry handcuffs. See-through nighties. Just thinking about it all made Laurel's face get hot and her insides turns to mush. The gift shop with anyone else, she could handle. The gift shop with Noah? She curled her fingers into her palms and wrapped her thumbs around them, fighting to regain control.

Walking into Maisie's gift shop with Noah would be like walking through Yellowstone Park with a Hi Bears! I've Got Food sign around her neck.

"Grandma, I—"

Before Laurel could say another word, the front door popped open and a familiar voice echoed through the inn. "Where's my little honey bunch?"

At the sight of Dr. Sam Ross, Maisie's cheeks got a little rosier and her twinkle intensified. Doc Ross was a mainstay on the island, a general practitioner who had been treating everything from broken bones to tourists who had partied a little too hardy, for as long as Laurel could remember. He'd retired four years earlier and much to Laurel's delight, he had accepted her offer to buy his practice. Doc Ross was a big, blunt man with a ruddy complexion and iron-gray hair. In the over-seventy crowd, he was the pick of the litter, the bachelor most sought after by the island's blue-haired matrons. Much to their dismay, Doc only had eyes for Maisie.

There was no doubt that Maisie returned his affections, but no chance, or so she said, that she was looking for anything permanent. Not at this stage of the game. That didn't stop Doc from trying. Even though it must have been the third or fourth time that week he'd seen her, he carried a dozen red roses and a bottle of champagne, and when he got to the front desk, he presented them to Maisie with a flourish.

"Oh!" Maisie twittered like a schoolgirl. She introduced Noah quickly, right before she took Doc's arm and headed toward the back of the house and her private rooms.

She called to Noah over her shoulder, "Laurel will take care of you!"

"Oh, no, you're not getting away that easily." Laurel went after her grandmother. She untangled her from Doc's grip and pulled her into a corner. "What's going on here?" she asked.

"I don't know what you mean, dear." Maisie had the nerve to look straight into Laurel's eyes and smile. She giggled, and the color rose brighter than ever in her cheeks. "If you're talking about me and Doc, you know the answer. A woman has needs." She gave Laurel a broad wink and when all Laurel did was stare at her in wonder, her grandmother tapped her on the arm and leaned close. "All women do, sweetie. Maybe it's time you remembered that."

"You know that's not what I'm talking about. I'm talking about him." Laurel shot a look over to her shoulder at Noah.

"Yes, I know," Maisie said. "That's exactly what I'm talking about, too. Good night, dear."

Too stunned to move, Laurel watched Maisie and Doc disappear into the long hall past the kitchen. A second later, the door to Maisie's private rooms closed and the muffled strains of *La Bohème* started up from Maisie's CD player and seeped through Cupid's Hideaway.

Needs?

Laurel was perfectly willing to accept that she had needs. Nobody had to point that out. She'd even indulged them a time or two in the years since she'd returned to the island and opened her practice. It was never anything serious. How could it be? Except for the small population that stayed on the island year round, most of the men she met were tourists. And there was one thing about tourists. They never stayed around.

Kind of like Noah.

The thought vibrated through her, deep, undeniable and bitter. But before she had a chance to remind herself this was not the time and place to think about it, the air warmed around her. She didn't need to turn around to know Noah had come nearer.

A second later, she felt the brush of his hand against her shoulder.

"You still wear the same perfume," he said.

Chapter Two

Seeing Laurel again was a lot like getting sucker punched.

That would explain why Noah's gut was tight. Why his head was buzzing. Why it felt as if the wind had been knocked out of him. She wasn't supposed to be there, and to say he'd been caught by surprise was the understatement of this, or any other, century.

When Maisie called him earlier that morning, she said Laurel was cruising. And when Noah thought of cruising, he thought of big ships, rum drinks and steel drum music. When he thought of cruising, he thought of far, far away.

Which Laurel definitely was not.

Noah had spent a whole lot of time in the last four years telling himself that he didn't miss Laurel. Not even a little. There were times when he even believed it.

Funny how fast all the positive reinforcement could go out the window. Funnier still that the warmth of Laurel's skin against his could throw him back in a time warp and make all the old emotions feel new. The sensation was like a drug that lulled him into la-la land at the same time it zipped through his bloodstream and set it on fire. Allowing himself a long, slow smile, he took a step closer. He let his eyes drift shut, and drank in the scent and the warmth of Laurel and the amazing connection he'd thought he'd never be lucky enough to feel again.

It was all a big mistake, of course. Letting her know he remembered her jasmine and roses perfume. Getting close enough to feel the electricity that buzzed in the air between them. Touching her. In light of the games that former lovers played, he had to be making the strategic blunder of all times.

He supposed he could chalk it up to shock. Or an overactive imagination. Or just plain, old stupidity

But, God, it felt good to be so near her again.

"And it still smells wonderful." Noah didn't realize he'd spoken until he heard the sound of his own words whisper on the air between them. "Your perfume."

"Of course I'm still wearing the same perfume." It wasn't so much the snap of Laurel's words that brought Noah out of his daze as it was the fact that she stepped away from him. By the time he opened his eyes, he found himself holding nothing but thin air.

Laurel was already an arm's length away. Her feet were apart. Her arms were tight against her sides. Her hazel eyes flashed lightning. "I'm still doing a lot of things I used to do," she said. "But then, I'm not the one who changed."

"So much for the formalities, huh?" Noah pulled his hand to his side. He supposed he should be grateful that Laurel reminded him of what he should have remembered in the first place. But then, she always was good at setting ground rules. Almost as good as she was at igniting his fantasies, his emotions and his libido.

Good thing she broke the spell before he could act

like even more of a bonehead. Good thing she reminded him that history or no history, she was—thank goodness—strictly off-limits. He didn't come three miles from the Ohio mainland into the middle of Lake Erie to have his ego crushed, and he didn't need to give her any more of an opportunity to do it. Already he was sure she was marking her mental scoreboard: One to nothing, Laurel Burton.

Noah promised himself he'd even the score. Sometime soon. But if he was going to do that, he'd need to catch her off guard. Waiting for his opportunity and using the time to get himself and his thoughts on solid ground, he rolled back on his heels and took a look around the Cupid's Hideaway lobby.

"So she finally did it, huh?" Noah asked, his voice as neutral as his look. "Maisie always talked about opening up a place of her own. It's—"

"*Amazing* is sort of the all-purpose word I like to use to describe it." Laurel's explanation was as quick and efficient as her movements. Chin down, steps quick and sure, she headed to the other side of the big front desk. To get something? Or to put as much distance as possible between herself and Noah? He knew the first scenario was probably true. He chose to believe the second. It played better with his plan.

She scooped a strand of her shoulder-length hair away from her face and tucked it behind her ear. Her hair was the same color as the old mahogany desk, rich with red undertones and colors that, in the soft light, reminded him of the leather covers on his collection of antique anatomy books. She was wearing it longer than she had in medical school, and Noah watched it swing against her back as she walked. He supposed here on the island, with its slow pace and its minimal demands on her education and her skills, she had more time to mess with her hair. At least more time than she'd had in the old days, when the only time she had was for her work and the only thing she messed with was Noah's life, his career and his heart.

Not a good thing to think about. At least not with Laurel only a couple feet away. Except for the one time it really mattered, she always had the uncanny habit of reading his mind.

Telling himself it was something he couldn't afford to forget, Noah glanced around, from the frothy paintings on the ceiling to the chintz-covered furniture and the pink lightbulbs in the fixtures on the wall in back of the desk.

"It is an amazing place, and Maisie is an amazing woman to keep it all going." Laurel said exactly what he was thinking. No surprise there. It was a knack they'd always shared. "The people who come to visit appreciate it for what it is," she said. She ruffled through a pile of the day's mail and sorted each letter into one of five cubbyholes. "Quirky. Different. Fun in its own weird sort of way. They're nice people." She stopped and reached for another pile of mail and as she did, she allowed her gaze to travel to Noah. She looked him up and down. "At least most of them are nice."

Noah could ignore a lot of things. This wasn't one of them. He was at least willing to act civilized. She, it seemed, was just going to be Laurel. He didn't need to remind himself what that meant. Laurel could be bullheaded. She could be opinionated. She could be as tough as nails and as hard as rocks and as determined as anyone Noah had ever met.

Another whiff of perfume drifted by and reminded Noah of something else.

She was also the most sensual and passionate woman he'd ever had the misfortune to fall in love with, and she'd never been afraid to show that side. At least not to him. He'd spent plenty of time trying to forget that. He wondered if Laurel had, too.

A slow smile brightened Noah's expression. She wanted to play hardball? Maybe he'd just found a way to score some points of his own.

He waited until Laurel started sorting a second pile of mail, and when she was paying more attention to the latest sale circular from the local grocery store than she was to him, he flattened his hands against the desk and leaned forward. When she was done, he was ready for her. He was only inches away, and when she looked up and realized it, she caught her breath. Her pupils widened. Her breasts pressed against her sweater. Noah allowed himself one quick look of appreciation before he raised his gaze to hers.

"You used to think I was nice people," he murmured.

"Yeah, I did." Laurel skimmed her tongue over her lips. Caught by the warmth of Noah's look or maybe by the pull of the same memories that threatened to turn him upside down and inside out, she leaned closer. Closer still. Her lips a heartbeat from his, she gave him a one-sided, cynical smile. "What the hell was wrong with me, anyway?"

"Right." Noah pulled back and gave her a smile that was so stiff and artificial it hurt. Make that Laurel Burton two, Noah Cunningham nothing. He watched her ruffle through four sets of keys.

"What will it be?" she asked. "You're Maisie's only guest for the night so I suppose you get your pick of the rooms. They're right up the stairs." She pointed.

"And they're all marked. You in the mood for a tropical paradise?" She jingled the key, and when he didn't reach for it, she held out another. "A flashback to the sixties? A little rock and roll? Or a whole bunch of red velvet and gold paint?"

"I'm in the mood…" Noah thought long and hard about what he was going to say next. Well, maybe not too long or not too hard, but he did think about it. He thought about what Maisie had said earlier about getting the things he needed, things like a toothbrush and a comb. And when he thought about that, he thought about the way Laurel's cheeks went dusky at the mention of the inn's gift shop. He was looking for a way to break down her legendary self-control? Maybe he'd just found it.

"I'm in the mood for a toothbrush." He sang the words in a low, pure baritone and when he did, he knew he hit the mark. Laurel stiffened and that nice, dusky color in her cheeks went a little ashen.

"Toothbrush. Fine. Sure." Laurel's fingers fumbled over the keys. She glanced across the lobby toward a room that looked innocuous enough. The door of the room was closed but Noah suspected it had once been an enclosed porch. The door had an oval glass insert that was covered from the inside by a lace curtain. On the outside of the glass in a beautiful flowing hand were written the words Cupid's Love Shack.

Noah's eyebrows rose along with his expectations.

"That's the gift shop," Laurel said. "Right over there. You're looking right at it. We never lock it. Go on in. Get the stuff you need." She headed to the other side of the desk. "I'll just go upstairs and make sure your room is—"

"Oh, no!" Before she could zoom out of his reach,

Noah grabbed her hand. "I think you'd better help me out."

"Help? You?" Laurel made an effort to sound cocky. It might have worked if her eyes didn't dart toward the Love Shack. If her pulse wasn't beating double-time against Noah's hand. "Since when does the great Dr. Noah Cunningham need help from anybody? I think you can handle it, Doc. There aren't a whole lot of choices you need to make. Green toothbrush. Blue toothbrush. Crest or Colgate. Small decisions. The kind you should be able to handle all on your own." She stopped and her eyes widened, as if she'd just remembered something. "No. Wait a minute," she said. "The way I remember it, you were pretty good at handling even the really big decisions all on your own."

If she was trying to distract him, it almost worked. Almost. They'd talk about the decisions each of them had made some other time. Now was not the time for soul-searching or introspection or regret.

It was time for a little sweet revenge.

Being as gentle as he was sure to let her know he wasn't going to change his mind, Noah wrapped one arm around Laurel's shoulders. "I just wouldn't feel right going into Maisie's gift shop and taking things," he said. "If you're with me, you can keep a list. You know, help Maisie out when it comes to inventory."

Laurel took one more look at the closed door of the Love Shack. She drew in a long, shaky breath and gave Noah a sidelong look. "All right," she said, and he felt her stiffen against him. "If that's what you want."

They walked across the lobby, Noah's arm looped over Laurel's shoulders. No big deal in the great scheme of things. At least it shouldn't have been. At least it wouldn't have been if every step they took didn't make

Noah remember how perfectly they fit together. Laurel's blue jeans scraped against his cashmere suit. Her hip swayed against his. Her hair spilled over her shoulder and brushed his neck. By the time she swung open the door to the Love Shack and flicked on the lights, Noah's skin was buzzing as if he'd been loofahed from head to toe.

"Toothbrushes." Like a sentry on duty, Laurel stood in the doorway, her back to the open door, her spine as rigid as if a broom handle had been shoved up her sweater. She pointed to a display on a glass counter to her left. "Lots of toothbrushes. Pick one. And a comb." She pointed to another display. "Heck, throw in a bottle of mouthwash if you like." She smiled a toothy, stiff smile. "Get what you need and let's get out of here."

"What's the hurry?" Humming softly to himself, Noah did a turn around the tiny gift shop. What was the word Laurel had used to describe Cupid's Hide-away? Amazing? *Amazing* didn't begin to describe the Love Shack.

On first glance, the place looked about as normal as every gift shop in every hotel Noah had ever been in. Next to the rack of toothbrushes was one of those spinning wire racks full of postcards, islands scenes mostly, though he saw some that were sepia-toned, Victorian reproductions that showed everything from ladies in lacy underwear to a man and a woman in what must have been—at least for the time—a torrid embrace. Cute. Sentimental. Romantic, he supposed, in a fluffy, old-lady sort of way.

At the far end of the room was a display of scented candles, soaps in packaging that was tied with ribbons and a variety of massage oils in colored glass bottles arrayed on the windowsill.

"Oh," Noah cooed, picking one up and reading the label. "Love Nibbles."

He wiggled his eyebrows in as near as he could come to a lecherous look and got no response at all from Laurel. Too bad. There was a time when she would have been as interested in a little love and a little nibbling as he was. A time when they would have laughed over the name and hurried home with a bottle to find out if it was as delicious as its label promised.

Regret wasn't a pretty feeling to experience or to watch, and before Laurel could suspect how hollow his stomach felt and how empty his arms had been for the four long years they'd been apart, he replaced the bottle and continued with his tour. At the door, he stopped to examine a glass display case.

The case was about five feet long and three feet high, pretty ordinary, really. The kind of display case he'd seen in bakeries and clothing stores and bookstores all over the country. But one look and Noah knew this was no ordinary display. He whistled low under his breath and bent to take a closer look. The case was filled with the most amazing variety of sex toys he'd ever seen.

Noah's temperature shot up a degree or two. Right along with his fantasies. Most of the stuff looked pretty familiar, but there was one especially extraordinary-looking object that even he, with his medical background, wasn't exactly sure how to use. It was hot pink and about a foot long, no bigger around than a pencil. One end of it was crowned with a flamboyant pink feather.

Imagining the possibilities, he stared at the object for a moment or two before he glanced at Laurel. "I don't suppose you—"

"Demonstrate?" She pulled her shoulders back and

marched over to the counter. "Isn't it just like you to ask. That's the most immature, sexist, inappropriate—"

"I was going to say gift wrap." His hands against the counter, Noah stood and gave her a smile that was as innocent as it was wide. "I was going to ask if you gift wrap."

"Oh." A blush rushed up Laurel's neck and stained her cheeks, but he had to give her credit, she kept her cool. Crossing her arms over her chest, she stepped back, her weight on one foot. "It's not working," she said.

"It's not?" Noah gave her a wink. "It used to work really good."

"That's not what I mean, and you know it." Either she was one heck of an efficient worker or she was looking for something to do. On the counter was a stack of flyers advertising an upcoming sale at the Love Shack. Laurel grabbed them and carefully folded one after another. "You're not going to embarrass me, Noah. So don't even try. We're both medical professionals. And we're both adults. How about you cut the crap and we get down to business."

Noah grinned. "And that business is…"

"Toothbrushes."

"Toothbrushes. Yes, ma'am." He nodded, the picture of compromise. "Can I get a bag or something?" he asked.

Laurel reached under the counter and came up holding a small pink shopping bag. "Here. Your bag." She opened the bag and waited for him to fill it.

Noah took his time. He walked around the gift shop once more, checking things out. He was tempted to take a look through the antique wardrobe that took up most of one wall. The doors of the wardrobe were open, and inside was a variety of lacy lingerie. Pink. White. Lavender. Black. The colors and frothy fabric begged to be touched.

He didn't. It was one thing teasing Laurel. It was another teasing himself with the memories the filmy clothing conjured. Laurel in lace. Laurel in satin. Laurel in nothing at all.

Shaking off the thoughts, Noah went to the toothbrush display. He plucked one from the rack and dropped it into the bag. He added a travel-size tube of toothpaste and a tortoiseshell comb, but it wasn't until he reached for a small bottle of minty mouthwash that he realized there was a display he hadn't noticed. A rack of condoms.

Noah glanced over his shoulder to where Laurel was waiting, the shopping bag open, her gaze fixed on the far wall.

Yeah, they were both medical professionals.

Yeah, they were both adults.

But that didn't mean he couldn't have a little fun.

He grabbed a pack of condoms and walked to the counter. It wasn't until right before he dropped it into the bag that he read the package and saw that the condoms were glow-in-the-dark.

When Laurel looked at him, her eyebrows raised, he shrugged. "What? You never know."

"Right." She tapped her foot. "Are you done?"

"No." Noah grinned and continued to explore. When he came to a display of edible underwear, he couldn't resist. They were packed in plastic shrink-wrap, each pair different, each hung from a little satin hanger. He considered a bright pink bra, but one look at the expression on Laurel's face and he knew she was right. It was too sexist. He thought about a purple G-string, bubble gum flavored, according to the packaging, and decided that was too blatant. The only thing that seemed just right was a pair of man's briefs. Brief briefs. They were bright red and, if the package could be believed, tasted like candy apple.

Prolonging the moment, Noah strolled to where Laurel was waiting. He dangled the package over the counter between them, crooking his finger just enough to make the briefs swing back and forth. He watched Laurel's gaze dip to the briefs and up again. He watched two spots of color rise in her cheeks. He watched her catch her breath.

"So," he said, "what's a nice doctor like you doing in a place like this?"

"Funny, I was going to ask you the same thing." Laurel plucked the underwear out of his hand and tossed it into the bag. "I'm here because tourist season is over and the clinic isn't as busy now. That gives me some time for myself. And it gives me some time to stop by once in a while and see if Grandma needs anything. When she's busy, I try to help out as much as I can. And you're here because…"

Her question hung on the air between them. When the silence dragged out to one minute, then two, she tossed the shopping bag on the counter.

"I can't believe you just stopped by, Noah. No one just stops by an island in the middle of a lake in the middle of the fall. What's going on?"

He gave her a lopsided grin. "A guy can't get nostalgic?"

"A guy? Sure. A guy can get plenty nostalgic. But you're not just any guy. You don't do anything unless you've thought about it six ways and sideways."

Noah let his gaze slip from Laurel to the case of sex

toys. Her hand was on the counter, and he slid his over hers. "I've thought about you six ways and sideways."

"No. You haven't." Laurel shook her head, but she didn't pull her hand away. "You haven't thought about me, and I haven't thought about you. I thought we made that pretty clear the last time we saw each other. We promised—"

"We didn't exactly promise." Noah barked out a laugh. "I have a photographic memory, remember? Even if I didn't, I think I'd remember that *promise* is way too nice a word to describe the things we said to each other. The way I remember it, you said you'd never waste another minute thinking about me," he reminded her.

"And you said you were glad," she countered. She pulled back her shoulders and looked him in the eye. "You said you'd already spent enough time worrying about a woman who wasn't worth worrying about."

"And you said you didn't care because you didn't want me worrying about you, anyway." Noah skimmed his hand up her arm. "You said you could look after yourself, that you didn't need anyone to tell you what you wanted out of life."

"And you said that was just fine, because you weren't going to tell me, anyway." Laurel's voice rose along with the tempo of her words. "You said that was great. It was terrific. It was really, really good. You said I should grow up and figure out what was really important. What was important to you, you said, was your career. And you weren't going to throw it away on some backwater island where—"

"Where the only thing a doctor ever got to treat was broken bones and beestings. Yeah, I know." Noah had no intention of getting pulled into an argument. Not the same argument. Not all over again. But if that was the case, why was his voice as loud as Laurel's? He found himself clutching her arm a little tighter. ''You said you were happy to finally get things out in the open.''

''And you said goodbye.''

Their words hung in the air, as bitter and painful as they had been four years earlier. Nothing could change the things they'd said or done. Noah knew that. Nothing could erase the pain or the regret. Nothing could bring back the years and the happiness they might have shared.

Nothing.

Noah loosened his grip on Laurel's arm. He couldn't change the past but he could, at least, do something about the present. The moment. The instant. And in that one instant, Laurel's eyes were as pretty as ever, her lips were as full. Her breasts were as lush, and when she pulled in breath after shaky breath and they strained against her sweater, he knew it was one moment he couldn't let pass.

As quickly as he loosened his hold, he reached for her again, and leaning over the counter, he brought his mouth down on Laurel's.

Chapter Three

Big mistake.

As soon as the thought formed in her head, Laurel amended it.

This wasn't just a big mistake. This was a whopper. A screwup. The mother of all mistakes.

Which explained why she felt like a complete idiot.

Which didn't explain why she was enjoying Noah's kiss quite so much.

The thoughts tumbled through her head at the same time a riot of sensations assaulted her body. Lips that were skilled. A taste that was unique. A certain heart-stopping sizzle that bubbled through her bloodstream. And the heat.

Laurel tipped her head back, and when Noah parted her lips with his tongue and deepened the kiss, she heard a moan of pure pleasure rise from deep in her throat. The heat of Noah's hand seared her skin even through her sweater. His lips scorched hers. An answering heat built inside her. She leaned closer. The hard edge of the glass display case poked her in the ribs, and Laurel cursed her luck. If it wasn't for the display case, she'd be feeling Noah's arms around her. If it wasn't for the display case, she'd be pressing her body against his. If it wasn't for the display case, she could get closer still and let her hands roam over him, exploring and remembering.

If it wasn't for the display case, she'd be making an even bigger fool of herself than she already was.

The heat that pounded through her veins froze with the icy realization, and Laurel flattened one hand against Noah's shoulder and pushed away from him. "What the hell do you think you're doing?" She stopped just short of screeching the question and struggled to collect herself. With any luck, he was as confused as she was. As overwhelmed. As flustered. Otherwise, he might catch on to the fact that she wasn't sure if she was asking the question of him or of herself.

"Are you nuts?"

Another question she could very well have aimed at herself. Instead, Laurel ran a hand through her hair and moved back a couple steps. It might have been easier to ignore the thread of desire wound tight inside her if she didn't find herself with her back against a display of itty-bitty panties and teeny-tiny bra tops and eentsy-weentsy wisps of lace that tickled the back of her neck and her imagination in ways it shouldn't have been tickled. At least not when Noah was in the room. Or at the Hideaway. Or on the island.

Beyond the point of knowing or caring if what she was about to do looked as much like a retreat as it felt, Laurel darted from behind the counter and headed for the door.

"Where are we going?" she heard Noah call from behind her.

On her way past the front desk, Laurel grabbed the first set of room keys she could get her hands on. She glanced at the name etched into the heart-shaped brass key chain. "Almost Paradise," she told him.

Behind her, she heard Noah's footsteps against the antique Oriental rug. She felt his arms go around her waist, holding her in place. At the same time, his breath brushed against her neck, soft and warm. "Cool," he murmured. "I have to admit, I wasn't really planning for that little kiss to turn into a full-scale seduction, but if you're willing..."

This time, Laurel did screech. She screeched her annoyance and her frustration. She screeched not because of Noah's suggestion, but because what he was suggesting sounded good to her. Way too good.

"You are crazy." Laurel spun and darted out of his reach. She slapped the room keys into Noah's hand. "If you think I'm going to go up to that room with you and—"

"Isn't that what you just said?" Noah looked from the key to the stairs that wound to the second floor to Laurel. He gave her a lopsided, devilish smile, the kind that in the old days packed the magic punch that could make her do anything. "Let me get this straight. You kiss a guy—"

"I didn't kiss you, you kissed me."

"You kiss a guy and you're having a really good time and—"

"I wasn't having a good time." Laurel set her jaw. "You're imagining that part of it."

"You're having a really good time and then you make a move. Not just any move. You move quickly, conclusively, dare I say..." He wiggled his eyebrows. "Enthusiastically toward the lobby."

"Not enthusiastically," she insisted. "I was never enthusiastic."

"You move enthusiastically, a woman with a mission. You can't wait. You can't wait to get out of the gift shop. You can't wait to get across the lobby. You can't wait to—"

"Oh, I can wait, all right. I can wait until hell freezes over."

"And you grab a set of room keys and you tell me we're headed to paradise and you mean... What?" He looked at her, his expression hovering halfway between *I dare you to try and talk your way out of this one* and *Go ahead, make my day.*

"What I mean..." Laurel moved back one step. Two steps. It was well past time to put some distance between herself and Noah. Some distance between herself and the memories he had a way of evoking, like a magician conjuring something beautiful and tempting where only moments before there had been nothing but thin air. "I mean it's time for you to go to your room and stay there."

"You mean..." Noah gave her the sort of wide-eyed, dramatic, smart-aleck look that told her he was going to milk her discomfort for all it was worth. "You mean...good night?"

"I mean good night. What else would I mean? How could any woman in her right mind mean anything else? I mean good night. I mean goodbye. Because I won't be here in the morning, and that's when you'll be leaving." She hurried to the other side of the front desk. At least with a few hundred pounds of solid mahogany between herself and Noah, she felt as if she stood a fighting chance. "You'll find everything you need in your room," she told him, using the kind of honeyed tones that seemed to suit an innkeeper. "Towels. Soap. Shampoo." She glanced at the little pink shopping bag he'd managed to bring along with him from the Love Shack. "I see you've got everything else covered."

"I do." Noah moved toward the desk, and Laurel found herself automatically moving back. Even then, he managed to reach across the sign-in book and the room keys and the pile of mail she hadn't finished sorting. Gently, he touched her arm. His cocky grin softened and so did his voice. "Take it easy, Laurel," he said. "It was only a kiss."

Only a kiss?

Laurel could hardly believe her ears. Only a kiss? That? What happened between them in the Love Shack was only a kiss like Pavarotti was only some Italian guy who liked to sing in the shower.

She shook off the thought. And the memories. And Noah's hand. She supposed she should be grateful that he'd laid it on the line. It was only a kiss. At least to him. At least she knew where he stood. At least she knew where she stood, and where she stood was on the edge of an abyss. She could take a step forward and free-fall headlong into the void. She knew what waited for her there. For a while she'd feel as if she was floating, as if she was flying, and while it lasted, it would be awesome. Like the feeling she had the first time someone called her doctor and the buzz of Fourth of July fireworks and Christmas morning all rolled into one.

But sooner or later she'd land, and when she did, she knew she'd land hard. There was nothing waiting for her but a rocky pit and nothing as sure to make her forget the good times as the bad times.

She had to choose and she had to do it right here and now. She could take the step and start on a dizzying trip that was sure to end with nothing but heartbreak.

Or she could convince herself that Noah was right. It was only a kiss.

"Only a kiss, huh?" Laurel congratulated herself— she sounded nearly as nonchalant about the whole thing as he did. "That wasn't only a kiss, Noah. That was an aberration. A deviation. An anomaly. A freak of nature, like two-headed snakes and those fish that live deep in the ocean where there's no light so they have these antenna things..." She wiggled her fingers over her head. "And these sort of little lightbulb thingies that flash so they can see where they're going and—"

"I get the message!" Noah laughed and held up one hand in surrender. "I'm sorry. Honest. I wouldn't have kissed you if I knew it was going to make you so nervous."

"I am not nervous." Laurel tucked her hands behind her back before he could see that they were shaking. She forced herself to look Noah in the eye. "I don't get nervous," she told him. "Not about things as inconsequential as that."

"Of course not," he agreed. Looking at her looking at him, the smile faded from his face, and he glanced away.

That was a first. Laurel made a mental note. Noah was never the first to back down from anything. Interested, she tipped her head and watched him shift the shopping bag from one hand to the other. Was it her imagination, or had a little of the swagger gone out of Noah? It must have been a trick of the soft pink lighting. She could have sworn he looked as disconcerted by what had happened in the Love Shack as she was feeling.

"I don't want you to get the wrong impression," he

said. "I don't want you to think that I was expecting that you—"

"No!" Laurel jumped in to interrupt as quickly as she could. She didn't need Noah to spell it out for her. She didn't need him to detail exactly what he'd been expecting. She didn't want to think about what he'd been expecting. Or what she'd been expecting in return. Or what she'd been expecting him to expect.

"I mean, I don't want you to think that I thought I could just waltz in here after four years and—"

"Of course not." Laurel decided it was better to agree with him than it was to risk further discussion. Kissing her former fiancé within minutes of running into him after a long separation and a nasty breakup was not the kind of thing a woman wanted to discuss in detail. At least, not with her former fiancé.

Laurel wasn't prepared for the stab of regret that followed fast on the thought. She could take the surprise and the anger that was part of the package of seeing Noah again. She could deal with the embarrassment she felt at losing her head and giving in to the potent pleasures of his kiss. But regret…

She pulled in a slow breath and let it out.

Regret used to be her best friend. It was one friend she didn't want to get chummy with again.

Holding fast to the thought, she raised her chin. "Good night, Dr. Cunningham," she said.

For a second, it looked like Noah wanted to say something. She watched his lips part and his eyes spark, the way they always did when he was headed into some particularly interesting discussion. He apparently changed his mind. Hanging on to the shopping bag, he headed to the stairs. "Good night, Dr. Burton."

Laurel didn't watch him go upstairs. There was something just a little too twisted about enjoying the sight of that nice, tight rear of his.

"Don't need it. Don't want it," Laurel mumbled to herself. Maybe if she said it often enough, one of these days she'd finally convince herself it was true. Before she could forget it, she moved to the front of the desk and hurried through the routine Maisie had taught her to follow each night—check to make sure the fire was out, check to make sure nothing was cooking in the kitchen, check to make sure the doors were locked. When it was all taken care of, Laurel grabbed her car keys off the counter in the kitchen and her jacket from where she'd tossed it over one of the kitchen chairs. She thought about stopping to say good-night to Maisie and Doc Ross and decided against it. Something told her they had other things on their minds.

Things she refused to have on her mind.

Laurel headed out of the kitchen and across the lobby. She'd left her car parked in front of the inn so she decided to go that way and lock the front door behind her. On her way through, she flicked off the overhead chandelier and flicked on the couple small stained-glass lamps Maisie left burning all night. She slipped into her lightweight jacket, turned toward the front door and ran headlong into Noah.

"What are you doing?" Laurel pressed a hand to her heart and jumped back a step. "Are you trying to scare me to death?"

He gave her a small smile of apology. "What I'm trying to do," he said, "is get into my room." He jingled his key at her. "Doesn't work," he said.

"Doesn't work?" Laurel plucked the key chain out of Noah's hand and held it up to the light. "Almost

Paradise.'' She read the room name on the brass heart. ''Are you sure you were at the right room?''

''I can read signs,'' he said, a bit of sarcasm creeping into his voice. ''And I'm pretty good at unlocking doors. One of life's basic skills. But I've been trying the door for the last five minutes, and it's not working. I didn't want to bother you, but…well, I don't think the place will ever get a five-star rating if you leave your guests sleeping in the hallway.''

He was right. Or at least it looked as if he was right. Laurel gave Noah a quick once-over, as if the assessment would tell her if he was telling the truth. ''You're not trying to trick me, are you?''

''Scout's honor.'' Noah crossed his heart. ''Besides, what would I possibly be trying to trick you into? Get you up to the room? Lock you in? Take advantage of you?'' He laughed, and Laurel bristled at the sound. Was there something so ludicrous about the thought of him taking advantage of her? Before she could answer the question, Noah gave her a friendly pat on the back. ''Lighten up, Laurel,'' he said. He leaned a little closer and grinned. ''It was only a kiss, remember?''

''Right.'' Telling herself not to forget it, Laurel led the way up the stairs. Almost Paradise was the first room on the left, and she stopped outside the door. Maisie had opened the inn eighteen months earlier, and by now, Laurel was used to the place. She was used to the wacky decor and the titillating gift shop, used to her grandmother's sometimes screwy, sometimes explicitly suggestive gimmicks for adding a little romance to the lives of the people who came to stay there. But of course, Noah wasn't. While Laurel tried the key, Noah eyed the sign outside the door, the one that looked like it had been carved from a tree branch. The words Almost Paradise were engraved into the wood in undulating letters. They were partly obscured by the fat, satisfied-looking snake wound around the branch. Above the wooden snake on a second branch was a bright red apple.

Noah didn't comment. It was just as well. If he thought the sign was bizarre…

Laurel set aside the thought and turned the key in the lock. It worked just fine. But the door didn't open.

"That's funny," she said. She wrinkled her nose, thinking through the problem. "This door never sticks. The door in Love Me Tender, now that door always sticks. But this one…" She tried turning the handle again, lifting a little this time, thinking that might help. It didn't.

"The key works." She locked the door, then used the key again to show Noah there was no problem there. "But the door…" She put her shoulder to the door and pushed. "It's stuck."

"Here. Let me help."

Before Laurel could decide it was a bad idea for Noah to step up right beside her and lean against the door with her, he was already doing it. "On three," he said. "One…two…three!"

They pushed together, and the door popped open. Unfortunately, neither Laurel nor Noah was ready for it. They staggered into the room together, and Laurel fought to regain her footing. It would have worked nicely if someone hadn't left one of the tropical plants that should have been by the window in the middle of the floor.

The force of opening caused the door to slam against the wall, then swing shut behind them. Even though two of the walls in the room were floor-to-ceiling glass blocks, it was past sunset, and they were facing the lake. The room was dark. Laurel saw the plant at the last second. She sidestepped it, pivoted. She would have been fine if she hadn't tripped over her own feet. She heard herself let out a yelp of surprise, felt herself falling. She braced her arms to stop herself from hitting the floor and waited to feel the impact.

It never happened.

From behind her, she felt Noah's arms go around her waist. He caught her so fast, he knocked the wind out of her, and while she struggled to catch her breath, he lifted her, held her. And completely lost his balance.

"Hang on," she heard Noah warn, but by that time, it was too late. Fortunately for her bones, she landed on her back on the bed. Unfortunately for the rest of her, Noah landed on his stomach right on top of her.

Above her, she heard Noah try to catch his breath. She saw him smile. He adjusted his weight against her. "You folks have a great way of making guests feel welcome. Is this what you call room service?"

"This is what I call annoying." Laurel tried to squirm out from under him. It was a bad plan from the start. Squirming only made her breasts scrape against Noah's rock-hard chest. Squirming only made her legs tangle with his. Squirming brought her hips in direct contact with his, and direct contact told her more about the situation than she wanted to know. Noah hadn't changed. He'd always told her that she could arouse him at the drop of a hat. There were no hats dropping at the moment, but that didn't seem to make much of a difference.

"It's only a bed," Laurel told him, the emphasis on *only*.

"Uh-huh." Noah settled himself more comfortably,

his hands on either side of her. "And it's only a little physical contact."

"You bet." Laurel hoped the breathy voice she heard wasn't coming out of her. It was hard to be sure when she was feeling so light-headed. Hard to get her bearings when her heart was pounding so violently she was sure the entire island could hear it. "Only a little physical contact," she agreed. "And it's going to stop right now." She braced her hands against Noah's chest and pushed, and when he sat up, laughing, she thanked her lucky stars and whatever guardian angels watched over doctors with more lust in their hearts than they had brains in their heads.

Laurel tugged her sweater into place and sat up. She knew Cupid's Hideaway as well as she knew her own house in town and she knew there was a lamp close by. She leaned forward, reaching for the lamp on the bedside table. "Let's get some lights turned on," she said, and even to her own ears, her voice sounded too tight and her words sounded a little too rushed and formal. "Then you can get settled for the night." She turned the switch on the lamp, and nothing happened.

"What the heck?" Laurel tried again. "The bulb's burned out," she grumbled. Moving carefully in the dark, she stood. "Maisie keeps more lightbulbs in the bathroom," she told Noah. "You stay here. I'll just go... Ouch!" Her shin slammed into a second potted plant, one she swore wasn't in the middle of the floor the last time she'd been in the room. She rubbed the spot where she knew there would be a bruise by morning. "I'll get a bulb."

Carefully, Laurel negotiated her way through the room. Even in daylight, finding a path through Almost Paradise could be a challenge. The room had been de-

signed by Maisie and brought to life by an architect who
was skeptical at best. Not a romantic and not possessing
Maisie's imagination or her fondness for fantasy, he
didn't understand why a room needed winding paths
covered with carpet that looked like grass and bordered
with tropical foliage. He didn't understand about the
waterfall, either, and listening for the gurgle so she
could maneuver around it, Laurel headed into the bathroom. She hit the light switch at the same time she heard
a splash. Noah barked out a curse.

Laurel spun around just in time to see him ankle-deep
in the pond that took up one corner of the room.

She fought to control a smile. "I told you not to
move," she said.

"You told me not to move. You didn't tell me there
was a lake in the middle of the room. Damn!" Noah
lifted up one foot and watched water drip off the leg of
his expensive trousers.

"You didn't hurt any of the fish, did you?"

He glanced at the water, then at Laurel, and even
though the room was bathed only with the light that
seeped from the bathroom, she could see the flush of
anger and embarrassment that stained his face. "The
fish are fine." He shook one leg and stepped out of the
pond. "I don't suppose you could toss me a—"

"Towel." Laurel already had one in her hand. She
lobbed it to him before she turned to look for a lightbulb
in the vanity below the sink. Retrieving one, she headed
into the bedroom.

"What the hell kind of place is this?" She found
Noah looking around the room, his expression as in-
credulous as his pant leg was wet.

Smiling, Laurel got rid of the old lightbulb, screwed
in the new one and flicked on the lamp next to the bed.

The light brought the room to life, and just as she expected, Noah looked more amazed than ever.

Not only were the walls made out of glass blocks, the ceiling above the bed was a skylight. There were tropical plants everywhere, and as Noah had already discovered, a small pond in the corner, complete with a waterfall and a family of goldfish.

One eyebrow raised, Noah glanced Laurel's way. "You're kidding, right?"

"Not me." She smiled. "Maisie. And Maisie's never kidding. Not when it comes to Cupid's Hideaway. This is her version of paradise."

"More like—" Noah didn't finish the comparison. He didn't have to. He untied his wing tips, stepped out of them and poured the water that filled his right shoe into the pond. He peeled off his sock and laid it on the rocks that surrounded the pond.

"I didn't bring a suitcase, remember?" He undid his belt while he gave Laurel a beseeching look. "I don't suppose you folks have bathrobes or something for guests to use."

The request echoed in Laurel's head. She might have been listening to it if she wasn't so busy watching Noah. She'd forgotten how sure and capable his hands were. He unfastened his belt with the kind of quick economy of movement he used to do everything else. His fingers were long and tapered, the kind of fingers she'd always thought would be better suited to a surgeon or a musician than they were to a professor. She'd forgotten that, too. Too bad she hadn't forgotten the little thrill she'd always felt as she watched him get undressed. Or the tiny flickers of desire that always followed when she thought that Noah getting undressed usually meant her

getting undressed. And when they were both undressed…

Laurel yanked herself back to reality. Just in time to
keep herself from succumbing to too many vivid memories. Not in time to keep Noah from knowing exactly
what she was thinking. He'd stopped what he was doing—thank goodness—and he was looking at her, his
eyes sparking a suggestion and his lips quirked into a
smile that told her the suggestion was suggestive.

The very thought was intriguing. And as bad an idea
as Laurel had ever had.

Apparently, Noah felt the same way. At the same
time she pulled herself from the brink, he turned his
back on her to unzip his pants.

"Bathrobes. Check." Before she could convince herself there was any merit in doing anything else, Laurel
darted into the bathroom. Maisie was especially proud
of the Hideaway's bathrobes. She didn't scrimp when
it came to the Hideaway, and the bathrobes were a perfect example. They were thick and comfortable, and
each one had a cute little cupid embroidered over the
heart. They were supposed to be for her guests' use
while they were at the inn, but more often than not, her
guests purchased them before they left.

The bathrobes were always hung in the same place,
on hooks behind the bathroom door. Laurel reached behind the door and grabbed what was hanging there. She
knew from the start that what she'd retrieved wasn't a
bathrobe. It wasn't big or heavy or plush enough. In
fact, it was positively tiny. But she was already on her
way to the bedroom before she realized exactly what
she had in her hands.

Under normal circumstances, Laurel didn't embarrass
easily. But ever since she'd walked into the lobby and

found Noah at the front desk, her life had been anything but normal. She looked at what she was carrying, and her cheeks shot through with heat. Her stomach clenched. Her heart pounded once, twice, and she swore it stopped.

"I'm wet and cold," she heard Noah say. "Hurry up with that bathrobe, will you." He glanced at her over his shoulder, and before Laurel could tuck it behind her or make up an excuse that sounded even a little adequate, he saw what she was holding. Noah's mouth dropped open, and he turned. His belt was on the bed next to him, his pants were already unzipped, and a hint of green-and-white checked boxers showed at the fly. He held up his trousers with one hand and pointed at Laurel with the other.

"That's not—"

Laurel squeezed her eyes shut and forced herself to take a deep breath. That might have been a whole lot easier if the breath didn't wedge against the ball of panic in her throat. "No bathrobes," she told him. "At least not that I can find. This is the only thing here for you to change into." She held out the bit of green fabric. "I can't say for sure. I don't know if I've ever seen one before. I think…" She looked again at the triangular wedge of fabric. It had straps sewn to it, like a thong, and it was embroidered to look like—

"I think," Laurel said, "it's a fig leaf."

She didn't wait to see how Noah might respond. She didn't want to know. Her cheeks on fire, her heart in her throat, her knees as wobbly as if she'd run a couple miles, Laurel thrust the fabric fig leaf into Noah's hands and headed for the door. She bolted into the hallway and slammed the door closed behind her.

Out of the corner of her eye, Laurel caught sight of

the wooden snake carved into the sign. Its grinning face and flashing eyes told her it knew exactly what had happened inside the room. Exactly what she was thinking. Exactly how close she'd come to ignoring all the good advice she'd given herself over the past four years.

"What are you looking at?" She glared at the snake right before she pushed away from the door and headed downstairs, far from Almost Paradise and all the temptation that lay just on the other side of the door.

Chapter Four

Noah didn't need a lot of sleep. Which was a good thing for a guy with a schedule as hectic as his. More hours in the day—and the night—allowed him time to travel, lecturing at all the medical schools that were chomping at the bit to get the hottest internist in the country on their schedules. More hours in the day—and the night— allowed him to catch up on his reading and the lecture notes he was usually preparing and afforded him the opportunity of meeting with his students, his colleagues and reporters from medical journals who were, more and more lately, requesting interviews with the doctor many other doctors considered to be one of the most gifted instructors in the business. More hours in the day—and the night—gave Noah the luxury of having a social life, too. Not that he was a wild man. He knew his limits—physically as well as emotionally. He also knew that even a doctor with a reputation as good as his and a future as bright as any, needed to blow off a little steam now and again.

But even a guy who didn't need a lot of sleep needed some sleep. And some sleep was exactly what Noah didn't get in Almost Paradise.

Grumbling, he rolled over onto his stomach and took

his pillow with him. He clamped it over his head, doing his best to shut out the morning light that filled the room thanks to the overhead skylight and the glass-block walls. It didn't work. The pillow didn't block out the funny, gurgly sound of the waterfall, either, or the now-and-again plop of the fish as they swam around in the little pond across the room. It sure didn't do a thing to stop the memories that had kept him tossing and turning all night.

Noah knew a losing battle when he saw one and he flipped over and chucked the pillow aside, a kind of overstuffed surrender flag. There was no use trying to sleep, just like there was no use trying to forget everything that had happened since he walked into Cupid's Hideaway, so he kicked off the blankets. Scraping his hands through his hair, he sat up and looked around.

It wasn't just a bad dream.

The tropical plants were real. The winding paths were real. The faint background noise was real, too, a recording of roaring lions and squawking birds that must have been on a timer because he hadn't—thank goodness—heard it during the night.

As if he needed more proof that he was smack-dab in the middle of a situation he wasn't exactly sure how he'd gotten himself into, Noah saw the fabric fig leaf on the bed beside him. No doubt, the fig leaf was Maisie's idea of a joke, a little prop never meant to be worn but rather to be used as a kind of trigger designed to titillate the imaginations of the couples who stayed in Almost Paradise. Like the entire Cupid's Hideaway concept, the fig leaf was clever and bizarre and a little corny. In its own warped way, it was also very funny.

So why hadn't he and Laurel done any laughing?

Not a question Noah wanted to consider.

Hoping to get rid of the memories as easily as he got rid of the kink in his neck, he stretched and got up, headed to the bathroom. He was done asking himself questions. It was bad enough he'd spent the night second-guessing his handling of the situation and wondering where he got off thinking he could waltz into what was essentially enemy territory and come out without being handed his head, or at least his heart, on a silver platter. It was even worse realizing that four long years of telling himself he'd done the right thing—both for himself and for his career—didn't amount to a hill of beans. Not when Laurel was stretched out on the bed and he was lying on top of her.

Halfway down a winding path lined with flowering orchids, Noah stopped, nearly upended by the thought. He sucked in a long, slow breath, willing his heartbeat to slow down, telling himself to remember that there was more to any relationship than simply sex.

An easy enough concept to understand. Or at least it should have been. But try as he might, he couldn't forget that in the months he'd shared with Laurel, simply sex wasn't so simple. With Laurel, it was more like great sex. Mind-numbing sex. Heart-pounding, better-than-ever-before-or-since sex. He also couldn't forget that in that one moment, there in the dark in Almost Paradise, when Laurel's breasts were pressed to his chest and Laurel's breath was warm against his skin and Laurel's heart beat to the same manic rhythm as his, he'd wanted her again. Wanted her more than he'd ever wanted anyone. Or anything. At anytime. Ever.

The thought was enough to send Noah's temperature soaring, and that was enough to convince him he was in deep trouble. He knew what he had to do. He was a man of science, one who was the first to sneer at the touchy-feely stuff so many pseudoprofessionals advocated. But this time, he knew he had to make an exception. This time, it was time to listen to his instincts.

And his instincts told him to cut and run.

He knew exactly what he had to do. Get the Golden Apple and get out of there. After all, it was what he'd come to the island for in the first place.

Even after all these years, just thinking about the prestigious award he'd been presented by his medical school graduating class never failed to stir a curious brew of emotions in Noah. Pride, sure. How could he not be proud of the fact that he'd been honored as the most successful, the most competent, the most admired student in his class? It was a mark of distinction he hadn't been about to turn down. Not even when he found out Laurel had come in second for the award.

But there was something else tangled up with the pride, some emotion that was hard to define but impossible to ignore. Part anger, part disbelief, part baseball-bat-to-the-side-of-the-head surprise. Every time he thought about the fact that when Laurel walked out on him, she had the audacity to take the Golden Apple with her.

Four years removed from the incident and the residual effects still burned through Noah like acid. All the more reason he needed to get away from Cupid's Hideaway. And get away fast. He'd take the ferry to the mainland. He'd get back to his life as he knew it. It was all he ever wanted.

No. Noah corrected himself. Not precisely true. Today he wanted something else, too—a long talk with the fluffy little old lady who'd played him for a patsy.

Once he was done, he'd get out of there. The sooner he was off the island, the better. It was time to put some distance—and all the water in Lake Erie—between himself and Laurel. Just the way he'd done four years earlier.

Satisfied that he'd reasoned through the problem and come up with a solution guaranteed to preserve his self-respect as well as his self-esteem, Noah stepped behind the screen of living tropical plants that served as a shower curtain. He lathered down with a bar of soap that looked like a miniature pineapple, washed his hair with shampoo that smelled like coconut. Considering all that had happened in the last fourteen hours or so, he had to admit he was pretty pleased with himself.

Which didn't explain why his mind kept wandering. Or why every time it wandered, it wandered straight to Laurel. Or why, every time it did, he found himself turning down the water temperature.

HALF AN HOUR LATER, Noah was downstairs in search of coffee. And answers. What he found instead was an empty lobby. There was no fire dancing in the fireplace as there had been the night before, no tea on the buffet. He heard some off-key singing coming from the kitchen but he knew the voice didn't belong to Maisie, not unless her tastes included vintage Rolling Stones along with her *La Bohème*. He headed down the long hallway beside the front desk. The first door past the kitchen had a pink-feathered wreath hanging on it and a dainty needlepointed picture to the left of the door, one of a fleshy cherub with a naughty smile on his face. He knew he'd found what he was looking for.

"Good morning!" Maisie chirped in response to Noah's knock. He pushed open the door and found her looking as perky as the birds that darted around the patio outside her office. She was dressed in a pantsuit that perfectly matched the last of the summer's hot pink geraniums growing in pots around the patio door and she was bent over what looked to be a set of blueprints. When Noah walked in, she rolled up the blueprints, tied them with a red velvet ribbon and stashed them in the corner.

Maisie's smile was as bright as the sun that filtered through the lace curtains. "Sleep well?" she asked.

"Frankly, no." Noah didn't need to remind himself that he was fond of Maisie. He always had been. But as much he liked Laurel's grandmother, he couldn't afford to be hoodwinked by that sunny smile or the old-lady act. Not again.

He crossed his arms over his chest and pinned her with the kind of look that had been known to make even third-year medical students shake in their shoes. "You want to explain what this is all about?"

"This?" Maisie's eyes went wide, and her hand automatically went protectively to the blueprints. "I'm afraid I can't tell you. A woman has to have her secrets."

"That's not what I'm talking about, and you know it." Noah pushed off from the door and ventured into the room that was, in its own way, as bizarre as Almost Paradise. But instead of plants and tropical bird calls, Maisie's office was filled with cupids. There were glass cupids on the bookshelves directly across from Noah, silver cupids and porcelain cupids arranged on the windowsills. There was a candle cupid merrily burning and making the room smell like roses, a cupid carved out of wood that apparently doubled as objet d'art and doorstop and, on the table next to the brocade couch, another cupid that looked to be made of solid chocolate and had one wing bitten off.

The cupids shared table space with candles of all shapes and sizes, potpourri, bunches of brightly colored fresh flowers and more lace then Noah had ever seen at one time in one place. There was a thick Oriental rug on the floor and the kind of white-and-gold furniture he had always associated with fussy old ladies and the French bordellos he'd seen only in the movies. The walls were a color that reminded him of shrimp. The woodwork was gold, a color that was repeated in the picture frames, Maisie's desk accessories and her old-fashioned, ornate telephone.

Refusing to get distracted—again—Noah turned. "What I mean," he said, "is—"

"Coffee. Yes. Of course." Like a butterfly on speed, Maisie flittered to the front of her desk and headed through a doorway that apparently led to the kitchen. She was back in a minute carrying a thermal carafe decorated with bright red hearts. She handed the carafe to Noah and disappeared again. This time when she came back it was with a tray that contained a coffee cup that matched the carafe, along with a crystal sugar bowl and cream pitcher and a porcelain plate filled with what looked and smelled like freshly baked blueberry muffins. "One lump or two?" she asked, setting the tray on her desk and taking the carafe from Noah.

"We weren't discussing coffee."

"*We* weren't, no." Maisie filled his cup, adding one sugar and no cream, just the way he liked it. "But I was," she said, handing him the cup. "I'm the inn-keeper, and my guests' comfort is my utmost concern. Especially when the guest in question is such an old and dear friend. How did you like your little piece of paradise?"

It was on the tip of Noah's tongue to tell Maisie that

one man's paradise was another man's perdition. He didn't, but only because she was so sincere and so darned pink and fluffy, he didn't have the heart. He swallowed his words along with a sip of coffee.

"I know, I know." Maisie patted his arm. "It's a bit much at first, isn't it? I mean, all that beauty. It's enough to take your breath away, and I can understand why you're not thinking clearly. And then there's the temptation..." She sighed. "Overwhelming."

"Right." As soon as Noah set down his cup, Maisie filled it. "It's a great room, Maisie, but I—"

"That's a given, isn't it? Almost Paradise is...well..." Maisie giggled, and the sound reminded Noah of the bubbling water in the pond upstairs. "It's paradise!" She leaned forward as if sharing a secret. "It's my favorite room here at Cupid's Hideaway, though I don't let any of the guests who like the other rooms know that. They each have their own tastes, of course, and who's to say that one person's taste is better than another's? But, you see, when I mentioned beauty and temptation, I wasn't talking about the room."

Noah hadn't realized how hungry he was until he saw the muffins. He had one in his hand, and he stopped and glanced over his shoulder toward Maisie. "Not talking about the room? Then what—"

The answer struck with all the subtlety of a meteor crash landing, and suddenly a muffin didn't seem like such a good idea. He set the muffin on the plate and brushed his hands together, getting rid of the bits of sugar that had stuck to his fingers. He wished it was as easy to brush off the disturbing images of Laurel that Maisie's comments had conjured. Laurel's beauty was enough to take his breath away. And as for the temptation...

Noah braced himself against the memories and reminded himself that Maisie was the last one who needed to catch on to the fact that thinking about Laurel left him feeling as if he'd been plugged in to a two-twenty line. Correction. Maisie was the second last one who needed to know.

Noah was determined to keep to the subject he'd come to discuss in the first place. "Look," he said, "why you decided to lie to me about Laurel being on the island is your business."

"Lie?" As if he'd spoken in another language, Maisie peered at Noah, her eyes narrowed. "I'd never do such a thing. I said she was—"

"On a cruise."

Maisie clicked her tongue. "Not precisely, dear. I said she was cruising. Two entirely different things." Looking more than ever like the bunny in the battery commercial, Maisie scooted to the other side of her desk, going in her own direction in spite of how Noah tried to keep the conversation on track. "And wasn't it a nice surprise to see her again?"

Noah set down his coffee cup a little faster than he realized. Coffee splashed over the side and onto the silver tray, and he wiped it up with the napkin that had been left next to the plate of muffins. "It was a surprise, all right."

"And I do so like surprises!" On the other side of the room, Maisie bustled around, opening cabinets and closing them again. By the time she was finished, she had a linen cloth in one hand and a basket with a handle in the other. She put the cloth into the basket and piled the muffins into it. "And Laurel likes surprises, too." Smiling, she held out the basket to Noah. "Which is why she'll be so pleased when you show up at the clinic with breakfast."

"Oh, no!" Noah stepped away from the basket of muffins, the twinkle in Maisie's eyes and her ridiculous suggestion. "I'm not here to renew old acquaintances," he reminded her. "You know that. I told you that when you called yesterday." He glanced at his watch. "It's almost ten, and the way I figure it, there's got to be a ferry over to the mainland soon. I'm going to be on it."

"Yes, yes. Of course you are. I can understand that. It's just that..." Maisie chewed the shocking pink lipstick off her lower lip. "Well, I hoped you'd take these muffins to Laurel. She doesn't always remember to eat—"

"Laurel's dietary habits are none of my business."

"—and she doesn't always keep sensible hours—"

"Neither are her work habits."

"—and she did mention that she hoped she'd see you again before you left."

"She did?" The simple statement caught Noah completely off guard and started a kind of buzzing in his bloodstream. He knew why. It was all the fault of Almost Paradise. He knew that for a fact. If it wasn't for the wacky room with its heady, earthy scent, its winding paths and the plants that were where plants weren't supposed to be, he and Laurel never would have ended up tumbling onto the bed together. And Maisie's announcement wouldn't have left him feeling so weak-kneed.

But they had tumbled on the bed together, and in those few, electrifying moments Noah wondered if Laurel was just as interested and just as aroused as he was. Looked like he just might have the opportunity to find out.

Noah sucked in a sharp breath, fighting to control the mixture of white-hot heat and frosty-as-ice disbelief that collided inside him like a cold front moving across the Texas panhandle in the dog days of August. The results were the same. A tornado that stirred his blood and turned what had been a well-ordered world on its head.

He took a minute, letting the thought settle and getting used to the feel of it. Not exactly easy when he considered that he'd spent the last four years learning to live with the idea of never seeing Laurel again.

Not that he thought there was any future in it. For either one of them. He knew some wounds were too deep to heal. Some hearts could never be resuscitated. No matter how skilled the doctor.

It was a fact. And facts were impossible to dispute. Which explained why Noah found the whole thing so impossible to believe. It didn't explain why the next thing he knew, he had the basket of muffins in his hand and was headed out to find Laurel.

"I WISH I could help, Laurel. Honest. But…"

Gilly Wilson's face was an unbecoming shade of green. Understandable considering that Gilly was not only six months pregnant, but had the flu, as well. The fact that she'd had the energy to pack her husband's lunch before he left the island for his job on the mainland that morning and get her three-year-old to day care on time impressed the heck out of Laurel. In spite of everything, Gilly had also managed to get her five-year-old twins to the clinic for their annual checkups. No doubt about it, Gilly was a candidate for Mother of the Year. At least in Laurel's opinion.

Which was the only reason—besides the fact that Gilly just happened to be her best friend—Laurel didn't beg, plead and offer Gilly bribes not to leave the room while she examined the boys known around town as the Wild Wilsons.

"It's the shots," Gilly said, her voice breathy even at the mention of the word. "I just can't stand the thought. And if I watch..." She fanned her face with one hand. "I'm afraid I don't know what might happen."

"I do." One arm around Gilly's shoulders, Laurel led her to the door. "And I don't need pregnant women fainting in my examination room. I'll tell you what." She opened the door and escorted Gilly into the waiting area, glancing at little Max and his partner in crime, Alex, with a look she hoped told them to stay put and behave. "I'll do the boys' checkups and I'll bring them home. How does that sound?"

"I couldn't let you." Gilly's protest didn't sound very convincing, which was fine with Laurel. She wasn't about to be convinced.

"Sure you can. It's no big deal. This won't take long, and they'll be home in plenty of time to get to school this afternoon. Besides, I don't have any other appointments this morning. I even sent Carole home." She glanced at the empty desk where her receptionist usually worked. "Tom's getting their boat out of the water, and I could tell she would rather be helping than sitting here waiting for the phone to ring."

Gilly looked toward the examination room where the boys were busy seeing which of them could scream the loudest. "They're a handful," she said, as if Laurel didn't already know that.

"Even a handful of trouble sounds like a pretty good idea this morning," Laurel admitted. When Gilly looked at her in wonder, Laurel smiled. "Not today."

She opened the door that led outside. "You're too sick, and I'm not in the mood. I'll explain everything when we're both feeling better."

"You're sure? About them?" Gilly glanced toward the exam room, then at the door and the freedom—however fleeting—that waited just beyond, and though she wasn't sure, Laurel knew she couldn't deny her friend a couple minutes of peace and quiet.

"I'm sure," she said. She ushered Gilly out, closed the door and turned to the examination room.

Any other day the very thought of being left alone with Max and Alex Wilson would have been enough to make Laurel as green as poor Gilly. But this morning was different. This morning, she needed something to distract her. Something to keep her mind on medicine. And off a certain medical practitioner.

But as she headed to the exam room, something told her even going a couple rounds with the Wild Wilsons might not be enough to banish the memories that had been careening through her head all morning. Or quiet the voices that had kept her awake all night. The ones that reminded her over and over that the best thing she could do for her sanity and her well-being was to forget last night ever happened. The same ones that told her she was a fool because she knew she never could.

Max and Alex were exactly what she needed.

Laurel pulled back her shoulders and pasted a smile on her face. When she heard a crash from the exam room, the smile didn't last.

Lucky for the Wild Wilsons, no one got hurt and nothing got broken when they decided to see how fast they could push the low-wheeled stool Laurel used for rolling around the exam room into the wall. Rather than being intimidated by the crash or the fact that Laurel came running, the boys were delighted by the noise and the attention. They shouted and laughed, and as soon as she was inside the door, Laurel picked up the culprit who had obviously pushed the stool and set him on the exam table next to his brother.

She stepped back. "Okay," she said. "Who's first?"

The question was enough to get their attention. Max looked at Alex, Alex looked at Max, and as if they had choreographed the moment, they both burst into tears.

Laurel wasn't sure how she got through the next half hour. She quieted the boys enough to start their examinations. But when she examined Max, Alex climbed on the desk and tried to take the pictures off the wall. While she examined Alex, Max nearly fell headfirst into the tall swivel-top trash can. By the time she was ready to give the boys their shots, the neat braid she'd managed to wind into her hair earlier that morning wasn't so neat anymore, and she was breathing as hard as if she'd run a marathon.

"All right, you two." Laurel pushed a curl out of her eyes and turned to get the shots. "We're almost done. Then I'll take you home."

"Don't wanna go home." Max folded his arms across his chest and scowled at her.

"Don't wanna go home." Alex echoed the words and the gesture of defiance.

"But you have to." She drew up the shots and turned to her patients. "Because I have to work and—"

One look at the syringe was all the boys needed. Alex was the less rambunctious of the two. All he did was scream his head off. Max was the bold one. He jumped off the examination table and headed out the door.

"Oh, no, you don't!" Laurel ran after him. Which would have been a whole bunch easier if she didn't have to keep an eye on Alex at the same time. Hot on Max's trail, she darted into the waiting area. She almost had him when he dumped the magazine rack on the floor in front of her. Max got to the door and pulled it open just as Laurel's foot hit the slick paper. She did a belly flop and skidded toward the door. She made a wild grab and caught nothing but thin air at the same time her nose slammed into a leg clad in navy-blue cashmere.

"Well, well. What do we have here?"

Her lips pursed, Laurel blew a strand of hair out of her eyes and looked up just in time to find Noah grinning at her. "Hello, Dr. Burton. Looks like you could use some help."

Chapter Five

Help was not what Laurel needed. What Laurel needed was a hole to crawl into. A deep one.

Holding on to what little was left of her pride, she propped herself on her elbows. "Max," she said, tipping her head toward the little redhead who was even now trying his best to squirm away from the hold Noah had on his shoulders. The crashing sound of medical instruments hitting the floor came from the exam room and made Laurel groan. "That's his twin," she said, glancing toward the room. "Alex."

"Twins. That explains it." Noah crouched down, eye-to-eye with Max. "Go see what that brother of yours is up to, will you? Sounds like he needs some help."

"Sure," Max agreed and with a look as angelic as it had been devilish only moments before, he headed to the examination room.

Noah watched him go, then stuck out a hand to help Laurel up. She had just reached to wind her fingers through his when he said, "You know, you really need to keep control of your patients."

Laurel pulled back her hand. She glared at Noah at the same time she braced herself against the three-year-old copy of *National Geographic* lying on the floor next to her.

"You're asking for an accident." Noah slipped the magazine from under her. "It will slide, and you'll—"

If Noah heard the word she grumbled from between her gritted teeth, he didn't show it. Still spouting what sounded like a public service announcement about office safety and a doctor's responsibility toward his—or her—patients, he stepped back and watched her maneuver so she was sitting on the floor. Not exactly easy considering she was biting her tongue at the same time. Too early in the morning for a fight with Noah, she reminded herself. Too early in the morning to get sucked into the kind of one-upmanship that had them competing against each other from day one. Too early for Noah, now that she thought about it. Too early and—

"What are you doing here, anyway?" Laurel asked.

Was it her imagination, or did something spark in Noah's eyes? She dismissed the reaction as a trick of the light, and because she supposed she looked less than professional sitting on the floor in the middle of her own waiting room, she pulled herself to her feet. Her gaze went to the basket in Noah's hands. "Don't tell me, let me guess. Maisie sent you."

"Maisie sent muffins." Looking as much of an enticer as the snake who decorated the threshold of Almost Paradise, Noah held the basket out and nudged back the cloth. Before Laurel had a chance to register how delicious the muffins smelled or how she hadn't eaten any breakfast because she hadn't slept a wink and had an extra-hard time getting herself together that morning, the sounds of a brother-on-brother scuffle erupted from the examining room. She raced that way, too worried about the Wild Wilsons to care that Noah was right beside her.

"What are you trying to do?" he asked, and as had happened so many times before when they worked together, she didn't need him to elaborate.

"DTP," she said, "and polio injections. They don't think it's a very good idea."

"Their mother should be here."

Laurel didn't explain. She didn't have time, and besides, it was none of Noah's business. She headed into the exam room, scooped Alex in her arms just in time to keep him from punching his brother in the nose and sat with him on her lap. Across the room, Noah did the same thing with Max.

"So what's up, guys?" Noah asked the boys, and damn him, but he didn't look winded or flustered or nearly as upended as Laurel felt. Aside from the fact that the right leg of Noah's navy suit pants looked like it had been thoroughly soaked, dried over the back of a chair and not pressed, Noah looked as together and as in control this morning as he had the night before. His hair was perfectly combed—thanks to the comb Laurel had given him from the Love Shack—his smile was as bright as the sun outside the clinic windows—thanks to the toothbrush and toothpaste Laurel had given him from the Love Shack—and there was a gleam in his eyes—no thanks, she sincerely hoped, to the kiss Laurel had given him in the Love Shack.

He was wearing the same shirt he'd worn the night before, but he made even that look more like a calculated move than a fashion faux pas. He had rolled the sleeves above his elbows, gotten rid of the expensive tie and undone the button at his throat. Informal chic. Country comfort. Business casual, as only a man with

Noah's innate sense of style could pull off business casual.

Laurel fingered the braid that was in even worse shape after the spill she took in the waiting room. She glanced at her lab coat, less than pristine thanks to her skid across the floor. As if all that wasn't bad enough, the Wild Wilsons were taking to Noah like Yogi Bear going after the biggest picnic basket in Jellystone Park.

The twins gazed at Noah with nothing short of hero-worship. They laughed at every joke he told them, even though most of them were lame. They answered every question he asked about school. They told him what kind of pizza they liked best.

On Noah's part, it was textbook-perfect bedside manner. The same textbook, as far as Laurel could remember, that didn't bother to mention infamous five-year-olds with a sparkle in their eyes and mayhem in their hearts, or mothers with morning sickness.

When Noah finally slid Max off his lap and onto the examining table and told him to stay put, Max listened. Alex fidgeted off Laurel's lap and jumped up next to his brother.

All of which should have made Laurel feel better. All of which might have made her feel better if she wasn't so busy feeling as if her clinic had been snatched out from under her nose.

Even while Laurel was considering what was happening and all that it meant, Noah was up and rummaging through her equipment. "Okay, who's the bravest?" he asked. Max looked from the syringes Noah was holding to Alex. Alex looked from the syringes Noah was holding to Max. Laurel braced herself, ready for the screams.

"I am," Max shouted.

"I am," Alex chimed in.

And before Laurel could even get out of her chair to help, Noah had given both boys their injections and helped them off the table.

"Easy as pie," he told Laurel, watching the boys head to the waiting room. "You might want to consider—"

"You might want to consider not walking into my clinic and acting like you own the place."

Okay, so she was overreacting. So she was taking things a little too personally. The way Laurel figured it, she had the right. It was her clinic. At least last time she looked, it was her clinic. And that was something very personal.

She grabbed a prescription pad on the table near her right hand. "Ross-Burton Clinic. See that?" She pointed to the name across the top of the pad. "You're not Ross, pal, and I think I can say with some authority that you're sure not Burton. What makes you think you can—"

"Oh, come on, Laurel." Noah shook his head, honestly amazed. "You ought to be thanking me."

"Really?" She held on to her anger. But just barely. "Thank you," she said, and she didn't even try to control the acid in her voice. "Thank you for showing up out of nowhere and acting like you own my clinic."

"I could have owned your clinic."

The comment was below the belt, even for Noah. Rather than telling him so and risking having her temper snap along with her composure, Laurel slapped the prescription pad on the table and headed out to see what the Wild Wilsons were up to. Better to find them swinging from the swag light over Carole's desk than to stand

there and be reminded of the one thing she'd been trying to forget for four years.

In those times when she indulged in self-analysis and
managed to do it without getting her once-upon-a-time
feelings for Noah all tangled up in the sticky web of
her psyche, Laurel had come to grips with the fact that
it took more than one incident to blow a relationship to
smithereens. It was a cumulative kind of thing. First the
little things, then the big ones. Then the Big One. The
straw that broke the camel's back. The match in the
powder barrel.

. In her case, that was the Ross-Burton Clinic.

Marching through the wood-paneled hallway toward
the waiting area, Laurel nearly laughed. The clinic had
two less-than-state-of-the-art examination rooms, a
storeroom filled nearly top to bottom with the collection
of toy trains Doc Ross swore he'd move to his house
one of these days, a linoleum-floored waiting area complete with the requisite outdated magazines and a cli-
entele limited to the couple hundred permanent island
residents and the tourists who came and went, mostly
on summer weekends. With limited facilities and a staff
that consisted only of Carole and Maureen, an RN who
had a summerhouse on the island and who helped out
in rare busy times, Laurel wasn't equipped to handle
really serious medical conditions. Those went to the
mainland, more often than not by airplane. At the clinic,
she concentrated on the kind of medicine that was often
lacking in places far from a major metropolitan area.
She sewed up cuts and she bandaged sprains. She took
care of the occasional broken bone and gave talks to
health classes at the local elementary school. She gave
yearly physicals, kept an eye on chronic conditions,
made sure her elderly patients took their medicine and

ate right, and talked to her younger patients about the dangers of smoking.

Not exactly the stuff dramatic, end-of-the-love-affair combat was made out of.

Enough to tear Laurel and Noah apart.

Laurel pushed the thought aside. Not the time, not the place, she reminded herself. It was too depressing to add that it would never be the time or the place, not as long as Noah was anywhere within a three-thousand-mile radius.

Because the clinic wasn't any more large than it was prestigious, Laurel got to the waiting area in no time. She found Max and Alex sitting at the kid-size table she kept for her pediatric patients. They had their heads together, busy examining something Max had taken out of the pocket of his pint-size denim shorts. They were as happy as clams. And more well-behaved than she'd ever seen them.

If she wasn't so amazed and so busy wondering what Noah had put in their shots, and how they could bottle it and become billionaires, she might have noticed him come up behind her.

He touched her elbow, and Laurel jumped. "That was out of line. I shouldn't have mentioned it."

She raised her chin. "You did mention it."

She heard Noah let go a sigh of impatience. She didn't bother to turn and look at him. She didn't need to see his expression. She remembered how often he'd been able to detour her with a look, how many times he'd been able to make her worries or her anger evaporate with something as simple as one of the smiles that crinkled around his eyes and tugged at the tiny scar at the right corner of his mouth, the one he'd gotten when he fell out of a tree he was climbing when he was ten.

She wasn't in the mood to be conciliatory. Not when he'd barged in and made her look like an intern in her own clinic. Not after lying awake all night, wondering what might have happened if he hadn't been so quick to give up when they landed on the bed together the night before. If she hadn't gotten as far away as she could—as fast as she could—from the fabric fig leaf and the sultry atmosphere of Almost Paradise and from the way being that close to Noah reignited about a thousand different fantasies she thought she'd been strong enough and smart enough to quash a long time before.

"I'm leaving this morning."

Laurel couldn't help but think he was fishing for a reaction she couldn't give him. She glanced over her shoulder only long enough to let him know it. "Would *yippee* be an appropriate response?"

"I just thought…" Noah shrugged. "I just wanted to say goodbye."

Laurel turned to face him. "Why? You didn't bother to say goodbye last time."

Noah's jaw tensed. "You never gave me a chance to say goodbye last time. By the time I got home—"

"By the time you got home, you had made up your mind. You weren't going to listen so why did I want to stay around to talk?"

"So maybe that means—"

"Dr. Noah?" Max interrupted whatever it was Noah was going to say, tugging at his pant leg. "Dr. Noah, look what I found on the way over here. Wanna see?" He held something up, and automatically Noah reached for it.

Just as quickly, he winced, and his mouth dropped open. "Ouch!"

Laurel looked at Noah's hand. The thing Max handed

him was a small, sharp piece of metal, rusted around the edges. At least Laurel thought it was rusted. It was hard to tell with Noah's blood all over it.

"They're lucky they didn't cut their fingers off." Laurel looked at the Wild Wilsons who, sensing something was wrong, immediately retreated and circled the wagons. They scurried to the door, hanging on to each other's hands. "It's okay, guys." Laurel gave them a smile she hoped looked chipper enough to calm the panic she saw rising in their expressions. "Dr. Noah cut his hand. That's all."

"That's all?" Noah gazed at the blood pooling in his palm. His face looked a little pale, but Laurel had to give him credit. Rather than frighten the boys or make them feel as if they'd done something terrible, he cupped his hand so they couldn't see the blood. "What do you mean, that's all?" he asked Laurel. "Easy for you to say. This isn't your blood—"

"Blood!" Max wailed.

"Blood!" Alex echoed.

And Laurel knew she had to get them out of there fast.

"Come on, boys." She grabbed their hands and headed out the door. "Dr. Noah's going to be just fine. But he needs to get into exam room number one." She tipped her head, showing him which door. "There's a supply cabinet in there, and he'll find everything he needs to take care of his hand. He needs to irrigate the wound with normal saline. Then when Dr. Laurel gets back, she can take a look at the cut."

"Dr. Laurel doesn't need to take a look at the cut. Dr. Noah is a doctor, too. Dr. Noah knows he has to irrigate the wound with normal saline," Noah protested. Of course, Noah protested. But even before she nudged

open the door and stood with her back to it so Max and
Alex could head outside, Laurel knew he wouldn't let
his pride get in the way of his common sense. At least
not this time. He was already headed toward the exam
room. As the door swung shut behind her, Laurel heard
the sounds of him rummaging through the supply cabinet.

It didn't take more than a couple minutes to get the
boys home. On the way, Laurel gave them a matter-of-
fact lecture about picking up rusty or sharp objects, and
once she got there, she gave Gilly a quick version of
the story, just so there were no surprises if the boys
started talking about blood. She left out most of the
details, especially the one about the patient—the one
who'd cut himself—being Noah. No use having Gilly
ask a million questions. Especially when Laurel didn't
feel like answering them. Especially when Laurel didn't
know the answers.

By the time Laurel walked across the waterfront park
in the center of downtown and got to the clinic, Noah
had the cut cleaned. He was dabbing at it with a sterile
four-by-four. Watching him, she paused in the doorway
of the exam room. "Think you'll live?" she asked.

Noah didn't bother to look up. He gave the cut one
last wipe. "Pretty sure," he said. "Though it was touch
and go for a while. Did you tell the boys—"

"About the dangers of sharp, rusty objects? You
bet." She strolled into the room and stood behind Noah.
He had rolled the wheeled stool close to the examining
table, and he had his hand propped on the table. The
light was good there, and in it, Laurel got a better look
at the damage caused by the piece of metal.

"Lateral anterior aspect, just below the fifth phalange
on the right hand," she mumbled. She looked at Noah's

palm under his little finger. The wound wasn't bad enough to need suturing, but it did look deep.

"I'll need to approximate the wound edges and hold them in place." Laurel reached toward the cabinet behind her and pulled out the supplies she needed to accomplish the task. "You'll want to keep from bumping it, too, so we'd better bandage it. Cushion it, you know?"

"I know." Noah held out his left hand for the supplies, and automatically, Laurel found herself clutching everything close to her chest.

"My clinic, my Steri-Strips," she told him.

"Oh, come on, Laurel." With a long-suffering sigh, Noah stood and nudged the stool out of the way with one foot. He winced a little when he put his hand down. "I know what I'm doing. I can bandage a cut. "

"What, now you're not just perfect, you're left-handed, too?" The comment was ill-timed. Not only was it unfair to pick on a guy who only a short while before had been bleeding all over her waiting room, it was a little too close to the truth for Laurel's comfort.

Of course Noah knew how to bandage a cut. Noah knew how to do everything. Noah did everything better than anyone else.

She'd been thinking medicine. At least that's what Laurel thought she'd been thinking. But thinking about the way Noah did things better than anyone else naturally made her think of *all* the things he did better than anyone else. And a whole bunch of those things had nothing whatsoever to do with medicine.

Unless the medicine in question was the kind that warmed her heart at the same time it sent the rest of her into nuclear meltdown.

Not a good thought. Not with Noah standing less than

two feet away. Not when suddenly Laurel's heart was pounding so hard she swore he could see the Steri-Strips and stack of four-by-fours jumping where she had them clasped to her chest.

Maybe he did. Or maybe he was just a mind reader. Noah's eyes lit. "You think I'm perfect?"

The comment and the cocky smile that went along with it were enough to shake Laurel back to reality. She dumped the supplies onto the exam table. "Perfectly annoying."

"But perfect. You think I'm perfect at being annoying, right? Which means that technically, you do admit I'm perfect at something."

"You're perfect at a lot of things." There was no use beating around the bush. They both knew it was true. "But one of them," she said, glancing to where he was cradling his right hand in his left, "isn't bandaging a wound with your left hand. Besides..." She reached for the Steri-Strips. "It's my fault and I feel responsible. I should have kept a better eye on the Wild Wilsons. I owe you."

Noah hesitated, and for one second, Laurel wished he'd snatch everything out of her hands and take care of the wound himself. Not the best course of treatment, medically speaking, but at least then she wouldn't have to worry about what was going to happen when she touched him.

No such luck. He gave her a one-shoulder shrug along with a tiny smile that told her he knew exactly what she was thinking. "All right." He held out his hand. "I'm all yours, Doc."

She'd won. At least this round. Funny, Laurel always supposed besting Noah at anything would feel better than this. Setting the thought aside, she caught one leg of the stool with the toe of her sneaker and slid it closer. She was already sitting down and had gently laid Noah's hand on the exam table in front of her by the time she realized she was eye level with his belt buckle. Not the best vantage point, considering she was trying to keep her mind on medicine.

Reminding herself not to forget it, she turned her attention to bandaging his hand, a procedure that should have been nothing more than routine. A procedure that would have been nothing more than routine if not for the fact that the second she touched him, she felt Noah tense. In the great scheme of things, Laurel should have been thrilled to realize she wasn't the only one who was disconcerted by the feel of flesh against flesh. It meant Noah didn't have nearly the power over her he thought. But what should have been a clear-cut victory was hardly that simple.

When she smoothed her fingers over his to straighten his hand, he flinched, and Laurel felt the tiny jolt down to her toes. When she dabbed at the last of the blood on his hand, the muscles in his arm bunched, and she caught herself holding her breath.

Anxious to get the procedure over and done with and get some relief from the heat that was somehow penetrating every inch of her body, Laurel carefully closed the edges of the wound and held them in place with the Steri-Strips. She cushioned the whole thing with four-by-fours and wrapped it carefully.

It wasn't until she was done that she realized Noah hadn't spoken a word throughout the entire procedure.

She glanced up and found him looking down, but not at his hand. At her. He looked a little chalky, and instinctively Laurel knew it had nothing to do with his injury. When it came to the blood-and-gore parts of medicine, Noah was as tough as any. Which didn't explain why he looked like someone had whacked him on the head with a ton of bricks.

Then again, it didn't explain why Laurel was feeling the same way.

"So…" She sucked in a long breath and let it out slowly, fighting to calm the sudden, wild tempo of her heartbeat. "Does it hurt?"

"Not anymore." Laurel's hand was on the table next to his, and Noah closed his fingers over hers. "Did you do some kind of mumbo-jumbo painkilling spell over my hand while you were bandaging it? Or are you just very good?"

"I did some kind of mumbo-jumbo painkilling spell." Laurel didn't move her hand away from his. She didn't get flustered, either. She knew that was exactly what he wanted. Instead, she stood and looked him in the eye. "And I'm very good."

"I know." He didn't smile, and he didn't say if he was talking about medicine. Or something else. "Which is why I was happy to hear it when Maisie said that you didn't want me to leave until you had a chance to say goodbye."

The comment was like cold water on the heat inside Laurel, and just like cold water colliding with heat, it left her steaming.

"Maisie?" She was careful to school her anger. It wasn't easy. First she needed to decide who deserved the brunt of her wrath—her grandmother for cooking up another one of her off-the-wall romantic fantasies, or Noah for being egotistical enough to believe it. "Maisie told you…"

"How you wanted to see me before I got on the ferry. Sure." Noah looked so matter-of-fact about the whole thing, Laurel nearly laughed. She might have laughed if she wasn't so busy being totally irritated. Of course, Noah never noticed. Noah never noticed anything Noah didn't want to notice.

He shuffled a couple steps closer and lowered his voice. "If I knew you were that anxious to see me again, I would have stopped by sooner."

"Lucky me." Laurel gave him a big, toothy smile at the same time she backed away from the magnetic field that hummed around him. Out of the range of danger. Away from the force of the gravitational pull that was Noah Cunningham. "You are without a doubt the single most conceited human being I have ever met."

"Conceited?" As if he'd never heard the word before—or at least as if he'd never associated it with himself—Noah crinkled his nose and looked at her in wonder. "You think I'm conceited because…"

"Because Maisie dangled that little morsel in front of you and you jumped at it like a trout to a well-tied fly."

"So you're telling me you didn't want to see me before I left?"

"I didn't want to see you before you got here. I didn't want to see you while you stayed. No, I didn't want to see you before you left."

"I don't believe you."

Laurel threw up her hands in exasperation. "Of course you don't believe me. You don't want to believe me. Don't you get it, Noah?" She whirled and stalked to the supply cabinet that took up the far wall of the room. Whether Noah realized it or not, they weren't done with his treatment. She opened the top drawer of the cabinet, looking for what she needed. When she found it, she set it down within easy reach before she whirled the other way and leaned against the cabinet, her arms crossed over her chest. "You can't just walk back into my life and expect things to be the way they were four years ago. The world doesn't work that way."

"Who said I wanted it to?" He closed the distance between them. "Did I say I wanted it to? Or did I just assume, since Maisie said you wanted to see me—"

"That I was ready, willing and able to throw myself at you."

His eyebrows slid up along with his smile. "Aren't you?"

Of course she wasn't.

The words were there, right at the tip of Laurel's tongue. She was certain they were true. Yet for some reason she couldn't fathom, she couldn't get them out of her mouth.

Of course, she wasn't ready to set aside four years of heartache. Of course, she wasn't willing to forget that Noah had chosen a hot job offer over marriage, a home here on the island and a partnership in the clinic.

Of course, she wasn't about to let him know that.

Laurel decided it was time to fight fire with fire. In Noah's case, the fire was mighty hot. But then, the way she remembered it, he'd always told her she could be plenty hot herself.

Trying not to forget it, she propped her hands on either side of the cabinet behind her and leaned forward just a little. She lowered her voice to a seductive purr.

"There's only one thing I have to say to you, Noah Cunningham," she told him.

Noah grinned. "What's that?"

"Pull down your pants."

Chapter Six

In his wildest dreams, Noah had never imagined things would progress this far, this fast.

And he'd had some pretty wild dreams.

As surprised as he was intrigued, as intrigued as he was suddenly and fully aroused, he found himself staring at Laurel. He imagined that her lab coat had been crisp and clean when she shrugged into it earlier that morning. Not anymore, and he could understand why. Going a couple rounds with the Wilson twins was enough to take the starch out of anyone. The coat was pulled to one side so it hung higher on her left than on her right. There was a glob of something sticky across the front, a smudge of dirt on one sleeve.

Beneath it, she was wearing a dark green, long-sleeved T-shirt, one that hadn't survived the onslaught any better. Once, the shirt had been tucked into her khakis. Now it was pulled out of the waistband, tugged up on one side to reveal a strip of skin.

There was nothing Noah wanted more than to reach out and run one finger across that little bit of bare skin, to feel the heat that rose off Laurel's body the way the scent of something herbal rose from her hair and perfumed the air around her. His body urged him to go for it, to give in and give himself up to the desire pulsating through every inch of him. His body told him to take advantage of the situation—quick—before she came to her senses. Before she changed her mind. His body voted fast and furious.

His common sense warned that if he listened, he might ruin what could turn out to be a very good thing.

For a couple seconds, it was touch and go.

His common sense won. Not because he didn't want to satisfy the craving that made him ache from needing her but because he knew they'd both have a better time if they took this slow.

Wondering if he had the strength and the stamina to keep his good intentions, Noah forced his gaze up. He skimmed it over Laurel's breasts and neck. Though she had recovered as much as it was possible to recover from the effects of twin tornadoes, Laurel's cheeks were still flushed, her breathing was fast, and her lips were parted.

Which, now that he thought about it, might have had a whole lot more to do with Noah than it did with Max and Alex.

The thought was enough to kick up his fantasies a notch. Smiling at the thought, he glanced at the riotous disarray that had apparently once been a braid in Laurel's hair. There was a single curl hanging like an upside-down question mark over her right ear, and as eager to discharge some of the electricity that had built inside him as he was to touch her, he brushed it back with his left hand.

Laurel's eyes widened at the contact, but she didn't move. She didn't flinch. It was clear she'd been expecting this reaction from him, clear she knew exactly what she was getting into the second she issued her invitation, and just knowing that excited him more than ever. So did the tiny flicker of light in Laurel's eyes, the one that came and went like summer lightning as she watched him carefully.

If this was one of his wildest dreams, Noah knew exactly what would happen next. There would be that one, pristine moment of awareness, that one second when their gazes locked and their minds clicked, when who they were and what had happened to them four long years before didn't matter nearly as much as what they wanted right here and now. There would be that first tentative touch, the one he'd skim along the path the sunlight splayed across the pocket of her lab coat. And when he nudged the coat aside to trail his fingers over her breasts, Laurel would shiver with the same anticipation that pumped through him.

Just like he had so many times in so many of his wildest dreams, he imagined the way he'd kiss her and the way she'd respond. Eager. Urgent. Reckless. In the wildest dreams he'd been having since the day Laurel walked out of his life, he knew he'd be feeling all the same things. But in his wildest dreams, he never thought it would all happen in the exam room of the Ross-Burton Clinic.

The thought brought Noah up short, and he pulled in a sharp breath that made him hurtle back to reality. "You kind of caught me off guard," he admitted. As if he had to tell her. As if he hadn't been gaping at her as if she'd just confessed to an Elvis sighting. "You want to repeat those orders, Doc? And you'd better say it slow because I think my hearing might be a little off. I could have sworn you said—"

"Pants off. I said, pants off." Laurel allowed herself the smallest of smiles.

"You're the doctor." Noah couldn't help himself—he had to smile, too. He shuffled a step closer at the same time he automatically reached for his belt buckle with his right hand. Pain shot through his hand, and he winced. He'd been so wrapped up in the sensations pounding through his body, he'd forgotten about Mad Max and his deadly piece of metal.

He glanced from the bandage on his hand to Laurel and gave her a meaningful look. "Still a little sensitive," he said, holding up his hand. "You want to do the honors?"

"I don't think so." She shook her head and sidestepped around him. How she made herself sound so matter-of-fact when Noah could barely breathe from wanting her was a mystery to him. "You want to go over to the exam table?" she asked.

"The exam table?" Noah glanced that way. It didn't look comfortable and it wasn't nearly big enough for everything he had in mind, but he supposed they could make do if they had to. The way he remembered it, he and Laurel had made good use of a lot less accommodating places. Grappling with his belt buckle with a left hand that wasn't used to doing the brunt of the chores, he glanced over his shoulder. "You want to shut the door?"

"I don't think we need to." Laurel dismissed the suggestion with a shake of her head that loosened the strand of hair he'd just brushed back. "I don't have any other appointments scheduled this morning, and it's not a busy time. We won't get interrupted."

"Good thing." Noah smiled. "I'd like to take my time."

"You would?" She cocked her head, thinking it

over. "I thought you'd want to get it over with as fast as you could."

"Oh, come on!" Noah laughed. How could he not? He was feeling as if he'd just mainlined a lifetime's worth of high-test exhilaration. His skin tingled, and his blood rushed in his ears. Impatient to touch Laurel, even if it was only with his left hand, eager to feel her touching him, anxious to fulfill four years of fantasy, he undid his belt. He drew it out of the belt loops and tossed it on the chair in front of the desk across the room. He unbuttoned his pants. "You might be able to accuse me of a lot of things, but getting it over as fast as I could was never one of them."

"Okay." She shrugged, obliging. "If that's the way you want it." She looked him over carefully and, seemingly satisfied with what she saw, she said, "Now turn around. And drop the pants."

"Turn around?" The directive struck Noah as a little odd, but he wasn't about to argue. From the no-nonsense look on her face, it was clear that Laurel wanted to be in control, and if that's what made her happy, he was a good enough sport to give whatever she had in mind a try. With a good-natured shrug, he did as he was told, turning toward the exam table at the same time he unzipped. He let his slacks fall around his ankles.

"Your right hand still hurts, I'm sure." Laurel came up behind him. "So let's use the left side. Pull your boxers down over your left hip, please."

"But what about—"

What about at least a kiss? That's what Noah wanted to ask. *What about gliding my hands under that green T-shirt of yours? What about taking you into my arms*

*and holding you close so that I can feel the heat of your
body and remember the way your hips fit against mine?*

Sure, he'd decided to let Laurel take control, but
Noah wasn't sure how long he'd be able to keep the
promise to himself. She was going to miss out on an
awful lot of good stuff if she wanted to do this fast and
furiously.

Noah's heart beat double-time. Then again, fast and
furiously didn't sound like such a bad idea. He grabbed
the elastic waistband on his boxers and pulled them
down.

For a couple seconds, all Laurel could do was stare.
Silly. She knew that for a fact. Silly to stand there with
her mouth open and her eyes wide and her heart slam-
ming so hard against her ribs it felt like it would crack
right through them. It wasn't like she'd never seen a
guy's bare rear end before. Heck, it wasn't even like
she'd never seen *this* guy's bare rear end before.

Knowing that was one thing. Keeping it from turning
her upside down and inside out was something else.

Something that inched through Laurel like warm
honey and filled the places inside her that had been
empty for four long years. Places she hadn't even
known existed until right then and there. That same
something started a buzzing in her brain and a humming
in her bloodstream, a noisy chorus of what-had-beens
and could-have-beens that drowned out the voice of her
common sense.

For one split second, she considered reaching out and
touching him. She thought about cupping her hands
around his behind, about stroking his skin and enjoying
the feel and texture of his bare hips. For one split second, she nearly gave in to the deafening chorus that told
her it wasn't just a good idea, it was a great idea. A

once-in-a-lifetime opportunity that, lucky her, had come around twice.

She might have done it if she wasn't convinced Noah was so hot, she'd get burned.

In the tiny portion of her brain that was still functioning—the part that hadn't been overpowered by out-and-out lust—Laurel supposed she should be two-stepping her way through a victory dance. She wanted to get even with Noah for the way he'd barged into her clinic and taken over? She wanted to show him who was boss?

She'd done that, all right. Done it in spades. The only proof she needed was Noah's reaction. The good doctor might be thinking, but it sure wasn't with his head.

Laurel's cheeks flushed with heat and her insides caught fire. She never imagined that getting even with Noah would mean putting herself at risk, and right about then, the risk was very real. If she wasn't careful, she'd find herself giving in to the fantasies that whispered sweet nothings in her ears. And once she let them start whispering, it wouldn't be long before they were shouting. And once they were shouting, they'd join that chorus, too, the one that told her to throw caution to the wind and herself into Noah's arms.

Not smart. Not smart at all.

Laurel held on tight to the thought. As tight as she held on to what was left of her common sense, her pride and the beyond-a-doubt awareness that if she let Noah into her heart again, she'd wake up one morning and find it had been shredded into a billion tiny pieces. Again. Her mind made up, even if the rest of her didn't agree that it was such a good idea, she reached over to the supply cabinet.

By that time, Noah was tired of waiting, and Laurel

couldn't blame him. In spite of his promise to take it slow and easy, there was only so much patience a man could have, especially when his pants were down. She timed the move carefully, and when he glanced over his shoulder to see what she was up to, Laurel had a syringe in her hands.

"What—" Noah's voice vaporized at the same time the buzz of exhilaration in his blood congealed. Before he realized it, he whirled to face Laurel. He swallowed his surprise and the momentary panic that blocked his breathing. "What are you doing?"

"Doing?" Laurel looked at the syringe. She looked at Noah. "What does it look like I'm doing? I'm going to give you a tetanus shot." She let her gaze glide over his white shirt and beyond, down to the glaring evidence that he had more on his mind than eradicating any bacteria that might have decided to take up residence in his bloodstream thanks to Max's piece of rusted metal. "What did you think I was going to do?"

"Tetanus. Shot." Noah's stomach bunched like a bad home perm. Even though he knew it was too late, he turned his back on Laurel and grabbed for his boxers. He tugged them up as fast as he could and hoped against hope that Laurel hadn't noticed what he was afraid she noticed.

No such luck.

"If I needed proof, I guess I've got it," she said, and Noah held his breath. Whatever tirade was about to escape her, he supposed he deserved it. He deserved it for falling for a stunt that should have been obvious from the moment she told him to drop his pants and gave him that crafty little smile of hers along with the order. He deserved it for thinking Laurel of all women would settle for a slam-bam-thank-you-ma'am encounter in the middle of her place of business. He deserved it for looking like a jerk and for acting like a jerk, and most of all, he deserved it for caring so much.

"Proof." Laurel leaned over and purred the word in his ear. "You are the most conceited person on the face of the earth. Otherwise you never would have assumed what you obviously assumed." Before Noah could open his mouth to dispute the claim, she continued. Good thing. Because he didn't know what he was going to say.

"And you are also the most gullible person I've ever met. Let me guess. Maisie told you I've been pining away, right? Just waiting for you to walk back into my life. Maisie told you, and you believed her."

"Never did." Instinctively, Noah fought to save face. As if there was any way he could. "I only came over here to make her happy. She told me you wanted to see me before I left but I never believed her. Not for a moment."

"Uh-huh. It's sad, Noah. That's what it is. Sad, sad, sad. Now…" She moved back to give him a little elbowroom. "Pull down those boxers again, and let's get this over with. I'm feeling more and more like I'd like to see the end of you. No pun intended."

"I don't need a tetanus shot." Noah ground the words from between clenched teeth.

"Really? When was the last time you had one?"

"I don't remember, but I—"

"If you don't remember, then you need one."

"I don't have to agree to treatment."

Behind him, he heard the toe of Laurel's sneaker tapping against the linoleum floor. "No. You don't," she admitted. "But in spite of how you've been acting, I don't think you're that dumb. You know this is nothing to fool around with, Noah. That little trinket Max had was plenty rusty, and remember, thirty percent of tetanus patients die from the toxin.''

"So now you're going to throw statistics at me?''

"I'm going to throw common sense at you. Common sense. Remember? Something you seem to be sorely lacking.''

She was right, and Noah knew it. A tetanus injection was the best course of treatment.

It was the best thing to do, the smartest, the safest. Which didn't mean he had to fold like an origami stork. With his left hand, he pushed the right sleeve of his shirt further up his arm. "Deltoid,'' he said, holding his arm straight out at his side. "Give me the injection in my arm.''

"Good, but not good enough, and you know it. More blood flows in the gluts,'' she said, and Noah didn't have to look over his shoulder to know she was giving his the once-over. "Better absorption. Less irritation. Less painful in the long run.'' She leaned over his shoulder. "You'll thank me for it in the morning.''

"I'll bet.'' This time, Noah was a little more discriminating. With a sigh of surrender, he pushed down the elastic waistband of his boxers, but exposed only enough skin for the injection. "Let's get this over with,'' he grumbled.

Laurel laughed, a sound that didn't do a thing to brighten Noah's spirits. "What happened to slow and easy?''

"Slow and easy is for—'' Noah winced when she swiped a swab of cold alcohol across his behind. "Slow and easy is for—'' He flinched when, without warning, she poked him with the syringe.

"Slow and easy is for what?'' she asked, withdrawing the needle and backing away. "Long-lost lovers? Old and dear friends? Two people with more lust in their hearts than brains in their heads? That leaves us out on all counts. Especially the part about the brains. I'm convinced that you don't have any."

"And you do?" Noah grabbed his pants and tugged them up. With one hand, he did his best to stuff his shirttail into his trousers. The look wouldn't pass muster with *GQ*, but right about then, that was the least of his worries. Better to save face than try to make a fashion statement. "If you had any brains," he told her, "you wouldn't have pulled that little stunt. What were you trying to demonstrate? That you could get me all hot and bothered? Consider it done. But maybe you ought to ask yourself why it was so important to prove you could do it. Been wondering, Laurel? Been wondering if I still found you attractive?"

The color drained from Laurel's cheeks. "Absolutely not!" She backpedaled her way across the exam room. "You don't think I care, do you? You don't think I care if you do or don't find me attractive? The fact that you…that you…" As fast as it drained, the color rushed up her neck and into her cheeks. "The fact that you had the reaction you had… Well, you assumed things you shouldn't have assumed and just because you assumed what you assumed doesn't mean you should assume—"

"Oh, dear! I haven't picked the wrong time to stop in, have I?"

The soft, sweet voice that interrupted Laurel could only belong to one person. She turned to find her grandmother standing in the doorway of the exam room. With a practiced glance, Maisie gave Laurel the once-over. When she switched her attention to Noah, it was more like a twice-over. Her eyes as wide and innocent-looking as the eyes of an incurable meddler could be, she looked at his pants—still unbuttoned—and at the belt he'd flung over Laurel's desk chair. Maisie's cheeks turned a shade of pink that matched her pantsuit.

"I suppose I should have called before I came over," Maisie said. "Sorry."

"Sorry?" Laurel would have laughed if there was anything funny about the situation. Instead, she sighed with resignation. "You've never been sorry a day in your life," she told her grandmother. "And you wouldn't be sorry now except that you think you missed something. News flash! You didn't. You didn't miss anything. Hate to disappoint you." If the syringe she held in one hand wasn't clue enough for Maisie, the look she gave her grandmother should have been. "It's not what you think."

"It's not?" Laurel knew her grandmother well enough to know that it would take more than strong words to convince her. Not that it mattered. What Maisie wanted to believe was Maisie's business. Just like what Noah wanted to believe was his. And if he wanted to believe Laurel had gone through with that little ruse just to see if she could get a rise out of him…

She cringed at her choice of words.

If he wanted to believe she still cared, that was Noah's business. Noah's business and Noah's mistake.

She set the thought aside as easily as she went to the supply cabinet and disposed of the syringe. Behind her, she heard Noah zip his pants. He reached for his belt, and his arm brushed her back. Instinctively, Laurel tensed. She hid the reaction behind a frosty look and as professional a demeanor as she could muster consider-ing she'd been thrust smack-dab into the middle of a scene straight out of a bad—and not very funny—sit-com. Laurel turned and leaned against the cabinet. "What can I do for you, Grandma?"

"Oh, it's not you I'm looking for." Maisie swung around and gave Noah a look that hovered somewhere between regret and anticipation. If he knew her as well as Laurel did, he would have known what the look meant. Whatever Maisie was here for, it wasn't good news.

Maybe Noah knew more about her grandmother than Laurel gave him credit for. He stepped forward. "What is it?" he asked. "What's wrong?"

"Well, wrong isn't exactly the right word. If you know what I mean." Maisie clutched her hands at her waist. "It's just that I heard from Doc a little while ago. He was over on the mainland and...well..."

Before Maisie could find the words to finish her story, they heard the outside clinic door slam.

"It's me," Doc Ross called, and the next thing they knew, he was standing in the doorway behind Maisie. He was holding one brown, very expensive leather suitcase in each hand.

"Hey!" One look at the suitcases, and Noah shot forward. "What are you doing with my luggage? How did you get it? I left it in the car at the—"

"The ferry dock. Yes. We know." Maisie nodded. "And it's a good thing Doc just happened to be going by."

It was Doc Ross's turn to nod. The big man set down the cases. "Good thing," he said, echoing Maisie's sentiments. "Before the car was towed."

"Towed?"

Laurel wasn't sure who asked the question. The single, shrill word might have come from her. Or it might have erupted out of Noah. Either way, by the time she recovered, she realized that both she and Noah were staring at Maisie, fists on their hips.

"You'd better have a good explanation for this, Grandma," Laurel warned.

"Explanation?" Maisie waved away the word. "There's no explanation. Not one that doesn't make perfect sense. Doc was at Catawba. Over on the mainland. He saw the police getting ready to tow a car, and since there weren't many cars parked at the ferry dock—"

"He naturally assumed it was my rental car?" The expression on Noah's face reminded Laurel of the way Gilly had looked earlier that morning. She almost felt sorry for him. Almost.

Noah looked from Maisie to Doc Ross. "My car? My rental car was being towed?"

Doc shook his head solemnly. "Smack-dab in the middle of a no-parking zone," he said.

"But I—" As if he was trying to picture the small gravel parking lot at the ferry dock, Noah squeezed his eyes shut. Apparently, he didn't call up any memories that told him he'd parked illegally. He dismissed the matter with a shake of his head. "So you saw a car being towed and you assumed it was my rental car and so you stole my luggage?"

"Of course not!" Doc Ross laughed, a booming sound that vibrated through the little room like thunder. "Didn't know it was a rental car. Didn't know it was yours until Todd Rumminger ran the plates."

"Todd is the sheriff over on the mainland." Maisie supplied the explanation.

"And when I found out it was yours, well, that's when I put two and two together. I knew you wouldn't want to be left high and dry without your things. Talked Todd into prying open the trunk and rescuing your suitcases." He gave Noah an ear-to-ear grin. "You can thank me for it later."

"He can thank you for it never." Laurel stepped forward. "So his car was towed. So what? He'll just go over to the mainland and get it out of the impound lot and—"

"Sorry." It was the second time in as many minutes that Maisie used the word. The second time in as many minutes that Laurel wondered if she knew what it meant. "It's Friday, after all, and you know that Hank over at the impound lot likes to close early on Fridays. Especially in the off-season. He fishes," she told Noah. He didn't look like he cared.

"So?" Noah did his best to get a grasp on the situation. "So the impound lot is closed, I don't have a car and—"

"And Frank at the airfield…well, I heard he had one too many at that party last night. He won't be back for hours. There's always the ferry, of course, but…well, something's not working quite right. At least that's what they told Doc on his way back over. The ferry isn't running anymore today."

The news didn't sound any better to Laurel than it did to Noah. He held up his good hand to stop the flow of bad news at the same time she felt her stomach lurch.

"Are you saying…?" She gave Maisie a look along with a silent plea. *Please say you're kidding, Grandma,* her look seemed to say. *Please say you're not saying what I think you're saying.*

"I'm saying that things have worked out perfectly." Maisie patted Noah's arm. "Isn't this fun? It looks as if you'll be able to visit with us for the entire weekend."

Chapter Seven

By the time Laurel got everyone calmed down and out of the clinic, she decided to call it a day. It was just after noon, and the way she figured it, there was only so much excitement anyone could pack into one morning. On a typical morning, the Wild Wilsons would have been more than enough to fill the bill. Today, she thought as she flicked off the waiting room light and locked the clinic door behind her, was anything but typical.

Just knowing Noah was on the island was enough to make her as jumpy as a june bug all night. Then having him show up at the clinic...

Laurel pulled in a deep breath and let it out slowly.

Having Noah show up at the clinic was nothing compared to having him take over the treatment of her patients. Having him take over the treatment of her patients was nothing compared to him getting injured. And Noah getting injured...

Though Laurel was sure one deep breath should have been enough to last, she found herself fighting for another.

Noah getting injured was enough to cause a commotion. Treating Noah's injury was enough to take commotion and turn it on its head. Commotion in the clinic, confusion in Laurel's head, a flurry in her heart, an out-and-out fracas battering her insides.

She shook off the thought and the tiny tingles of electricity that danced through her body by reminding herself that she didn't have the luxury of enjoying such sensations.

The thought caused a very different kind of sensation to rocket through Laurel's brain, one that advised caution. One that told her her grandmother was up to something. No way had Doc Ross just happened to be at the ferry dock in time to see Noah's rental car being towed, her common sense told her. No way had the impound lot been suddenly closed for the weekend. If Laurel was a betting woman, she'd place a huge stack of chips on the fact that she'd see both Sheriff Todd Rumminger and Hank Adams, the man who owned the impound lot, at Cupid's Hideaway sometime soon, enjoying dinner— and probably a room—compliments of the house. Maisie never let a favor go unreturned.

A chill scooted up Laurel's spine, and she pushed off from the clinic door and headed toward home. One of these days, she'd have a long talk with her grandmother about the perils of interfering in other people's lives. One of these days. As soon as Noah was gone, and it was safe to go near Cupid's Hideaway again. She'd explain how some people—Laurel, for instance—didn't need other people deciding what was good for their love lives. She'd point out how some people—Laurel, for instance—were perfectly happy without the kind of romantic fantasies that were as second nature as breathing to Maisie. She'd mention that some people—Laurel, for instance—didn't appreciate being thrown together with certain other people. Certain other people who should have been part of the past and not of the present. Certain other people who should have been nothing more than dim memories and not very real, here-and-now temptations.

In the middle of the sidewalk in front of one of the businesses that rented golf carts and bicycles to tourists, Laurel stopped. Across the street and a couple storefronts down, she saw Noah headed the other way. He hadn't seen her, but that didn't stop her stomach from jumping or her temperature from shooting up a notch or two. Yes, Noah was the most aggravating man on the face of the earth. But there was something about a guy in green-and-white boxers…

Something about *that* guy in green-and-white boxers…

And a whole lot of something that was a whole lot more than something when he was out of those boxers.

Laurel groaned and, for her efforts, got a curious look from the two gulls sitting on a nearby fence post. Bad enough that she was having to defend herself, her right to remain emotionally uninvolved and the impenetrability of the cocoon it had taken her four long years to build around her heart from her grandmother's wild and crazy romantic notions. Worse—much worse—that every now and again she was close to succumbing to those very notions.

"No way." Laurel grumbled the words, startling the gulls at the same time she dared the universe to oppose her. "Been there, done that," she reminded herself. At the same time, she reminded herself that she'd better not ever forget it.

As if she could.

Her mind made up, her resolve as in place as it could be with the memory of those green-and-white boxers still fresh in her head, Laurel got herself moving again. To keep her mind on Maisie's treachery—and off Noah—she practiced the lay-it-on-the-line speech she'd give her grandmother someday soon. She outlined it on her way across the park, refined it as she passed the marina. She reworked the how-dare-you-decide-what's-best-for-me part when she marched past the gift shops that were mostly closed now that the tourists were gone. By the time she had every last word of it right, she was passing the grocery store and she remembered she needed to stop for bread and milk for herself, and food for her dog, Felix.

Inside the store, she waved to Anita, the head cashier, and stopped to say hello to Stan, the retired Detroit cop who lived on the island now and kept himself busy stocking the shelves when he wasn't out fishing on his thirty-foot cruiser. The most recent medication Laurel had prescribed for Stan's seventy-five-year-old arthritic knees was having a couple surprising side effects. They discussed alternatives, and Laurel adjusted the dosage and made a date to meet Stan at the clinic right after lunch on Monday so they could look into the matter more completely.

Mrs. Wrentworth, former school principal and now a wanna-be mystery writer, was looking over the selection of bottled pasta sauces. She caught sight of Laurel and called her over, and they ended up conferring about the advantages and disadvantages of starting the newest Wrentworth grandchild on solid foods. Laurel saw Bobby, the bag boy, and reminded him he had to faithfully take his acne medication. She talked to Marcie, a divorced mother of four who made ends meet by working at one of the island's busiest bars, and asked how everything was going.

By the time she turned into the dairy aisle, she'd nearly forgotten the hubbub at the clinic, which was the only reason she stopped dead in her tracks when she saw Noah looking over the selection of yogurt.

Some people—Laurel, for instance—shouldn't have been bothered by the sudden and completely unexpected appearance of the man she'd been thinking about not thinking about. At least that's what she told herself.

Which didn't explain why she ducked down the snack-food aisle as fast as she could. Or why she decided she could go one more day with the slightly fuzzy bread that was living in her bread box and the slightly funny-smelling milk in her refrigerator. As for Felix…well, he'd understand. He was the only male in her life who always did. She set down the five-pound bag of his favorite kibble she was carrying and made a beeline for the door.

Safely on the sidewalk, she considered her options. Home was the safest bet. Behind the faded pickets of the white fence that surrounded her pint-size yard, she could pull inside her cocoon and work on making sure its walls were strong. She could muster her defenses the way she had so many times in the last four years, and with any luck at all, by the time she was feeling in control of her career, her world and her heart, it would be Monday morning and Noah would be long gone.

Good plan. It might even have worked if not for the fact that she kept thinking about that fuzzy bread.

With a sigh, Laurel gave in to the pangs of hunger crawling through her stomach. In the summer, there would have been a dozen places she could have stopped for lunch at the center of town. This time of the year, her selection was a little more limited. As they had for as long as Laurel could remember, the restaurant owners who stayed on the island after the season was over took turns opening for those few residents hardy enough to live there through the winter.

"If today's Friday…" she mumbled, and headed to the town's oldest hotel. Once she was inside its restaurant, she exchanged greetings with Cindy, who was working as the lunchtime cook as well as the cashier now that the crowds were gone. She chose an out-of-the-way booth in the corner, ordered one of Cindy's island-famous avocado salads and had already put three sugars in her iced tea when Noah walked in.

"Hey, Cindy, can I get that to go?" Laurel called into the kitchen at the same time she slid out of her booth. Before Noah even looked up at the sound of her voice and registered the fact that she was among the smattering of patrons in the restaurant, she snatched the to-go container out of Cindy's hands, grabbed a fork from the rack of plastic utensils near the door and headed outside.

She crossed the street and went into the park. There was a bench on the other side of the stone fountain, and she plunked down on it and stared at the avocado salad staring at her from inside the clear plastic container. The next thing she knew, Noah was sitting beside her.

"This is a little ridiculous, don't you think?" Laurel's words surprised even her. They sounded pretty calm for a woman whose stomach was flopping around like the fish the guy she could see at the marina across the street had just pulled out of the water.

"What?" Noah had a brown paper lunch bag with him, the kind Cindy used to pack to-go orders when the person placing the order was patient enough to wait. He reached into the bag and pulled out a sandwich wrapped in waxed paper. "I heard the ham and cheese was good. You don't think the ham and cheese is good?"

"I don't think—"

There was no use even trying. No use mentioning what she thought and what she didn't think. Noah wouldn't listen anyway. Noah never listened to anything he didn't want to hear. And with the way her blood was rushing and her heart was pounding, Laurel doubted that even she would be able to hear whatever wisdom she was about to spout. Rather than try, she got up and walked away.

There was an old wooden carousel on the far side of the park, and she headed for it. It was closed for the season, and there was a waist-high fence around the platform, but Laurel had lived on the island long enough to share its many secrets. The gate was locked but she, like so many of the island's permanent residents, knew exactly where to jab the bottom of the padlock. The lock popped, and she swung the gate aside and went into the enclosure. She locked the gate behind her and sat down next to her favorite of the carousel's animals, a brightly colored unicorn decorated with carved flowers and ribbons.

She wasn't very hungry, but just to prove to herself how little she cared that Noah was following her and how much she refused to let him influence her life, much less her eating habits, she snapped open the salad container and scooped up a mouthful. She refused to look toward the park to see what Noah was up to.

She didn't have to.

She heard him come up the sidewalk, toss over his lunch bag, hop the fence. The next thing she knew, he was standing right in front of her.

"Hey, fancy meeting you here!" Noah plopped down

beside her on the wooden carousel deck. "Come here often?"

"Only when I want to be alone."

"When you want to be alone. I get it!" He chuckled. "You're trying to avoid someone?"

"Noah…" As hard as she tried, Laurel couldn't control the sigh of frustration or the emotions that made the marinated avocado chunks taste like sawdust in her mouth. She closed the salad container. "You're not really staying the weekend, are you?" she asked him.

"Why shouldn't I?" Noah chewed a mouthful of ham and cheese. He tipped his head, looking at the carved canopy that circled the carousel. "The sun is shining, the sky is blue. All is right with the world. Except for the part about my rental car, of course." He gave Laurel enough of a glance to make sure she was paying attention. "Looks like I don't have much choice but to stay."

Laurel didn't like to beat around the bush. Especially when her peace of mind was at stake, not to mention her self-respect and what was left of the pieces of her heart. The ones that had been crushed, smashed, crumbled and scrambled the last time she'd let this man within arm's length. She stood and tossed her salad container into a nearby trash can. "It's a big island," she said, brushing off the seat of her pants. "And Monday is only three days away."

"And you didn't tell me you had a dog."

"A dog?" When Laurel realized he must have seen her in the grocery store, that he must have noticed she was too shook up to face him after the fiasco at the clinic, her cheeks got hot and her throat got dry.

"Felix," she said, because there wasn't anything else

she could do. "I have a dog and his name is Felix. He's a two-year-old chocolate lab."

For a second, she thought she saw something very much like wistfulness in Noah's eyes. He stood and stuffed what was left of his sandwich in the bag. "You always said you wanted a chocolate lab. Remember? And you told me you wanted to name him Felix. You told me that night we—"

"That night we went down to the Chesapeake and ate crabs at that little place near the water. Yeah, I remember." Laurel looked away. She didn't bother to mention that she'd shared more than her dream of owning a dog with Noah that night. It was their first real date, the first time they went out alone together and not with a group of their peers, and neither one of them had ever intended it to be more than a friendly dinner between colleagues. It wasn't until they'd finished two buckets of crabs and told each other all about their hopes, their dreams and their backgrounds that they realized they had somehow stepped over the thin line that separated colleagues from friends. Later that night, at Laurel's apartment and in Laurel's bed, their relationship changed again. From colleagues to friends. From friends to lovers.

"I kind of always thought we'd own Felix together."

The sound of Noah's voice was enough to pull Laurel back to reality. She looked up to find him studying her, and the look in his eyes told her he hadn't forgotten that night on the Chesapeake, either.

There was something about feeling nostalgic that didn't sit right with the hollow feeling in her heart. She shook aside the memories. "What did you expect me to do, Noah? Put my dreams on hold until you were ready to help make them come true? No, thanks." She backed away from him, putting as much distance as she could between herself and the past, widening the gap between the present and that funny little restaurant on the Chesapeake where she'd indulged her love of crab and laid her heart on the line.

"If I waited for you, I'd never have Felix," she told him. "I'd never have what I have here on the island. My house. My dog. My clinic. The things that are really important to me."

He shook his head, and though she expected him to look at least a little sentimental and maybe even a little remorseful, he looked mighty satisfied instead. "Glad to hear it," he said. "Maybe that means you understand."

"Understand? I—" The truth hit Laurel like a freight train going full speed. Here on the island, she had what she wanted. She had her grandmother and her sister, Meg, close by. She had the small-town practice she'd always dreamed of owning, the house with a fireplace she used almost every day once the weather turned cold and a bedroom under the eaves where she lulled herself to sleep and tried not to think about everything she used to believe in. She had the dog she'd always wanted, the one with a name that made her smile every time she said it.

Across the waters of Lake Erie and all the miles that separated her life from his, Noah had what he wanted, too—the high-powered career, the pressure-cooker intensity of med school he'd always thrived on. He had prestige and he had the chance to use his considerable talents to make a real difference in the lives of his students and the patients they would ultimately serve. He was steadily gaining a reputation, and one of these days, soon, she had no doubt he'd have his pick of professional opportunities. In a world where intellect, skill and knowledge ruled and big egos were as common as sutures and stethoscopes, he'd managed to rise farther and faster than most. It was his dream as much as a life on the island was Laurel's, and for the first time, she fully understood everything it meant to him.

The awareness should have filled her with a little of the remorsefulness she was hoping to find in Noah. It might have, if she hadn't had one other thought. Noah had everything he ever wanted, all right, and all he'd had to do to achieve it was to give up everything they'd had together.

Not exactly a news flash, but that didn't stop the thought from cutting through Laurel like the wind off the lake in the dead of January.

Before the realization swamped her, before he could catch on, she moved away and hopped the fence. "I hear Frank over at the airfield is back from that birthday party," she called to him over her shoulder. Without bothering to look back, she headed toward home.

"GREAT. What's that supposed to mean?" As if Noah didn't know. Rather than admit he did, he grumbled the question at Laurel's retreating back. Rather than think about her anything-but-subtle message, he followed her example. He hopped the fence, but instead of going after her, he paused and watched her walk away. Laurel's shoulders were back. Her chin was high. Her arms were so tight against her sides, she looked like a toy soldier from a school Christmas pageant.

Not exactly the warm and giving woman he'd romanced over a couple of buckets of crabs, the one he'd bedded and bedded again that first crazy night. The one he'd been convinced he wanted to spend the rest of his life with.

Regret was not a pretty emotion and not one Noah indulged in often. He knew there was no use indulging in self-pity because it wouldn't get him anywhere. No use reminding himself that he'd turned his back on his heart once, because he knew what that meant. It meant he couldn't trust his feelings. Not then. Not now. Which meant he couldn't trust the hollow ache he felt inside as he watched Laurel walk away. Regret? Maybe. Maybe he was just hungry. Or tired of being held captive by his memories in a place where they seemed to be lying in wait around every corner.

Noah shook off the thought and tossed his brown paper lunch bag, left-handed, into the nearby trash container. He headed out of town on foot, grateful that Doc and Maisie had volunteered to take his luggage to the inn in the shocking pink golf cart that was Maisie's mode of transportation. He didn't see Laurel again, but that wasn't much consolation when it came to the memories department. He passed the island's only miniature golf course and couldn't help but think of the time they played there, wagering kisses on strokes and not caring who won. He passed the winery and thought about the weekend they'd flown in to meet Laurel's family and the party Maisie hosted at the winery in honor of their engagement and their announcement that they were buying Doc's medical practice.

That was the first time Noah realized he was getting more than Laurel in the marriage bargain. Along with the woman he loved, he would be getting a chunk of her life, and her life would be his life—the tiny island out in a lake that could be treacherous in the summer and unnavigable in winter, a group of isolated residents, a small clinic where the list of medical conditions they'd treat would range all the way from the mundane to the...

"Mundaner." Noah grumbled the word and did his best to shrug away the guilt that settled along his shoulders. It wasn't his fault. He'd told himself that so many times in the past four years, it was a wonder he didn't believe it yet.

It wasn't his fault his dreams led straight to the top of his profession. Any more than it was Laurel's fault her dreams led her nowhere.

It wasn't until he heard a droning overhead that Noah realized he'd walked all the way to the island's only airfield. In spite of himself, he looked over his shoulder toward town, remembering Laurel's comment at the carousel.

"It's not my fault, Laurel," he whispered. "It never was." And he walked into the airport.

"SO, WHAT do you think?" Laurel lifted a hamburger out of a frying pan, chopped it in tiny pieces and scraped it into Felix's bowl. "Think this will do until we can get to the grocery store?"

Felix wagged his enthusiastic acceptance of the offer, and she set the bowl on the floor and watched him dive in. When she grabbed a banana and a jar of peanut butter and headed to the backyard with it, he was too busy to care.

She settled herself on the swing that hung from the oak tree at the center of the yard, opened the peanut butter and peeled the banana. It was nearly two in the afternoon, and this was her breakfast and her lunch, which, as far as Laurel was concerned, was a good enough reason to ignore fat grams. Besides, everyone knew that peanut butter was comfort food. And right about now, she needed the comfort more than she needed the food.

Just the thought made the peanut butter stick in Laurel's throat. She swallowed around it and told herself to stop acting like the naive kid she'd been four years before. She was older. She was wiser. She was happy with her life and her career, content in all the things that really mattered.

Which didn't mean seeing Noah again hadn't thrown her for a loop.

There. She'd admitted it.

Laurel sat back, as relieved and as proud of herself as if she'd just confessed to a lifetime of chocoholism or an addiction to one of those cable channels where they sold everything from floor cleaner to gold jewelry.

She'd gotten over the seismic activity of Noah's passing through her life once. "I can do it again," she told herself. "I will do it again."

Her pledge would have sounded a lot more forceful if it wasn't lost beneath the sound of Frank's plane flying low over the island. Laurel looked up as it went over, thinking of the suggestion she'd made to Noah at the carousel, wondering in spite of herself if he might be on the plane, headed toward home and out of her life.

Just the thought should have made some people—Laurel, for instance—do the dance of joy. Just the thought should have convinced some people—Laurel, for instance—that things could finally get back to normal. As a matter of fact, she knew that some people—Laurel, for instance—should have been happy as clams that he was gone.

Funny, knowing all that didn't change a thing. It sure

didn't do anything to warm the ball of ice that suddenly settled in Laurel's stomach. It didn't help soothe the prickles of disappointment that jabbed at her. And it sure didn't quiet the voice that taunted her.

The one that reminded her that, in spite of her brave words, some people might actually be sorry to see Noah leave.

Laurel, for instance.

Chapter Eight

Too much self-pity was as bad as too much peanut butter.

Laurel ought to know.

She'd indulged in her share of both.

The results were predictable. She felt cranky, unsatisfied and out of kilter. And that was just from the peanut butter. The self-pity made her feel even worse.

By the next morning, she'd decided that enough was more than enough. She was ready to put the misery behind her, and she knew there was only one surefire way to do that. Just after the sun came up, she headed to the marina with Felix, a lunch that included yogurt and fruit for her and a hunk of cheese large enough to send the lab into doggy delirium, and an irresistible urge to get out on the lake to clear her head and cleanse her soul.

It wouldn't be so bad if she could get her libido under control, either.

It didn't take long for the water to work its magic. By the time she hopped on board the *Jade Moon* and stowed the food she'd brought in a shocking pink Cupid's Hideaway tote bag, she was already feeling as if the events of the past two days were no more real than the mirages that sometimes sparkled over the lake. It was a perfect October morning with a light, crisp breeze, a cloud-free sky and just enough snap in the air to remind her it wouldn't be long before autumn showed its ugly side. Knowing that the sailing season wouldn't last much longer was enough to add an extra dollop of sweetness to the day, and Laurel vowed she would enjoy it to its fullest.

Which would have been easier to do if she didn't keep thinking about the plane she saw flying over the island the afternoon before. If she didn't keep speculating about whether or not Noah was on that plane. If she didn't keep picturing him, already on the mainland, headed toward home. If she didn't keep wondering, what if…

Before she realized what she was doing and long before she could stop herself, Laurel sighed.

"Stupid reaction," she told herself. "Stupid and emotional and completely illogical."

There was nothing she wanted more than to see Noah leave, to know he was gone. This time for good. She should have been doing the jig on her teak deck, not sighing like a teenager and wondering if this time she really would never see him again. She should have been smiling. Dancing. Humming a tune. She should have been well on her way to putting her life back into the shape it was in before he barged onto her island and into her clinic and messed up her life. Again.

She should have.

That didn't explain the tightness in her chest or the funny, hollow feeling inside her that didn't respond, no matter how many spoonfuls of peanut butter she heaped onto it. And it sure didn't explain why, when she went on deck to disconnect the electrical cord that fed the boat power from a breaker on the dock and saw Noah jog by the marina, her heart didn't just thump. It pounded. Bumped. Stopped. And started up again with such a jolt, it nearly knocked her off her feet.

He saw her at the same time she saw him. He stopped and, his hands on his knees, he took a few deep breaths. He waved.

It didn't explain why she waved back.

As if the wave was an open invitation, some sort of semaphore flag that shouted, "Come on down!" like the guy on the TV game show, Noah jogged closer. His running stride was long and loose, relaxed and so easy, no one would have suspected he took his running as seriously as he took everything else about his life. Noah had to be first, in his academic standing, in his profession, even in something he had the nerve to call a hobby. More than one long-distance competitor had been awestruck when the doctor with the easygoing smile and the loose-wheeling stride had come out of nowhere and left his fellow runners in the dust.

Something Laurel better not ever forget.

Giving herself a mental nudge, she watched him make his way across the dock to where she kept her sailboat tied. He was dressed in loose-fitting black sweat shorts that proved once and for all everything she'd thought when she first saw him standing at the front desk of the Hideaway. He wasn't an occasional runner. He was running regularly and he was running long distances. Otherwise, his legs wouldn't be so trim. They wouldn't be so well-muscled. He must have been working out, too, or maybe lifting weights, and though one part of her was wondering how a sought-after lecturer like Noah ever found the time, a whole lot more parts of her were not caring. Noah's time-management skills were his concern. She was more interested in the fact that without the one-of-a-kind tailored shirt he'd worn with his cashmere suit, she saw that his arm muscles were well-defined. The T-shirt he was wearing, however, had seen better days. Somewhere along the line—and if she had to guess, she'd guess that somewhere was a long time before—he'd chopped off the sleeves. He'd used the shirt so many times for so many runs, it was pulled out of shape and drooping at the neckline.

He didn't look like the polished professional she'd run into on that fateful visit to see Maisie. He didn't look like the know-it-all professor who had horned in on her examination of the Wild Wilsons and taken over her clinic and influenced everything from her peace of mind to the green-and-white fantasies that had been steadily flitting through her imagination. With his shabby T-shirt and his hair drooping over his forehead and the morning sun shining full on his face, he looked like Noah the medical student.

And whether she liked it or not, Laurel's heart squeezed in response to the memory.

She did her best to sidetrack the thought by jumping onto the dock and turning off the breaker. She could only guess that Noah had run all the way from the Hideaway and was headed around Peach Point and across the other side of the island. Though he didn't look tired and he wasn't winded, he was breathing hard.

Laurel realized she was, too.

Maybe he noticed. Squinting against the sun, he gave her a long look. "You look a little like you got hit by a yardarm. Whatever a yardarm is. You okay?"

Noah's question was completely ordinary, and she might even have answered it if there wasn't suddenly a lump the size of a softball in her throat. "I thought—"

She looked at the sky, as if something there might explain the airplane she'd seen the afternoon before and the assumptions she'd made about its passenger.

"I almost did." Was Noah reading her mind again? Or was the look on her face so easy to interpret? Whatever the answer, he followed her gaze and knew exactly what she was thinking. "I almost left," he said. "Even went into the airport and asked about prices."

"But?"

"But…" He shrugged. As if that was enough of an explanation. As if anything could explain. "I decided to stay a little longer."

Laurel swallowed an emotion she didn't want to think about. It might have been relief. Or maybe it was the anger she felt at herself for feeling so relieved.

"I didn't think I'd see you again," she managed to say.

"You mean you were hoping you didn't see me again."

Not exactly something she could deny. Rather than try, and have him catch her in the lie, Laurel glanced at Noah's right hand. "How does it feel?" she asked.

He held up the hand for her to see. "Better," he said, flexing his fingers as if to prove they worked. "Not much pain. I think I'll be able to play the violin again."

She couldn't help but smile. "You never played the violin."

"So maybe I'll start." His smile mirrored hers. "Maybe you're a miracle worker. Maybe—"

Whatever he was going to say, he was interrupted by a series of barks from Felix, who was at the other end of the dock, checking out the latest and greatest smells.

"Hey!" Noah grinned. "It's Felix! What a great

dog!'' When he leaned forward and slapped his left thigh, the dog came running.

Like dog, like master.

The thought was unworthy of her, and Laurel knew it. She set it aside and promised herself nothing was going to ruin her morning. Not even a guy with abs like the slate she'd seen on nearby Kelley's Island.

He stooped and roughhoused with the dog for a while, and Laurel couldn't help it, she knew that this time, the funny little pang in her stomach had nothing to do with peanut butter. And everything to do with jealousy. Ten seconds together, and Noah had found Felix's favorite scratch spot. Right behind the ears. Felix, predictably, was loving it. He leaned his head against Noah's leg, and the look he gave Noah was nothing short of out-and-out adoration.

It was, no doubt, a look Noah was well acquainted with. Laurel knew for a fact she'd given him the same look a couple hundred times.

Annoyed with herself for allowing so many disturbing thoughts to ruin what she'd been convinced was going to be a perfect day, certain that if she didn't get rid of her emotional baggage it would sink the *Jade Moon* as soon as she set sail, Laurel hopped onto the boat and started the routine she followed each time she went out on the lake. She'd already taken the sail cover off the mainsail when she realized neither Noah nor Felix had made a sound.

She looked over and found Felix still gazing lovingly at Noah. And Noah looking over the boat. He had one hand to his eyes to shade them. ''Nice boat.'' He nodded, and she remembered that sailboats were something Noah always admired. And one of the few things he didn't know anything about.

"Thanks. You..." She hesitated, but even while she did, she knew exactly what was going to happen next. She was going to invite him aboard, and he was going to say yes. She wasn't sure what prompted her. She was pretty sure it wasn't a good idea. She did it anyway.

"On board?" Noah's expression brightened. "You mean, like, for a sail?"

She didn't, but now that he mentioned it, it was hard to tell him it wasn't what she had in mind. Laurel stepped around the cabin to the port side of the boat to help Noah on board, and something about seeing him on her boat, on her deck, caused her doubts to whack her the way the waves slapped against the sides of the *Jade Moon*.

She scrambled to offer him—and herself—a way out. "Of course, if you have something else to do..."

As if he did. As if he could. It was a Saturday. It was October. There were bound to be a few hardy tourists around who were there strictly to enjoy the quiet beauty of the island now that most of the boaters, campers and college kids bent on drinking their brains out were gone. But other than a jog or a bicycle ride, there wasn't much to keep an active guy like Noah busy on the island. Except for a sail.

She wasn't as much moved by sympathy for his plight as she was by the fact that he was already on board. And from the way he was making himself at home, messing with the wheel like a kid who'd been allowed to sit in the driver's seat of a car, it didn't look like anything short of tossing him over the side was going to get him off her boat.

Laurel crossed her arms over her chest. "You don't work," she told him, "and you swim all the way back to shore."

"Work?" Noah hopped to his feet and gave her a crisp salute, which must have made his hand hurt because he winced when he snapped it down. "Aye, aye, captain, sir, er, ma'am. What did you have in mind?"

"Sailor's work," she told him, and she motioned him forward and showed him how to remove the cover from the staysail and stow it with the cover she'd taken off the mainsail. He was a quick learner, and she let him take over while she got Felix onto the boat. Within a couple minutes the dog was settled in his favorite spot in the forward cabin and Laurel had Noah untying the dock lines while she started the engine.

"Now, you..." She pointed Noah toward the dock. "Get off. Walk along the dock and hold on to the shroud while I motor backward."

Noah hesitated, and she couldn't blame him. Yesterday she'd pretty much told him she wanted him off her island and out of her life—fast. Here she was with the boat engine running, the sails ready to go up, and she was telling him to take a hike.

"You can hop right back on," she told him, because in spite of herself, she couldn't stand to think that he might suspect he was being abandoned. "I just need to get her out of the slip."

Whether he believed her or not, she didn't know. But he did follow orders. He walked along the dock as the boat moved and at the last second he jumped on. He held on to the shrouds supporting the mast, watching as Laurel turned the *Jade Moon* into the wind and cut the engine, and when she instructed him to take the sail ties off the main, pointing from where she stood behind the wheel, he got the task accomplished in no time.

Though she hated to admit it, Laurel couldn't help but acknowledge that he was doing a good job. It shouldn't have surprised her. He was Noah, and as her mind—not to mention her body—had been reminding her for the past four years, Noah did everything well.

At the same time she told herself she was being petty, she reminded herself she should be grateful for his help. She could sail the *Jade Moon* single-handed, she'd done it hundreds of times. But it was always easier to have help. Even when that help was a man she knew she would have been better off leaving on shore. Or marooning on one of the tiny islands they were going to pass.

Since she was pretty sure she wouldn't do that—not unless he wore out his welcome quicker than she held on to her patience—she decided she might as well get as much work as she could out of him.

"One more thing," she called. "You're going to raise the sail."

Noah glanced at the mast, following it to where a wind-speed indicator spun high above the deck.

"Don't worry." Laurel laughed. "No crow's nest for you to climb up to. Just grab on. There." She pointed. "And pull." When he had the mainsail up and the right tension on it, she had him repeat the procedure with the staysail. She turned away from the wind, helped him with the Yankee headsail, and when she had trouble explaining what to do next, she went forward and took a couple turns around the sheet winch until the sails had a nice shape.

"Now," she said, giving him a smile, "we're sailing."

Noah grinned, and she knew exactly how he felt. Any boater knew the thrill of being out on the water with the wind and the sun warm against skin. But only a sailboater knew the satisfaction of getting the job done with the minimal assistance of fuel-guzzling engines. It took work to sail. It took skill. It was more art than it was science, more passion than it was hobby. And there was nothing except treating a patient successfully that had ever given her the same satisfaction.

"You're good."

Surprised by the compliment, Laurel looked over to where Noah was standing near the bow. He made his way aft, skirting the cabin, stepping a little uncertainly as he tried to get used to the feel of the deck rolling gently beneath his feet. He joined her in the cockpit behind the wheel, dropping onto the seat built onto the deck. "I'm impressed. You really know what you're doing when it comes to boats."

Laurel adjusted her hands against the wheel. "I really know what I'm doing when it comes to a lot of things," she told him.

She thought for sure he'd argue the point. He didn't. Instead, Noah sat back, his left arm draped over one of the lifelines. "I can't believe your parents didn't take the *Jade Moon* with them when they retired to Beverly Beach."

The comment caught Laurel off guard. Though she had never confessed it to anyone—and hardly admitted it to herself—there were plenty of times in the last four years when she'd thought about Noah. More times than she liked to remember.

She had pretty much convinced herself that he never thought of her.

Yet he remembered that her parents, who were both once teachers at the island's elementary school, were retired and living in Florida. He remembered that the *Jade Moon* was their sailboat and that it meant the world to them.

The realization left her feeling light-headed, like the waves used to do when she was a kid and hadn't gotten used to the feel of the deck tilting under her feet. She glanced to port, checking their position in relation to the northeast arm of Middle Bass Island. There was a shoal nearby, and it was shallow and rocky. Navigating around it took experience and concentration. A little luck never hurt, either.

Kind of like navigating through a conversation with Noah.

"My parents...they said they had their fill of sailing. Can you imagine?" She shook her head. There was no such thing as too much sailing. She firmly believed that. She knew she always would. Then again, there was a time in her life when she'd believed there was no such thing as too much love.

"Besides—" Laurel shook away the thought "—ocean sailing isn't anything like lake sailing, and they said they didn't want to start learning all over again. Pop has his garden. Mom is taking art classes at the local adult education center. They keep plenty busy without the boat."

"And you have the boat so you can keep plenty busy."

"What's that supposed to mean?" Laurel's reaction surprised her. Her temper swelled like the wave that came up suddenly and crashed into the bow, and it wasn't until it did she realized she'd been holding her anger inside since the moment she saw Noah. Big-city, big-time Dr. Noah Cunningham.

Big deal.

Laurel reminded herself it wasn't what she wanted. It was never what she wanted. She'd never been comfortable in the spotlight. She'd never gone looking for the glory. Not like Noah had. Which only made it harder to sit there and listen to him criticize the choices she'd made.

"If you're talking about my practice and about how you don't think it's busy enough or important enough to—"

"Whoa! Wait a minute!" Noah held out both hands as if he could stop her words. "Is that what you think? That I don't believe your work is important?"

It wasn't just what she thought. It was what Laurel felt down to her bones. She looked Noah in the eye. "It must be what you think. Otherwise you wouldn't have walked away from your chance to be a part of it. Unless—"

She nearly let the words slip. Nearly let her mind breach the barrier she'd built around the truth all those years before.

Unless when you said you didn't want to live on the island and be my partner in a small-time, small-town, small-potatoes medical clinic, you were just trying to soften the blow.

Unless you really called off the partnership—and the engagement—because you didn't love me.

The thought clutched at Laurel's insides like an icy hand. It wasn't something she could afford to think about. Not with Noah sitting hip-to-hip with her on the teak-planked seat and nowhere to run and hide if he saw the truth through the tears that suddenly filled her eyes. Not without letting all the doubts, all the uncertainty and all the misery she'd felt four years earlier come crashing around her again.

To give herself something to do, some way to account for her sudden silence and something to take her mind out of a place she'd promised herself she'd never go, she set the autopilot, then got up and walked forward, checking the sails—which didn't need checking—testing the rigging—which didn't need testing—and peering at the horizon as if she expected to see Moby Dick himself come leaping out of the lake with Captain Ahab attached.

Behind her, she heard Noah get up. The breeze was light, the lake calm. There wasn't much of a chop, at least nothing Laurel wasn't used to handling. Even so, she heard him shuffle against the deck as he tried to find his footing.

"Is that what you think?" She felt Noah's hand on her shoulder, and though she knew it was a mistake, she turned. He slid his hand from her shoulder to her neck and, cupping her chin, he turned her face up to his. "You've got me all wrong, Doc," he said, his voice husky with the same emotion that shimmered in his eyes. "Just because I decided four years ago that I didn't want to own a clinic on an island doesn't mean I didn't think the clinic, the island or the doctor who decided to stay wasn't important."

"Just not your cup of tea, huh?" Laurel congratulated herself. She almost sounded like she didn't care. Not an easy thing to do considering the feel of Noah's hand was causing her outsides to burn and her insides to melt. "Bad medicine."

"Wrong. Good medicine. Just not my idea of a career." There was as little satisfaction in Noah admitting it as there apparently was for Laurel in hearing it. Afraid that he might see some of the same hurt he was feeling in Laurel's eyes—afraid that if he did, he'd want nothing more than to take her into his arms and kiss it away—he looked over her head toward the shoreline.

Though they hadn't been out on the boat for long, South Bass seemed miles away. Against a brilliant autumn sky, the island looked like a watercolor painting, all misty blues with touches of gold and orange where the leaves were starting to turn. Far away, the big tourist draw on the island, the monument commemorating the naval victory of Commodore Oliver Hazard Perry over the British in the War of 1812, was brilliant white in the sun.

In the four years they'd been apart, Noah had convinced himself that South Bass was the Great Lakes equivalent of the Bermuda Triangle. Go there. Disappear. Never be heard from again. But in the past couple days, he'd learned how time, distance and a big dollop of the kind of ugly emotion that had ended their relationship could turn a guy's memories around.

Now that he was back, the memories were starting to come into focus. They were good memories—the people he'd met when he visited soon after he and Laurel announced their engagement, the places they'd visited, the things they'd done. But just because the memories were good didn't mean he was comfortable with the emotions they brought to the surface. No one was more surprised than he was to realize that coming to South Bass felt like coming home.

The realization hit him like the gust of wind that came up and slapped him in the face, and this time, Noah was the one who turned away. Searching for a way he could explain the thoughts that were as tangled inside him as his memories of Laurel were tangled around his heart, he went to the side of the boat. Port or starboard? He never could keep them straight. He only knew that when a wave came up and splashed the side of the boat, he was caught off guard by the spray that soaked his T-shirt and hit his cheeks. He was a smart guy, and the symbolism wasn't lost on him.

He was surprised by the sudden wave, surprised by the memories that seemed as much a part of the place as the jagged shoreline and the blue water of Lake Erie, and he steadied himself, feet apart, and hung on to the *Jade Moon* for all he was worth.

Kind of like he was hanging on to his vision of the world.

The one it had taken him four long years to build.

Even though he knew it wasn't a good idea, he glanced over his shoulder at Laurel who was busy doing something or another with one of the sails. How could he explain to her that four years before, he'd seen his career headed in another direction from hers, one that, on a clear day, didn't include a view of Canada? How could he make her understand that he was happy with his choice?

In the first few weeks after they broke up, he'd composed a dozen different arguments supporting his position. As if he thought he'd ever have a chance to explain. In each and every one of them, he defended himself cogently. Persuasively. In each and every permutation of the daydream, he made Laurel understand.

For a while, it was enough to get him through the empty hours. But the longer the time got, the emptier the hours got, the more Noah realized he wasn't trying to convince anyone but himself. His argument was rock solid. Sometimes a man had to let go of what he loved most in order to attain what he wanted most. For four years, it worked.

Until two days before, when he stood at the front desk of Cupid's Hideaway and saw Laurel across the lobby.

The heat that flooded through Noah had nothing to do with the morning sun. He braced himself against the impact of the realization at the same time he made up his mind. Maybe Laurel would never understand. Maybe she would, maybe she did, but maybe she didn't want to hear it. Whatever the consequences, Noah's speech had been four years in the making. He knew it was time to tell her.

He turned and leaned against the shrouds, watching as Laurel stepped off the hump-back bulge in the center of the boat and headed toward the wheel. Just as she made to slip by him on the narrow planking that edged the entire boat, he leaned forward and hitched an arm around her waist.

"You know," he said, "I've been thinking about what we talked about yesterday. About that night we went to that little restaurant on the Chesapeake."

Her cheeks were pink. It might have been from the sun. Or the memory. It would have been easier to tell if she would look at him. "Maybe we shouldn't talk about that night on the Chesapeake."

"Kept you awake all last night, too, huh?"

"Yeah." Laurel adjusted her stance against the deck, but she didn't try to move away. She didn't look at him, either. "Something like that."

With his other hand, Noah ran a finger across Laurel's cheek. Her skin was as smooth as he remembered it. As smooth as it had been in all the dreams that filled all four of those long, empty years. "You know, the first time I saw you, I fell in love with you."

"Not true." Laurel laughed. Not exactly the reaction he was hoping for, but at least she hadn't decided that a headfirst dive over the side was better than standing within inches of him. She turned, and automatically his hand found the small of her back. "The first time you saw me, we were in Dr. Drinker's anatomy rotation. You answered every one of his questions before anybody else had a chance."

"I was nervous."

"You were an egotistical, shallow jerk."

"I was a nervous, egotistical, shallow jerk."

"You were trying to show everybody else up."

"Hey, it was something I was good at!" He hoped to elicit at least another smile and got his wish. "I might have been answering all Dr. Drinker's questions, but I only had eyes for you. You were wearing that sweater, the blue one with the—"

"It was pink." Laurel didn't exactly look happy about correcting him. Not the way she usually did.

"Yeah, pink." He edited the memory. "It had a V-neck and long sleeves and..." Noah sucked in an unsteady breath. "I could tell you were one really smart lady."

Another smile came and went quickly, sparkling in her eyes. "You could tell I was smart? From looking at my sweater?"

"I could tell a lot of things from looking at your sweater." It was true, and Noah felt every one of those things crashing over him again. "I could tell you had great taste in pink sweaters." He grinned, lowered his voice and shuffled closer. "I could tell that someone with that good a taste in sweaters was smart and funny and was probably going to be one heck of a doctor. I could tell you were beautiful, too. And that's when I fell in love with you. You know what?" He brushed a strand of hair from Laurel's face and tucked it behind her ear. "I'm still falling."

In that one moment, it felt like the truest, most honest, most genuine thing he ever said.

Too bad he never had a chance to see how Laurel reacted to it.

Because he was so busy looking at Laurel, he wasn't ready for the wave that hit the side of the *Jade Moon*. Because he had one arm around her waist and one hand touching her cheek, he wasn't holding on to the shroud. Because he wasn't paying attention to anything at all— anything but Laurel—he lost his footing, and once he lost it, it was impossible to get it back.

Noah felt himself lifted in the air. In the next split second, he was on his way down. Only the deck wasn't under him.

The only thing that was, the only thing that was all around him and over him, was the lake.

He only had enough time to suck in one quick breath before he went under the water.

Chapter Nine

The last thing Laurel saw of Noah was his bandaged right hand disappearing beneath the two-foot chop.

It only proved how worried she was that she didn't immediately think she didn't have a thing to worry about. She didn't remind herself that Noah was an excellent swimmer—that Noah was excellent at everything—and the fact that she didn't stop to think about it or to compare herself to the paragon that was Noah Cunningham proved something. If she wasn't so busy being worried, she would have taken the time to figure out that.

Instead, she turned the *Jade Moon* into the wind and prepared to do a quick stop. It was a maneuver she'd practiced dozens of times, one she hardly ever used, and it might have been easier if Felix didn't sense the excitement and come running from the cabin. He ran from port to starboard and barked like mad as his new hero broke the surface and bobbed in the water. Or maybe he just didn't approve of Noah's dog-paddle technique.

Laurel was too busy to care. She threw the life sling over the stern and maneuvered the boat toward Noah, circling until she was close enough for him to grab on to the U-shaped piece of foam. As soon as he caught it, she stopped the boat, hung the boarding ladder over the side and reeled him in.

The man who climbed up the ladder onto the deck was an angrier, more embarrassed, much wetter version of the one who'd had the nerve to tell her he was in love with her.

Which, now that she thought about it, was something Laurel didn't even want to think about.

"What's wrong with you? Don't you know you have to be careful on a boat?" Yelling was better than thinking. Lecturing Noah about being boneheaded enough to let go when he wasn't sure on his feet was better than listening to the little voice inside her head that reminded her he'd let go of the shroud so he could take hold of Laurel. Better than listening to her heart, because her heart was being annoying enough to remind her that she enjoyed every second of it. "Don't you know you could have gotten hurt?"

"You think I planned that little stunt?" Noah and Felix must have been soul mates. He shook like she'd seen the lab shake when they came home from a walk in the rain, and beads of water splattered around. It looked like the better part of Lake Erie was sluicing off Noah's body and puddling around his feet. He scrubbed a hand over his face and through his hair, pushing it back. "You think I don't know I could have gotten hurt? I'm lucky I didn't break anything." He flexed his arms and bent his knees as if to prove it. "I'm lucky I didn't smash my head or loosen a couple of teeth or—"

"Or get eaten by a great white shark?" It was impossible to stay angry when he was being so dramatic. Laurel laughed. "That's a little overboard—no pun intended—don't you think?"

"Maybe." He admitted it with a begrudging shrug

that made his T-shirt stick to his chest like wet Kleenex. "But I'd say a guy is entitled to being a little dramatic when he's just had a near-death experience."

"I would, too. When a guy's had a near-death experience. I think what you had was more like a not-so-near-death experience."

"That didn't stop you from springing into action."

There was a little too much huskiness in Noah's voice to allow Laurel to stay as completely detached as she knew she should. She shrugged away the compliment and wished it was as easy to set aside the thrill of warmth that erupted inside her because of it. "It was nothing. Hey, I'm a doctor. We doctors are famous for keeping our heads in emergencies."

"Which works only if the doctor in question also happens to be the most coolheaded captain on Lake Erie. Good thing you weren't the one who fell in. I don't know a thing about boats."

"Obviously." They were on solid ground, or at least as solid as the ground could be when they were on the water, and Laurel's insides were jumping like the wall-eye she saw splash over on the starboard side. "You need a lesson in boat safety, Dr. Cunningham."

In spite of the fact that at this time of the year the lake water was still warm, Noah shivered. "What I really need is a towel. Notice I didn't ask for a bathrobe. With my luck, you'd produce another wacky little fig leaf and I—"

"Me?" The solid ground tilted, just the way the boat did when another errant wave raced by. This time, Noah had the presence of mind to hang on.

"You don't think I had anything to do with that fig leaf, do you?" she asked him. "Because let me tell you, I didn't. And as a matter of fact, I do have bathrobes.

Cupid's Hideaway bathrobes. There are two of them. And before you accuse me of anything, I didn't swipe them. I bought them, even if I did pay only wholesale. They're down in the aft cabin.'' She gave Noah a nudge toward the companionway that led below deck and when he got moving, she followed him to the top of the steps. ''There's a locker starboard. You'll find them stowed inside.''

Before he went below deck he had the good sense to sit down and slip off his running shoes, and for the second time in as many days, Laurel watched him get undressed. For the second time in as many days, she was swamped by the memories, scalded by the sensations.

And disgusted by the fact that she thought she was old enough and wise enough not to go into meltdown just because a guy happened to have a terrific body, a terrific smile and a terrific—if somewhat annoying— personality.

And did she mention a terrific body?

Rather than put herself through it all over again, she looked up, checking the wind in the sails. Which gave her a peripheral view of Noah while he peeled off his socks and laid them on top of the cabin and slipped off his shirt and wrung it out over the side. By the time he was done, she was tired of watching the wind-speed indicator twirling. It reminded her too much of the way her head was spinning.

''Two?''

''Two?'' Laurel looked at Noah in time to see him laying his shirt next to his socks and smoothing the wrinkles out of it. ''Two what?''

''Two bathrobes.'' He glanced at her just long enough to gauge her reaction. ''You said you had two bathrobes below deck and I wondered why two. Felix doesn't wear a bathrobe, does he?''

"Maybe he does." She wasn't about to start explaining herself. Truth be told, Laurel had two bathrobes because once in a while she had a guest on board. There were a couple times that guest had been a man, but more often than not it was her sister, Meg, or when she could get away from the swirl of life in the Wilson household, Gilly. She had two bathrobes because when she had a guest on board, she and that guest sometimes anchored the boat and went swimming. And it was none of Noah's business. So there.

"You're being nosy."

"Uh-huh." Noah nodded. "I figure being baptized over the side of the *Jade Moon* gives me certain privileges."

She crossed her arms over her chest. "You figure wrong."

He clapped both hands over his heart. "Shot down."

"Not exactly. As far as I can see, you're still standing." She allowed herself a look that skimmed his legs and skittered to where his hands were clasped. Nice view. Except that there were goose bumps on top of his muscles. And goose bumps on top of his goose bumps. "And you look like you're going to turn blue if you don't go below and get the rest of those wet clothes off."

Noah's eyebrows inched up. "I don't suppose you'd like to help."

"Get below deck," she ordered. "I've got some towels down there and there's a blanket in my berth and—"

"You going to join me?"

It wasn't the question that clutched at Laurel's heart as much as it was the smile Noah gave her along with it. The one that warmed her through and through. The one that reminded her there was a time when she would have taken him up on his offer. Cheerfully.

"I'd be out of my mind." She figured he already knew it. She was pretty much just reminding herself. "And you'd regret it."

"I know I'd regret it. Later. But between now and later…" He gave a long, low whistle and a look that was pure white heat. "I'll tell you what, captain, I think between now and later, we could get this boat rocking way more than any waves ever could."

"And we'd both find ourselves in over our heads."

"What a way to go!"

He waited. Maybe to see if she'd jump at the proposition. Maybe because he wanted to allow her the opportunity to be the one to back off. Normally, Laurel would have taken the move as a compliment. It proved that he trusted her judgment. It showed that he, unlike a lot of guys she knew, didn't see letting a woman have control as some kind of threat to their psyches, their manhood and their Me Tarzan, you Jane fantasies.

All of which would have made her feel a whole lot better if only she knew what do to.

It was an offer that was way too good to refuse. She knew that from experience and from the accumulated wisdom of enough lonely nights to fill up four whole years. She also knew that if she let it happen, this time she'd be lonelier than ever when Noah left.

"Belowdecks, landlubber!" Laurel tried for a pirate voice and didn't quite make it. "I'll be topside, getting us to port. And on your way up, bring the yogurt with you."

"Aye, aye, captain." Noah didn't salute. He didn't

move, either. He stood at the top of the stairs, waiting for something Laurel couldn't give him.

"And bring up the first aid kit, too, will you?" She managed to choke out the request at the same time she firmly ignored the glint in his eyes and the touch of sun that sparkled against the beads of water caught in the fine mat of hair on his chest. "We'll get a dry dressing on your hand."

He gave up with a one-shoulder shrug and headed downstairs with Felix at his heels.

Good thing, too. Laurel wasn't sure how much longer she could have held on to her dignity, her self-respect and her head. Not while she was standing there looking into Noah's eyes. Not once she started remembering all they'd once shared.

She got rid of the idea with a shake of her shoulders and a firm reminder that the place she was headed was as rocky as the shoal outside the South Bass harbor. But even that wasn't enough to keep her from looking over her shoulder to the cabin where she could hear Noah rummaging around.

As if he was waiting for the right opportunity, he chose that moment to toss his wet shorts up and out of the cabin. They hit the teak deck with a noise like a smacking kiss and jolted Laurel out of her daydream.

And that was a good thing, too, she decided.

Because daydreams were just that. Dreams. Not reality. And a smart woman knew the difference.

Even if, once in a while, that same smart woman was tempted to forget it.

BY THE TIME they got back to the island, Noah's clothes were mostly dry. Mostly. His T-shirt was fine, but the elastic waistband on his shorts wasn't, and he squirmed a little at the dampness as he pulled the shorts on.

From where he stood in the cabin at the bottom of the stairs, he could see Laurel doing whatever it was a sailboat captain did to get her boat into port. Whatever she was doing, she was doing it well, and for just a little while, he stood and watched her, admiring the way she performed each of her tasks with a certain smoothness as graceful as the waves that rocked the *Jade Moon.*

He'd always known she was beautiful.

In all the time they'd been apart, it was the thing he dreamed of the most. Laurel's eyes. Laurel's hair. The color that rose in Laurel's cheeks when she was angry or embarrassed, when she felt strongly about whatever topic they were discussing, when she was aroused. Which of those emotions had touched her face with color as they stood together on deck before Noah took his infamous dive into the drink?

"I'd pay a bundle to know the answer to that one, pal," he told Felix. Since the dog was lying on an upholstered settee, snoring softly and steadily, Noah didn't get a reaction.

He didn't need one. He'd brought the remnants of their lunch to the cabin with him, and as he'd promised Laurel after they were done eating, he stowed away a couple apples and the one carton of yogurt they hadn't finished. Lucky for him, from the boat's tiny galley, he could still watch its captain.

Laurel's hair was pulled away from her face and tied in a ponytail. It was not the kind of hairstyle Noah usually found attractive, at least not on women of Laurel's age and professional status. There was something a little too artless about a ponytail, something a little

too girls' softball league. Most days, he suspected he
would have felt the same way about Laurel wearing her
hair that way.

But out here on the water, the laws of nature—or at
least of fashion—didn't seem to apply. Laurel's ponytail, Noah decided, looked just right, even though most
of it was hidden beneath a Cleveland Indians baseball
cap. Her red shirt and navy shorts looked pretty darned
good, too.

Before he realized he was doing it, Noah found himself hauling in a steadying breath. He was standing at
the perfect angle to look up and admire Laurel's legs.
They were another of her attributes he thought he knew
and knew well, but somewhere along the line, he'd forgotten how well-shaped they were, how slim, how
tanned. They weren't long legs, but then again, Laurel
wasn't a tall woman. Yet they were perfectly propor-
tioned. Perfectly perfect.

He let his gaze glide up her legs and over her hips,
across her hips and to her breasts, and as silly as it
seemed, he found himself glancing over to make sure
Felix was still asleep. No use letting the dog know his
master was being ogled. Ogled by a man who felt himself tighten like a clock spring just from looking at her.

The thought was too delicious, not to mention tor-
menting, and Noah did his best to set it aside. He
watched Laurel work to bring the boat in. Each of her
chores was accomplished quickly and efficiently, and
now that he thought about it, he supposed that was
partly because on a sailboat—even one as comfortable
as the *Jade Moon*—there wasn't a lot of room to mess
around. The insight had a curious way of heightening
his appreciation of her skills at the same time it heightened his senses. Though Noah would have sworn he

knew Laurel as well as a man could ever know any woman, he realized there was more to her than he'd realized. More than he'd appreciated.

Laurel was smart. She was funny. In a crisis, she could handle herself like a champ. Though she hadn't planned on a passenger, she was gracious enough to share her lunch with him. They sat side by side, Laurel behind the big teak wheel and Noah wrapped in the hand-knitted blanket he'd found on her bed, and though she'd had more than one opportunity to remind him that falling overboard was the nautical equivalent of slipping on a banana peel, she didn't make fun of him even once. And more than once, she'd told him how grateful she was that he hadn't been hurt.

Her concern was enough to warm him even more than the blanket. Enough to keep him from trying to tease her into joining him in its fuzzy folds.

Not that he would have minded so much.

With a cough, Noah cleared away the sudden tightness in his throat and got his attention focused on Laurel and away from the fantasies she had a way of kindling. Away from what might have happened under that blanket. It was apparent from watching her that she adored sailing as much as she adored the *Jade Moon*. He could tell that from the look on her face. She was totally into what she was doing. In the zone. Focused. Centered. Completely consumed by her interest and her love.

There was a time when she looked at Noah that way.

Not that there was any place on board to hide a two-ton rock, but if there had been, Noah would have sworn that was what just hit him. He grabbed the edge of the built-in table to steady himself at the same time he issued his ego and his sex drive a warning. Nothing had changed.

Just because Laurel was more beautiful than he remembered, just because she was more together and more in control and more appealing than he would have thought possible, didn't mean the basic rifts that had pulled them apart could ever be mended. Life wasn't like a cut hand, he reminded himself, looking at the new dressing she'd applied with skill and care. There were no Steri-Strips that could hold together the tattered pieces of what had once been their relationship.

The reminder was enough to get Noah moving up the steps. He got onto the deck just as Laurel brought the boat into the dock. By the time she told him which lines needed securing and showed him the right way to do it, Maisie's voice was floating to them from the other end of the dock.

"Yoo-hoo! There you are!"

Noah looked up just as Laurel did. He saw Maisie headed straight for them, resplendent in pink capri pants and a white cotton top embroidered with hearts and edged in lace.

"Perfect timing!" She glanced at Noah, and her snowy eyebrows rose. Though his shorts and shirt were on, he hadn't bothered with his socks or his soggy running shoes. Not exactly scandalous, but leave it to Maisie to read something into his state of undress. Grinning, she grabbed one of the lines Laurel threw onto the dock and secured it with more ease than he would have thought possible for a little old lady who more often than not had nothing in her head but thoughts of romance schmaltzy enough to fill a dozen chick flicks.

"I was a little concerned. About you." Maisie glanced at Noah at the same time she brushed her hands together. "You went out running and you didn't come back. Of course, I had to investigate. It's an innkeeper's job, after all, to keep her inn and her guests. I came down here and saw that you were gone…'' This time, her expert, inquisitive gaze homed in on Laurel. ''Well, I'm as good as anyone at putting two and two together. Or one and one, in this case.'' She giggled, the sound mixing with the noise of the lake gulls who circled overhead. ''I figured you two were together. Did you have a nice time out on the lake, dear?''

''We had a terrific time.'' Laurel smiled, and something in her expression told Noah she meant it. And something that flared inside him told him he was glad she did. ''We had lunch, sat in the sun, had a nice, long talk. And Noah fell in and nearly drowned.''

''Fell in? Oh, dear.'' For the first time, Noah's state of undress made sense, and Maisie's face paled. ''I do hope you're all right,'' she told Noah and then, apparently deciding he must be or he wouldn't be getting out the sail covers, she breezed right on. ''Because I've got the tickets!'' Like a magician pulling a magic rabbit out of a silk hat, she reached into her pocket and produced two blue pieces of paper, each about the size of a dollar bill. She leaned over the water and waved them under Noah's nose, smiling all the while.

''Tickets?'' Because something told him he wouldn't get an answer out of Maisie—at least not a straight answer—he looked at Laurel. ''Tickets for what?''

Laurel didn't answer. At least not right away. She coiled some rope that was lying on the deck, called Felix and, once he was on deck, pulled closed the hatch that covered the steps to the cabin. When she was done, Maisie was still holding the tickets, and Noah was more curious than ever.

''There's a dinner dance at city hall tomorrow evening,'' Laurel explained. ''But Maisie couldn't possibly have tickets for that.'' She looked at her grandmother, daring Maisie to challenge her. ''Because two weeks ago when the good folks at the Chamber of Commerce announced they were going to have a dinner, my dear grandmother told me she was going to buy two tickets, one for me and one for a date. And I told her she shouldn't bother. That even if I went to the dinner, I wasn't planning on taking a date.'' Laurel tied another line, and when she motioned to Noah, he handed her the mainsail cover and together they slipped it over the furled sail and secured it. They repeated the process with the staysail and got Felix onto the dock before Laurel said anything else.

''My dear grandmother,'' she added when they were done, ''knows better than to try and make those kinds of decisions on her own. That would be…'' She glanced at the mast as if trying to find words, then at Maisie, who was standing on the dock looking as pink, as in-nocent and as adorable as a bunny on an Easter card.

''That would be the equivalent of sticking her nose in other people's business, and I know my grandmother would never do that.'' Laurel stepped aside and let Noah get off the boat first. He tossed his sneakers and socks onto the dock and followed them, being careful to hang on to the shroud as he stepped over the side.

''She never would have bought two tickets,'' Laurel said, following Noah and landing lightly on the dock next to him. ''Not for me.''

''Bosh!'' Maisie waved away the lecture with one hand. ''I didn't buy them for you, dear.'' She pivoted to face Noah. ''I bought them for Noah. He's my guest, after all, and an innkeeper has to look out for her guests. Besides, I suppose it's technically my fault that he's staying the weekend. After all, I'm the one who invited him here in the first place. That means I have every right to look after his welfare. And an obligation to make sure he isn't lonely." She shoved the tickets into Noah's hand and while he was still looking at her as if she'd handed him the paper equivalent of a ticking time bomb, she waved a cheery goodbye and headed toward dry land.

"She's incorrigible!" As if praying for strength, Laurel looked toward the heavens. It was obvious, though, that she wasn't aggravated. Maisie was one of a kind. That was for sure. But she was also kindhearted and as lovable an old lady as Noah ever met. It was clear that Laurel adored her grandmother.

Smiling, she started down the dock toward land, and Noah walked along beside her. "She's just looking out for you."

"You think?" She glanced at him. "I think she's trying to stick her little freckled nose where it doesn't belong."

"Which doesn't change a thing." Noah held up the tickets, and they ruffled in the breeze off the lake. "I'm still the proud owner of a pair of tickets to what sounds like the hottest thing going on around here."

Laurel laughed. "You've never been to a dinner dance at city hall."

"No. But I'd like to try." Once they stepped off the dock and onto dry land, Noah reached a hand out and touched Laurel's arm. She was surprised enough to stop. She turned to him, a look in her eyes that wavered between expectation and out-and-out terror. It was enough to make Noah smile.

"Come with me," he said.

"Oh, no!" Something told Noah her reaction was more instinctive than rational. No sooner were the words out of her mouth than she backed away. "I told Maisie and I'm telling you. I'm not taking a date to that dance."

"You're not taking a date." Noah waved the tickets under her nose. "I've got the tickets. I'm taking the date. Come with me, Laurel. Please."

The smile on Laurel's lips floundered, and Noah held his breath. "All right," she said. "I'll go with you. Felix!" she called, and the dog came running over. She went to meet him at the sidewalk, but once she got there, she hesitated and glanced at Noah. "I'll see you tomorrow night."

"Yeah. Tomorrow night." Noah knew he should have done something. Waved, maybe. Smiled. At least said goodbye.

Instead, he stood there watching Laurel walk across the park, her strides long and purposeful, her shoulders back, her head high. He might have followed if not for the fact that his knees felt week and his legs were shaky.

It was the water. That's what it was.

Always the scientist, Noah searched for the most rational explanation.

The fluttering in his stomach and the spinning in his head had to be a result of the hours they'd spent on the lake. It was an inner-ear thing. He didn't have his land legs back yet. That was why he was feeling so lightheaded.

It couldn't have had anything to do with the fact that he'd just asked Laurel out.

That she'd just said yes.

Could it?

Chapter Ten

The really weird part was that he was nervous.

Noah checked his reflection in the mirror in Almost Paradise and hoped the slightly green cast to his face had more to do with the evening light reflecting off the glossy leaves of the plants that surrounded him than it did the fact that he felt as jumpy as the fish in the nearby pond.

"Like a kid." His voice tight in his throat, he spoke the words to his reflection, trying to talk some sense into himself at the same time he ran a comb through his hair. "You're acting like a kid, not like a man. You're acting like a kid on his first date and I'll tell you what, pal, it is not a pretty sight."

Which didn't keep him from combing his hair again. Or checking—again—to see if the khakis and light blue business shirt he'd chosen to wear to the Chamber of Commerce dinner dance looked just right. He could have opted for something a little more casual, he supposed, and not for the first time, he looked through the clothes he'd emptied out of his suitcase and onto the bed.

Jeans and a sweater. Shorts and a golf shirt.

He picked up each outfit and discarded each with a shake of his head.

"Maybe not casual," he mumbled. "Maybe this isn't a casual sort of occasion." He went to the closet and got out the suit he'd worn when he checked into Cupid's Hideaway. Thanks to Maisie, it had been cleaned and pressed, and he knew he had a fresh white shirt in his luggage. He could add a tie, drag out his wing tips and—

Noah was not prone to flights of fashion. Never had been. Though he had been told any number of times by any number of people that he had a flair for clothes and a knack for starting trends among his students and his colleagues, he was convinced fashion was something that just happened, not something that was planned. At least not in his life.

Which was why he never worried about it. Not like he was worried about it now.

He gave the internal fashion police a mental slap at the same time he pulled in a breath to steady himself.

"This is nuts!" he groaned. He hung the suit where it belonged and went to the dresser to collect his wallet and the Almost Paradise key on its heavy brass key chain, vowing he wouldn't look in the mirror again. That he wouldn't drive himself up the wall and around the bend and over the edge. Not about this.

After all, it was just a dinner dance on a small island in the middle of nowhere. It was just a bunch of island residents, and no doubt they were all nice people. There was nothing for him to be afraid of, no one he was trying to impress.

Besides, it was just city hall, not some elegant country club. Just a social occasion, not anything to get all crazy about. It was only a date. That's all it was. A one time, tonight-only, sit-next-to-Laurel-and-eat-baked-chicken-and-roast-beef-and-have-a-couple-laughs sort of event, and it didn't mean a thing.

Which didn't explain why his palms were damp and his stomach was doing a cha-cha. It also didn't explain why, in the twenty-four hours or so since Maisie had handed him the dinner dance tickets, his mind had been so preoccupied.

The night before, he'd spent a quiet evening in his room going over some notes for an upcoming lecture.

And thinking about Laurel.

That morning, he'd spent an equally uneventful few hours on a bike supplied by Maisie, tooling around the island and enjoying the solitude.

And thinking about Laurel.

He thought about her while he ate a burger for lunch, and he thought about her again when he rode past the Ross-Burton Clinic and stopped to peek in the window. Just in case she had some work to catch up on and happened to be in her office.

He'd been thinking about Laurel a lot.

Understatement of the century.

He'd been thinking about Laurel and nothing but Laurel. About what they'd say to each other tonight. And what they'd do. About how when the band played a slow song and he asked her to dance, she'd say yes. In his mind, he could see the way they'd walk onto the dance floor, hand in hand, and the way they'd start out dancing the way most people did. Slow and easy, but with just that little bit of restraint, just that little bit of censoring that most people—at least most people their age—used when they danced in public. Close but not too close. Slow but not too slow. Fluid and effortless and provocative.

But not too.

As the music went on and they found the beat, they'd move as if they were one. Like they'd done so many times before. And he'd pull her closer, and closer still, until he felt the heat of her breath on his neck and the warmth of her breasts pressed against his chest and the way her thighs moved against his to the same rhythm that pounded through his bloodstream. And when the dance was over—

With a groan, Noah shook himself out of the daydream.

When it was over, he'd be a crazy man. Just like he was a crazy man now. Just like he'd been a crazy man each and every time in the last four years when he thought that anything could be different between him and Laurel.

Keeping the one-time-only, chicken-and-roast-beef reality of the situation in mind, he splashed on some aftershave and combed his hair one more time. Tonight was just tonight, he told himself, and two blue tickets that had been forced on him by an old lady who didn't know when to leave well enough alone weren't going to change a thing.

Even though he was sure he was right, Noah checked the mirror one more time. Just in case. He looked himself in the eye. "Time to get real, Noah Cunningham. Time to pull yourself together. Remember, it's only a date."

IT WAS ONLY A DATE, and Laurel knew it. It was only a date, and even if the circumstances were different— and they weren't—it wouldn't have meant a whole lot in the grand scheme of things. Noah didn't go out searching for two tickets to tonight's dinner dance with her in mind. Maisie gave him the tickets. Noah just happened to be standing next to Laurel at the time. Any guy would have made the offer. Even a guy with no class, no smarts and no clue.

None of which had ever been part of Noah's problem.

Frowning at the thought and at the tiny tingles of anticipation that fizzed through her because of it, Laurel looked from the brown loafer she had on her right foot to the black, open-toed pump she wore on her left, one of a pair she hadn't worn since med-school graduation.

It was only a date, she told herself, and to her way of thinking, that meant she shouldn't have been any more jittery than she ever had been about any other date. Which didn't explain why her bedroom was littered with the outfits she'd tried on, discarded and tried on again. Or why she was standing in front of the full-length mirror hanging from the door of her bedroom closet, trying to decide which shoes looked best with the soft, plum-colored skirt and sage-green-and-purple sweater she'd finally decided to wear.

"What do you think?" Her arms out, Laurel spun toward Felix, teetering just a little. "Loafers or pumps? Pumps or loafers?"

Felix, predictably, didn't much care. Though at the sound of Laurel's voice he opened one eye, he closed it again just as quickly, stretched and went right back to doggy dreamland.

"Thanks a lot, pal." She made a face at the dog. "Just when I need you, you take the chicken's way out. All right. I'll make up my own mind."

She studied her reflection, noting as she did that the woman staring back at her from the mirror looked vaguely familiar. Same color eyes as the Laurel Burton she knew so well. Same hair, though for once, it had been tamed into a braid and it looked like it might stay there. She had the same body, compact and slim, the same way of standing with her feet slightly apart, as if she was just itching to take on the world.

It was the heightened color in her cheeks when she looked in the mirror that struck Laurel as alarming. The light that sparkled in her eyes. She was Laurel, but she was a stranger.

Which, if nothing else, might help explain why she'd been so nervous all day.

Laurel reached for her blusher and brushed it on her cheeks. Maybe that was the reason this Laurel who wasn't Laurel felt a little light-headed, a little shaky, a little like she'd had too many cups of the too-strong coffee Carole made at the clinic.

That would explain it. The zinging in her blood. The buzzing in her head. The feeling in her stomach that made her think of the loopy bows Maisie added to each and every birthday gift she ever gave.

"Nerves." Laurel said the word to her reflection. It sounded right. It felt accurate. What it didn't do was make any sense.

She'd known the people on the island all her life, and while she liked most of them, respected some of them and tolerated others, she was way past the point of influencing what any of them thought of her. By nature, the people of South Bass were mavericks. If they weren't, they never would have been able to tolerate summers full of tourists and winters that, once the lake froze, included months of isolation.

So why was it suddenly so important to wear just the right thing to dinner?

Laurel glanced at her reflection in the mirror. "Why is it so important?" She barked out a sound that was halfway between a laugh and "get real," and peered at Felix's reflection in the mirror.

"You're not the only one acting like a chicken," she told him. But admitting she was a chicken was one thing. Acting any other way was something else.

Rather than think about it, she concentrated on her shoes.

"Loafers," she said, authority ringing in her voice. Just to prove she was a woman of decision, she kicked the pump into the bowels of her closet.

Right before she decided that she looked like a schoolteacher in her loafers.

"Not that there's anything wrong with schoolteachers," she told Felix. She kicked off the loafer. She bent to retrieve the right pump at the same time she realized she'd kicked the left one so far, she wasn't sure where it had landed. She got down on her hands and knees in her closet.

"Schoolteachers are fine people. Mom and Pop were both schoolteachers. But that doesn't mean..." She reached beneath a pile of clothes she'd put aside for the Salvation Army and came up with a strappy summer sandal. Grumbling, she threw it over her shoulder. "It doesn't mean I want to look like my mother," she told the dog. She could just make out the shape of a shoe in the farthest, darkest corner of the closet, and she stretched, reaching around a box of Christmas decorations, and grabbed it just as the doorbell rang.

"It's not time," Laurel groaned. "It can't be. I'm not ready yet!"

Felix didn't care. His doggy sense told him there was someone he liked at the door, and barking even before his eyes were fully opened, he scrambled to his feet and headed down the stairs.

Laurel had no choice but to follow. Kind of hard to pretend she didn't hear the bell when Felix was making enough noise to rouse the neighborhood.

Not that she didn't consider it.

She set aside the thought with a deep breath designed to calm her nerves. It didn't work, so she smoothed her skirt, ran a hand over the braid that she realized, too late, was already starting to come undone, and pulled open her front door.

WHEN LAUREL opened the door, Noah wasn't sure what to say. She stood in the splash of sunshine that burnished her front porch and snuck in the front door, and for what was probably only a couple seconds, but felt like a couple long minutes, he stared. She was wearing a skirt that was the exact color of the mums growing along the stone path to her front porch and a sweater that hugged her breasts with softness. Her cheeks were glowing. Her lips were red with a color that looked more like stain than lipstick. Her hair was pulled back and coiled into a braid that brushed the back of her neck. Already, a couple long strands of it had come loose, and he itched to brush them away from her face.

Only a date, huh?

The question bounced around inside his head like a racquetball gone bad. He'd been on *only* dates, been on quite a lot of them in the four years since he and Laurel had decided that far apart was the only way to be, and as far as he could remember, none of them had left him feeling like the blood in his veins had been replaced by Alka-Seltzer.

Only a date, huh? Instead of trying to plumb the depths of a question he knew he couldn't answer, he stuck out his right hand. "Here," he said. "These are for you."

Laurel glanced down at the single stem of bright magenta flowers he held toward her. "Orchids. They're orchids." She gave him a look he couldn't read. She might have been pleasantly surprised. Or maybe she couldn't believe her eyes. "You picked the orchids from Almost Paradise? Maisie will have your head!"

He leaned forward and gave her a sleek smile. "Not if you don't tell her. Besides…" When Laurel didn't take the flowers from him, he grabbed her hand. He would have wound her fingers around the stem if she wasn't holding a black shoe.

At his touch, she looked at the shoe as if she wasn't quite sure how it got there. She dropped it, slipped it on and accepted the flowers.

"I only took one stem. " Noah defended what he supposed was—at least in light of the fact that he was offering the flowers to the granddaughter of the woman they theoretically belonged to—a pretty indefensible position. "There were plenty of others and—"

"Never mind!" He never thought the flowers would get him a reward as special as a laugh. As a matter of fact, he wasn't sure what he thought when he snipped the flowers from the pot that sat outside the bathroom door of Almost Paradise. Maybe he figured Laurel would be less likely to spend the night battling with him if he came bearing gifts, even gifts as modest as stolen orchids. Maybe he was too nervous to walk all the way to her house from the Hideaway without juggling something in his hands. Maybe he was just being corny, which wasn't a failing he usually had. Or old-fashioned, which was never something he'd been accused of being. Or sentimental, which he knew he wasn't because a man wasn't supposed to get sentimental about a woman who had once accused him of making her play second fiddle to his plans, his career and his own—in her words—elephantine ego.

Whatever the reason, it won him a laugh, and Noah found himself smiling, too. When Laurel moved aside to allow him into the house, he stepped into a tiny ceramic-floored entryway and from there into the living room.

"Something tells me even if Maisie did find out, she'd say it was for a good cause." Laurel laughed again, and it might have been Noah's imagination, but he could have sworn she sounded just about as nervous as he felt. "Silly, huh?"

"Yeah, silly." It didn't sound silly. Not to Noah. It sounded like Maisie was clairvoyant. Like she knew how beautiful Laurel was going to look tonight. Like she knew how the moment he saw her, Noah's tongue was going to feel like it had been tied into one of the knots he'd seen Laurel use on the *Jade Moon* and how his gut was going to tighten and how his heart was going to speed up to a beat he'd never been able to match even when he was running a marathon. Like somehow, Maisie would know that the orchids weren't just for a good cause. They were for the best of causes.

Laurel twirled the stem that contained six half-dollar-size flowers. "I guess I'd better put these in water," she said. "Felix will keep you company."

She disappeared toward the back of the house, and Noah heard her rummaging around in a cupboard, no doubt looking for a vase. While she was gone, he gave Felix a good-to-see-you-again rub behind the ears and took a quick look around Laurel's living room.

There was no doubt Laurel thought the world of

Maisie. But though she loved the old lady to pieces, it was obvious they didn't share each other's tastes when it came to decorating. Not a cupid in sight. No pink lightbulbs. Noah peered into a lamp sitting on a sleek, mission-style oak table, just to be sure. No red velvet, no lace.

Instead, Laurel's living room—and, he suspected, Laurel's entire house—was a lot like Laurel herself. Practical and no-nonsense, but with a certain sense of style. The lines were clean, the colors were warm and muted. There weren't many pictures on the walls, but the ones that were there were well chosen. There was a watercolor of the South Bass shoreline, a small oil painting of a vase of flowers that picked up the soft blues, greens and browns in the sofa. There was a field-stone fireplace across the room, and the mantel was lined with photographs. Noah headed that way to check them out.

There were photos of Laurel and her sister, Meg, a couple of their mom and dad. There was one of Maisie with Doc Ross. The most ornate frame in the display held a photo of Felix romping with what must have been a favorite chew toy. There was one of Laurel on the *Jade Moon,* another of a set of grandparents Noah had never met and a last photo of a younger Laurel standing outside the entrance to the clinic. Above her head, two burly-looking workmen were putting the finishing touches on the sign above the door, the one that changed the name officially from the Ross Clinic to the Ross-Burton Clinic.

"I look like a kid, don't I?"

The sound of Laurel's voice made Noah jump. He hadn't realized he'd picked up the picture until he found himself with it in his hands. As if she needed to see it, he tipped it toward her. "You look like a happy kid."

Laurel looked thoughtful. She was carrying a tall, skinny vase with the orchids in it and she set it on the coffee table. Her gaze moved to the picture in Noah's hands. "It was what I wanted," she said. "What I always wanted. A dream come true, you know?"

"Yeah. I know." It sounded trite, but it was the absolute truth. Noah did know what it was like to have a dream come true because one of his was coming true at that very moment. It was a dream he used to have, one he hadn't allowed himself to even come close to imagining in four long years. The one in which he and Laurel were here, in this house, together. Only Noah's dream included more pictures on the mantel—a wedding picture, a couple from that honeymoon on Maui they'd always dreamed about, maybe by this time a couple baby pictures, too.

He wondered how many *only* dates progressed from arriving at the front door to planning where to put the pictures of the kids in such short order. And told himself to get a hold. Fast. Before he said something, or did something, that proved he had no business here in the first place.

He should have known Laurel wouldn't allow anything else. As if she could read each and every one of the thoughts floating through his head about wedding gowns, Hawaiian shirts and booties, she plucked the photo out of his hands and set it where it belonged.

"It's still my dream," she told him, brushing her fingers along the frame even though there wasn't a speck of dust on it. She turned to face him and looked him in the eyes. "My only dream."

"Got the message." Noah backed off, his hands in

the air in surrender. "Loud and clear. You don't think I was possibly going to suggest—"

"Of course not."

"Good."

"Great."

Noah punched his hands into his pockets. Laurel clutched hers behind her back.

"Cold out?" she asked.

SOMETHING TOLD HER he wanted to say that it wasn't as cold outside as it was suddenly in. He didn't. But only because he was looking a little peaked, a little pale. She supposed that's what happened when the woman he'd been kind enough to ask to a dinner dance invited him into her home and then practically accused him of messing up her life.

Which he had.

Which, she'd told herself about a thousand times since they'd jumped off the *Jade Moon* and into the thick of Maisie's romantic web, she wasn't going to let bother her. Not tonight.

Easier said than done.

Especially when the hum of the magnetic field that vibrated around Noah was making a racket in Laurel's ears.

Rather than listen to the chaos it was creating in her head, rather than try to fight its pull, she moved toward the door. She said good-night to Felix and reminded him that he had to be very good. She waited while Noah stooped in front of the dog and gave him a couple friendly scratches.

It was hard to stay nervous around a guy who was crazy about the dog she was crazy about, and before Laurel even knew she was doing it, she was smiling

again. Smiling and reminding herself that their time on
the *Jade Moon* had shown that she and Noah could
peacefully coexist. Heck, it even proved they could
have fun together. Just like in the old days. If for no
other reason, she owed him the courtesy of remembering the good times and not the bad. At least for tonight.

Feeling a little guilty for snapping at him but not
guilty enough to admit it, Laurel offered Noah a small
smile. "I just wondered if I should wear a coat."

Not much in the olive branch department but apparently enough. With an equally tentative smile, Noah
moved out of the room. "No coat. It's gorgeous out,"
he said. He opened the door and let Laurel walk out
ahead of him. It wasn't until she was nearly past him
that he added, "Besides, if you get cold, I can always
keep you warm."

Fiery words that stopped her cold.

Halfway in and halfway out of her house, Laurel
paused and glanced over her shoulder at Noah. "Is that
a promise or a threat?" she asked him, and while he
was still thinking about it and trying to interpret the
twinkle in her eyes that left him guessing which she
would have liked it to be, she walked down the front
porch steps.

Chapter Eleven

"You wanna dance?"

The question came from over Noah's left shoulder, and considering he recognized the voice as belonging to Doug, the owner of the local bait-and-tackle shop, it sure couldn't have been directed at him. He turned and found gray-haired, flannel-shirt-clad Doug shuffling from foot to foot and grinning at Laurel.

"Dance?" Choking over the word, Noah gulped the last of the ginger ale he'd been sipping during a break in the music. He turned to Laurel, and though he tried to keep the note of desperation out of his voice, something told him it wasn't working. "This guy wants to dance with you and—"

"Sure!" Laurel handed Noah her light beer at the same time she gave the bait-and-tackle guy a sunny smile. A glass in each hand and a hollow feeling in his stomach—in spite of the fact that he'd just eaten enough baked chicken and roast beef to keep him going for days—Noah watched Laurel and Doug head to the dance floor, chatting and laughing like old friends. Which they undoubtedly were.

"Good thing this is only a date," he grumbled.

"Talking to yourself?"

Too busy watching Laurel and Doug trip the light fantastic to realize anyone had come up beside him, Noah flinched.

"That noticeable, huh?" he asked Meg. Laurel's younger sister followed his gaze to the dance floor where even now Laurel and Doug were doing a kind of two-step waltz to something that sounded, at least to Noah's untrained ears, like classic Patsy Cline.

"Kind of hard not to notice a guy holding two drinks and standing over here all by himself mumbling at nothing but thin air." Meg laughed. Though she and Laurel were only two years apart in age, they were light-years apart in personality. Noah had met Meg only once before he and Laurel sat across the table from her at dinner, but he remembered the stories Laurel had told him. Remembered them well.

Laurel was crazy about her little sister, but she never denied that Meg was wild. Meg was the one who, in her high-school years, had given their parents more than their share of sleepless nights. Laurel was studious. Meg was the class cutup. Laurel was nose to the grindstone. Meg was more of a free spirit. While Laurel worked like a dog to get through medical school, Meg flitted from job to job, jobs that ranged from lifeguard to bartender, from fishing-charter-boat captain to operating the carousel near the park. She'd settled down, at least for now, working as the chef at Cupid's Hideaway and running what sounded like a thriving catering business.

Meg was taller than Laurel. Thinner. Her hair was redder. Her skin was paler and covered with far more freckles. She was an attractive woman prone to wearing bright colors, funky jewelry and lots of earrings. Truth be told, her freewheeling personality was probably much better suited to Noah's independent spirit than her older sister's by-the-book nature had ever been. Case in point—Laurel wanted nothing more than to live happily ever after on the island. Meg made no secret of the fact that she'd just as soon leave, and leave for good.

Meg was a beautiful woman, no doubt of that, and Noah enjoyed her company. But as long as the truth was being told, he might as well admit it to himself. His taste ran more toward shorter, darker-haired women. Or *woman,* to be more specific. One who, even now, was twirling around the dance floor with a guy twenty years older, light-years less sophisticated and way more fishy smelling than Noah had ever been.

"I haven't danced with her all night long." Noah didn't realize he'd spoken the words until he heard Meg chuckle.

"There aren't many of these dinner dances," she said. "And even when there are, Laurel doesn't always come. Folks are happy she's here, that's all. They're trying to show her a good time."

"I could show her a good time." He was sounding whiny. Petulant. Grouchy. Noah didn't much care. All this time he'd been fantasizing about that slow dance, the one he'd been planning since the moment Maisie slapped those two tickets in his hand. He'd been picturing the way Laurel would move, fantasizing about the feel of her against him. He'd been dreaming about the way he was going to hold her in his arms.

And he hadn't even gotten close to making the dream a reality. No closer than watching her dance by with just about every other guy in the place, all of whom seemed to have a talent for jumping in with both feet and asking Laurel to dance before Noah could put together the words that would get her on the dance floor and into his arms. She'd danced with the mayor and a couple members of city council. She'd danced with Doc twice and with some young guy named Ben who held Laurel way too close for Noah's liking. She'd danced with Tom, the husband of her receptionist. She'd even danced with both the Wild Wilsons. Simultaneously.

She'd danced with everyone but Noah, and while he didn't think it was an intentional slap in the face, he was getting tired of the occasional dance with Maisie or one of the other elderly women she shot his way. He was tired of standing on the sidelines watching while his date went around and around the dance floor and his dreams went up in smoke.

"Not much fun just watching, is it?"

Meg's question reminded him he wasn't alone. At the same time it reminded him he was being just about as impolite as he possibly could.

"I'm sorry. I should have asked sooner." He tipped his head toward the dance floor. "Do you want to—"

"Oh, no. Not me!" Meg's laughter rose above Patsy's plaintive tones. "I have two left feet," she said, pointing to them. "Honest. And you wouldn't want either one of them stomping on yours. It's better—and safer—for me just to watch."

"All right." Noah gave in with a shrug. "I'll just wait for the next song and—"

"Oh, no, you don't! The night is far from young. It's close to midnight. Things will be over soon." Meg put one hand on each of Noah's shoulders and gave him a good-natured push. "Go cut in!" she ordered him. "Now. You might not get another chance."

"You think—"

"I know she wouldn't mind." Meg sounded so sure of both herself and of what Laurel would want that Noah found it impossible to resist the suggestion. With

a deep breath, he headed across the dance floor and
tapped Doug on the shoulder.

"Can I cut in?" he asked, and it wasn't until he did
that he wondered how he was supposed to respond if
Doug said no. Lucky for him, Doug was a reasonable
fellow. With a brief jerking bow, he backed away from
Laurel and headed to where tables had been set up along
the perimeter of the dance floor and a friend was waiting
with an ice-cold beer

"Thanks." Laurel didn't exactly look relieved, but
she didn't look sorry to see Noah, either. A fact that
cheered him no end. "He's a nice guy," she said with
a look across the room at Doug. "But not much when
it comes to the conversation department. As a matter of
fact, we were talking about his hemorrhoids."

Noah laughed. He'd been there, done that. "The perils of dancing with a doctor."

"More peril for the doctor than the patient."

"I promise I won't talk about anything related to
anatomy," Noah promised, moving in a step closer to
her. "At least not until I get you alone. Will you—"

"Dance with you?" Laurel shook her head, and for
one second, doubt streaked through Noah like the wail
of the slide guitar in the song still playing. "It's about
time you asked." She held out her hand, waiting for
Noah to take it.

He didn't bother. Instead, he fitted an arm around
Laurel's waist and tugged her against him, close enough
to feel the swell of her breasts, near enough to realize
that when he did, her heartbeat sped up. Nearly as fast
as his own. They were swaying to the bittersweet song
before either one of them took their next breath.

It was just the way Noah had imagined it. Just as
intimate. Just as pulse pounding. Just as provocative as

a fantasy could be when it was coming to life in the middle of a room full of people talking and chatting and shuffling to the music. Not exactly as private as he would have liked, but he'd settle for it. At least for now.

He flattened his hand against the small of Laurel's back. "I never thought I'd get the chance to do this tonight," he told her.

"Dance?" She looked at him, a spark in her eyes that might have been the reflection of the fluorescent lights along the perimeter of the dance floor. "Looked like you were doing pretty well dancing with Maisie and her chums. They'll be talking about you for weeks."

"I didn't mean dancing. I meant dancing with you." Laurel adjusted her stance, and her thigh brushed Noah's. A feeling like electricity sparkled through him. "I've been waiting all night to hold you like this," he told her.

The last forlorn strains of the song ended, and though the other couples on the dance floor stopped, waiting for the next song to start up, Noah and Laurel kept moving, dancing to a rhythm no one else could possibly hear. The silence settled. One second. Two. The first notes of the next song started, and all around them, people yelled, "Chicken dance!"

"Chicken dance?" Astounded, Noah stopped dancing and looked around in wonder. The place had gone from mellow to madness in no time flat. Suddenly, chairs were scraping back from tables and everyone was on the dance floor. Kids bumped into him, old ladies twittered when they hurried to take their places, and guys who looked like they were more comfortable behind the wheel of a truck or at the business end of a bar brawl gave in with good-humored sighs to significant others who dragged them to the dance floor.

"Chicken dance?" Noah wasn't sure why he even bothered to wonder what was going on. The song started in earnest, and all around him, folks swung into a dance of sorts, flapping their arms and moving their feet through a series of silly dance steps that got faster and sillier by the moment. Suddenly Laurel wasn't nice and close, she was three feet from him, flapping her arms just like everyone else, and Noah's arms were as empty as his fantasy was shattered.

"Come on!" When Noah stood looking around the room, as stunned as if he'd just realized everyone there was an alien, Laurel gave him a nudge. "Like this." She mouthed the words and went through the motions of the dance, waiting for him to follow.

LAUREL FLAPPED her arms. She moved her feet. She hated the chicken dance. Always had. Always would, she suspected. It was goofy. Its repetitious steps were annoying. Because she'd watched it from the sidelines so many times, she knew that the people doing it looked silly.

None of which kept her from throwing herself into the dance in earnest. After all, the chicken dance had saved her.

All night long, she'd felt as if she was about to hop right out of her skin. She was as nervous as she could be, and she'd jumped at the chance of dancing with everyone from the mayor to Carole's husband, Tom, just so she could get away from Noah and take a break from the hum of anticipation that tingled through her every time he so much as looked at her.

As the night went on, things got worse. Every time

another song started, she was afraid Noah would ask her to dance. Afraid he wouldn't. Afraid if she didn't get onto the dance floor with someone else—fast— she'd tackle him and drag him out there just so she could feel his arms around her.

She was afraid that if she committed herself and gave in to the urges that were screaming through her body, he'd think she was delusional, that she didn't realize this was only a date. That she didn't have the sense to remember a dinner dance at city hall didn't mean a thing.

She was scared to death he'd ask her to dance just as John Richter, who was in charge of the CD player for the night, was playing something slow and sweet like Patsy Cline. That the music would be mellow and the moment would be just right, and that when Noah put his arms around her, everything she'd been thinking and feeling since he walked back into her life wouldn't just be noticeable, it would be flashing over her head like a neon Come and Get Me sign. She was afraid if that happened, Noah would be all for it, and that if he was, what started out as a simple dance would accelerate way past dancing. And way past simple.

"Thank you, chicken dance," she breathed, and when Noah looked at her as if he'd missed something important, she waved away his concern. Poor guy. He was trying to keep up with the steps of the dance and was always a couple beats behind. At least he got points for trying.

Something about watching Noah muddle his way through the dance made Laurel's nervousness throttle back. Something about swinging around the dance floor, acting more like a goofball than a chicken, made it disappear. Pretty soon she was laughing, and Noah was, too, and by the time the song was over and all the lights in the hall came on, signaling the end of the event, they had linked arms and were headed for the door.

They stopped outside to say their good-nights, and when they saw Doc and Maisie, Laurel gave them each a kiss on the cheek. By the time most of the other party-ers were in their cars and headed out of the parking lot, Laurel and Noah were walking toward home.

"That was nice." No one was more surprised than Laurel to realize it was true. Spending the evening with Noah had been more than just nice. It felt right.

"This is nice, too." He took her hand and twined his fingers through hers, and they walked along in silence, passing some houses that were closed up for the winter and others where their fellow partyers were just arriving home. They called out their final good-nights and kept walking, and the farther they got from city hall, the quieter it got. Laurel loved the tranquillity of the island in the fall. She breathed in the crisp air and the smell of the leaves and relaxed, enjoying the silence and the feel of Noah walking next to her.

"I used to think I'd hate it here."

His comment caught her by surprise, and she stopped and turned to him. "That's not exactly the way I re-member it," she told him. "Seems to me you used to think it might be nice to live here. With me. Until you got that offer to teach. Then all of a sudden, I was the last thing you wanted."

"You're wrong." Noah put a hand on her waist. "You were what I wanted. First, last and always. I just didn't think I could turn my back on a career opportu-nity as good as that. It meant giving up this place, and I've learned to live with that. It meant giving up you, too, and I'll tell you what, it's a decision I've regretted every day since.''

"Don't.'' Laurel pulled away from him and kept on walking. Better to get moving than stand there and fall under Noah's spell. Better for him. Better for her. Better than believing words that couldn't possibly be true.

"Don't what? Don't tell the truth?'' He caught up with her as she got to the picket fence that surrounded her front yard and stopped her, one hand on her arm.

"It can't be true, Noah, because if it was true—''

"If it was true, then we'd both have to admit we made a mistake four years ago. Is that what you were going to say?''

"I was going to say that if it was true, it would mean things could be different between us. And I think we both know that's not possible.''

"Why not? Why isn't it possible?''

"Because…'' Laurel shook her head. His words were coming at her too fast. The things they hinted at were too foreign. She couldn't fit them into the framework she'd spent four years building around her life. "Because you have your life and I have mine. Isn't that a good enough reason? Because there's no place we overlap. No place we touch. Not anymore.''

"We touch here.'' Noah's hand tightened around her arm. He slipped it up to her shoulder. "We touch here,'' he said, and he ran a hand over her hair. "We touch here.'' He brushed his hand down her neck and touched her heart. "And we touch here,'' he said, and he kissed her.

There was no way Laurel could resist. No way she wanted to. At the Love Shack, she'd given in to Noah's kiss, but only because she was too stunned to do anything else. Now, she tipped her head to allow him to deepen the kiss and arched her back just a little so that he could cup her breast in one hand. She heard him groan at the same time he tightened his hold on her. She heard herself make a noise deep in her throat when he skimmed his thumb over her nipple.

"See?" Noah moved far enough away to smile into her eyes. "We've been avoiding that for days, and it wasn't so bad, was it?"

"No." As much as she would have liked to say anything else, she couldn't lie. Not to him. Not to herself. "It wasn't bad at all."

"So you want to try it again?"

She didn't. She wanted to pretend none of it had ever happened. That he hadn't come back to the island. That he hadn't worked his way back into her life and her heart. That she didn't want him more than she'd ever wanted anything. That she didn't feel the need for him screaming through her body.

She couldn't lie. Not about something this important.

Instead, Laurel raised her mouth to Noah's, and when he kissed her, she opened her lips and touched her tongue to his, and when she felt a quiver of excitement shiver through him, she wound her arms around his neck and pulled him closer.

"Nice, huh?" Noah breathed the word against her neck while he trailed a series of soft, shimmering kisses to her ear. He kissed his way down to the hollow at the base of her throat.

"Very nice." Laurel tipped her head back, and when he skimmed his hand over her sweater and tugged it out of the waistband of her skirt so he could touch her bare skin, she held her breath. His fingers found the lace that edged her bra and nudged it aside, and he rolled her nipple between his thumb and forefinger.

"Noah." Laurel barely recognized her voice. It was too breathy to have come from her. Too reckless. There was too much urgency in the way she pulled in breath after breath. Too much desperation in the need that screamed through her. "Noah, I—"

"I know. Me, too." He tucked a leg between hers and kissed her again. Longer this time. Harder. And Laurel wrapped her arms around his neck and held on tight, certain that if she didn't, she'd lose herself in the kiss and her hold on reality.

"Noah, I…" Her words came out in gasps, each one punctuated by a kiss. He kissed her lips and her cheek. He kissed her neck and hiked up her sweater just enough to press a kiss between her breasts.

"Noah…" Laurel could barely do more than whisper his name. She pulled in another breath, trying to ignore the feeling that flashed through her when he trailed a series of kisses across her breasts and took one into his mouth.

"Noah, it's not going to work."

She pushed away from him while she still could. While her brain was still working. Before her common sense and her better judgment were lost beneath the sweetness of the feelings flooding through her. "This isn't just good, Noah. This is great. But it's not going to change a thing. It's not going to work."

"What are you talking about?" Even in the dark, she could tell he was looking a little stunned. He pushed a hand through his hair and reached for her, and Laurel took a step back, instinctively trying to preserve herself. "What do you mean, it's not going to work? It is working. It's working as well as it ever did. You said it yourself, you said it was nice."

"It was very nice." Laurel's heart squeezed with a

fondness for Noah she'd forgotten ever existed. She remembered that only four years earlier, he'd been her whole life. Noah was the reason she got up in the morning. He was certainly the reason she went to bed at night. He was her lover and he was her friend, and in the four years they'd been apart, she'd buried her feelings for him beneath the load of hurt they'd heaped on each other.

She cupped his cheek in one hand. "It's better than nice," she told him. "But it doesn't change a thing. I'm still the doctor with the clinic in the middle of nowhere. You're still the one who's leaving in the morning. There's no use fooling ourselves into thinking anything is ever going to be any different."

"It's—"

She silenced his protest, one finger to his lips. "It's not," she said, and before he could try to talk her out of what she'd had to talk herself into, she kissed him long and hard.

"Good night, Noah," she told him when she finished. She turned and hurried up the walk and into her house. "Goodbye."

Chapter Twelve

Even though the next ferry to the mainland wasn't scheduled to leave for another hour and a half, Noah was just about ready to go.

Nothing like being early when it was already too late.

He grabbed his running shorts and T-shirt from the chair where he'd tossed them when he got back from the *Jade Moon* and chucked them into his suitcase. He searched around the bed for his running shoes, and when he didn't find them, he looked behind a plant that reminded him of the people-eating one from that crazy fifties movie. Once he had his shoes stowed away, he closed his suitcase, zipped it and wondered when—and if—it would ever be as easy to pack away his memories of the last few days.

Something told him not.

He wasn't prone to sighing. It wasn't in his nature, and besides, it wasn't a guy thing to do. Which made it all the more disturbing to realize it was exactly what he was doing. Standing there, suitcase in hand while his other hand was on the Almost Paradise doorknob. Sighing. Like some lovelorn knucklehead in a made-for-TV movie.

Just because Laurel had the sense to call things off the night before. Before they went too far.

Bad enough for his ego, not to mention his libido. Worse, because he knew she was right.

Noah glanced over his shoulder one last time, giving Almost Paradise a final goodbye. "If I'm ever looking for a tropical nightmare…" he mumbled. But he knew he never would be. And he knew he'd never be back.

He set his suitcase down in the hallway and closed the door behind him. As he did, he caught a glimpse of the wooden snake carved above the Almost Paradise sign. The snake was grinning at him. Grinning, and looking as satisfied as the cat that ate the canary. Or in this case, the snake that dangled too much temptation in front of him. Too much temptation that was too good to pass up.

"Too bad, pal." He gave the snake a friendly pat. "You tried your best, but this time, Eve wasn't about to be tempted. Maybe next time, huh?"

But even as he asked the question, he knew there wasn't going to be a next time.

Funny, the thought should have cheered him no end. There wasn't going to be a next time. No next time for the island that time forgot. No next time for the home of Love Nibbles, red velvet and fuzzy handcuffs. No next time for flopping fish and trickling waterfalls and jungle noises that he swore he could still hear, even with the door to Almost Paradise closed.

He was getting exactly what he wanted. He was getting away from the island, escaping with his ambitions unshaken, his self-respect pretty much intact and his goals as clear-cut as ever.

And if his dreams had changed just a little since he

first looked across the lobby and saw Laurel standing there?

At the bottom of the stairs, he instinctively looked toward the place he first saw her the night he checked in to the Hideaway. The spot was as empty as his insides suddenly felt.

Something told him he should have been having a totally different reaction to the whole experience. The same something that made him wonder why he wasn't.

"You're really leaving, huh?"

Noah turned and found Maisie standing behind the wide front desk. She was dressed in a color that reminded him of cotton candy. Her slacks were cotton candy. Her blouse was cotton candy. Even the scarf she had tied jauntily around her neck was cotton candy, accented with splotches of deeper pink.

"Of course I'm leaving." He set down his suitcase in the middle of the lobby and went to deposit his room key on the desk. "It's Monday, and I think the impound lot should be open by now." He gave her a long look, waiting for her to display at least a little guilt about the fact that both he and his car had pretty much been held prisoner all weekend. She didn't, and he had to give her credit. Maisie didn't apologize to anyone. Not when she thought she was fighting the good fight.

"Thanks for trying," he said, and he couldn't help but smile. "Even if it is going to cost me a bundle in impound fees. For a little while there, I—"

"Thought it would work?" Maisie tapped one bright pink fingernail against her cheek. "I did, too. You know, it might not be too late."

"Oh, no!" His self-preservation impulse kicked in, and Noah pushed off from the desk, away from Maisie and her romantic illusions. "I'm done being a guinea pig in your little romantic experiment. I tried, Maisie. As much as I had no intention of doing it when I walked into this place, I tried to make Laurel understand that things could be different between us. That they could be like they used to be. She was smart enough to know it would never work. And I... Well, if nothing else, I proved something I suspected all along. I had a real chance for happiness once and I blew it.''

It was the first time in four years Noah had allowed himself to admit the fact. To himself. To anyone else. It felt good to get the painful truth out in the open where it belonged, and he pulled in a breath and wondered why the good feeling didn't last any longer than the words did. The aching feeling settled into place, and he welcomed it like an old friend. He might as well. He'd been living with it for four long years.

"I let my career get in the way of my heart, and that's that." He shrugged like it was no big deal at the same time he confessed to himself that it was. It was a very big deal. Too bad the past wasn't like a video, one he could rewind and replay. One he could change. "No second chances," he said, and he tried for a smile that proved it wasn't a big deal, either, and fell short. "Any guy dumb enough to let Laurel go doesn't deserve to live happily ever after."

"You have to learn to trust your heart." Maisie's voice was so soft, Noah wasn't sure he'd heard her. He didn't ask her to repeat herself. No use rubbing it in.

"What I have to do," he said, "is get away from here. Get back home. Get my life back in order. I was perfectly happy before I—"

"Were you?" This time, he heard Maisie loud and clear. He read the look that sparkled at him out of her eyes. It made him shift uncomfortably from foot to foot.

"I was content," he insisted.

"You were fooling yourself."

"I was happy fooling myself."

"But you weren't happy. Not really." She bustled to the front of the desk and came to stand in front of him, her arms crossed over her chest in as no-nonsense a pose as he'd ever seen from anyone. "What do you intend to do about it?" she asked.

"Do?" Noah looked at his suitcase. He glanced at his watch. In less than two hours, he wouldn't have to worry about what he was going to have to do. He'd be on the mainland, starting toward getting his life in order. "I'm going to leave. That's what I'm going to do."

Maisie had the good grace not to look disappointed. At least not too disappointed. That didn't keep her from shaking her head. "If that's what you think is best," she said. "I just thought…"

"What? That if I gave it one more try, I could get my heart kicked out again?" He grabbed his suitcase and headed for the door. "No thanks, Maisie. Once is enough. Twice is too much."

"Third time's the charm."

He stopped at the door and turned to her. "Do you really believe that?"

"I really believe that if two people are meant to be together, the universe will find a way."

"The universe has been strangely silent for the past four years."

"Maybe it was just waiting. For the right time."

"Maybe I'd be crazy to believe that."

"Maybe."

"Do you think…" Before he realized he was doing it, Noah found himself putting down his suitcase at the same time he picked up the threads of an idea. He wasn't sure where it came from. He wasn't even sure it qualified as a real idea and not just some sort of hiccup in his brain. "If I had more time," he said. "If I could stay around for a few more days, maybe she'd change her mind."

"Maybe." Maisie didn't look too sure. Which only made Noah more determined than ever to prove his point.

"Maybe we just haven't had time to talk things through, to hash things out. Maybe if she had a chance to spend a few more days with me…"

Barely controlling a smile, Maisie went back to the desk and reached for the Almost Paradise key. "Does this mean you're staying?" she asked.

"It means I've got to find a reason to stay."

Maisie's smile fell like a bad soufflé. "You've got a reason. You've got Laurel."

"Oh, sure. Laurel." Now that he'd talked himself into facing reality, he needed to think things through. Noah paced in front of the desk. "But I've got to have a reason. You know, for staying on the island. I've got to make it look like there's something keeping me here."

"You've got to learn to trust your heart."

It was the same advice she'd given him not three minutes before, but Noah knew it was just a lot of romantic hooey. He didn't need the kind of advice he expected to see embroidered along with hearts and flowers and hung on the walls of Cupid's Hideaway. He needed a plan.

"I know!" Inspiration struck, and he swung around and gave Maisie an ear-to-ear smile. "You could get hurt."

"Me?" She didn't look convinced. About the need

for a plan. Especially not about the need for the hurt part. She stared at Noah for a long while before her devious mind clicked with his. "You mean if there was some reason for a doctor to have to tend to me..."

"You've got it!" Noah waited to see if she'd buy into his plan. And why shouldn't she? It was a stroke of genius.

"I don't know, Noah." Maisie shook her head. "I think it might just be better if you would—"

"Oh, no!" There was no use debating. There was nothing to debate about. He needed to convince Laurel they had had something real four years earlier. That they could have it again. If he was going to do that, he needed to buy some time. "It's the only thing that's going to work, Maisie. You know that and I know that."

"But Laurel—"

"Laurel doesn't know what she wants." Noah thought about everything that had happened the night before. About the kiss they'd shared in her front yard. About the way his blood pounded when he thought that kiss might turn into something more. About the way it still did. Laurel might not know what she wanted, but she was on her way to finding out. Last night proved it. If he stuck around a while longer, she was sure to find out. He'd already figured out what he wanted, and what he wanted was Laurel.

"I know if I just give her a little more time, this will work. And if I can't do that, well..." He hated to admit it, but Noah was convinced as only a desperate man could be that he was right. "If you don't help me out, I'm not sure I can make this work."

"Well..." It was enough of a wishy-washy response to assure Noah he'd won Maisie over. Leave it to an incurable romantic to fall for the scheme of a guy who'd been convinced he was anything but. Until he walked into Cupid's Hideaway.

He gave Maisie a high five that she returned with equal enthusiasm, and they put their heads together. It was only a matter of moments before they hatched what he was convinced was a surefire plan.

LAUREL WAS NOT in the habit of stopping at the Hideaway most days. She visited Maisie at home a couple times a week and saw her a couple more times in town. Every Wednesday night, rain or shine, she and Meg took turns having their grandmother, and each other, over for dinner. When the call came inviting her to the Hideaway for lunch that Monday afternoon, she was skeptical at first. Until she looked at the clock.

It was past noon. She was safe. By now, she knew Noah would be long gone.

Laurel walked out of the exam room and slipped out of her lab coat, wondering why the realization didn't make her feel any better.

"Because you were all set to hop into bed with him last night, that's why," she told herself.

When Carole at the reception desk gave her a curious look, Laurel waved her concern aside and congratulated herself for being the one who had the sense to end things with Noah when she did. That proved it. Once and for all. She was the intelligent one. She was the right one. She was the one who deserved a pat on the back and the Smart Girl Award for pulling away at the very last second.

Which she nearly didn't do.

Which she didn't want to do.

Which she'd kicked herself about a thousand times for doing.

Which she knew she'd do again.

Not because she wanted to.

Because she had to.

The thought still too new and far too painful to come to grips with, Laurel mumbled a goodbye to Carole, hopped in her car and headed for the Hideaway. She knew there were guests scheduled to arrive at the bed-and-breakfast that afternoon, so when she got there, Laurel was surprised to find the lobby empty. She was even more surprised when she looked into Maisie's office and didn't see anyone. The kitchen was empty, too. When she peeked into the parlor and saw Maisie lying on the red brocade fainting couch with her feet propped up, her eyes closed and one hand thrown across her face, Laurel's heart skipped a beat and her blood ran cold.

"Grandma?" She hurried into the parlor and was relieved to see that Maisie's color looked good and her breathing seemed normal. She got down on her knees and grabbed one of Maisie's hands, automatically feeling for a pulse. "Grandma, are you all right?"

Maisie's eyes fluttered opened. "All right?" She did her best to sit up, and when she did, a wave of pain crossed her face.

"Grandma, what's wrong?"

"It's her ankle."

The answer came from over Laurel's right shoulder, and she didn't need to turn around. Even if her ears hadn't recognized the voice, the instantaneous, complete and completely illogical response from her body would have told her she was wrong about Noah. He hadn't been on the noon ferry.

She spun around and found him holding an ice pack in one hand and a towel in the other.

"What are you still doing here?" she asked him.

"That's a fine way to say hello." He walked right past her and to the end of the couch where he wrapped the ice pack in the towel and carefully laid it on Maisie's left ankle. "I'm here because—"

"Good thing he stayed." Maisie's voice was a little too weak for a woman who had apparently sustained nothing more serious than a sprained ankle, but Laurel reminded herself that her grandmother was up in years. No injury was too small to take lightly. She sprang to her feet and went to have a look.

And found her path blocked by Noah.

She supposed she should be glad she was seeing him again under such traumatic conditions, but that didn't make it any easier to look him in the eye. She forced herself to do it anyway, and reminded herself that there was nothing like a healthy dose of worry. At least if she was worried about Maisie—and she was—she didn't have to worry that Noah might be thinking about all the same things she was thinking about. About the night before and the way his mouth had tasted against hers. About the way she caught fire when he brushed his hand against her breasts. About the way she'd nearly been willing to throw aside every bit of self-esteem she'd built in the past four years. Just for the chance to make love to him again.

Nearly.

"Do you mind?" She stepped to her left at the same time he moved to his right. "I'd like to take a look at my grandmother's ankle. If she's hurt, I'd like to—"

"She's fine. At least for now. I've taken care of everything."

Laurel glanced from Maisie's ankle, nearly lost beneath the ice pack and towel he'd packed around it, to Noah. "Yes, I know you took care of everything. Thanks." A flood of guilt rushed into her cheeks, and she found herself swallowing hard before she looked at him again. "I appreciate the fact that you took care of her, that you stayed around and missed your ferry. But really, I'd like to—"

"Don't worry about it, dear. Noah's here. He'll take care of me."

She turned to Maisie in wonder. She tried to remind herself that Maisie had just been through a shock. That it was more than likely emotions were speaking louder than reason right now.

That didn't do a thing to relieve the sting when she realized her grandmother wanted Noah to take care of her injury. "But I'm your doctor." Laurel knew she sounded just a little too sulky. Well, chalk another one up to emotions running high. If Maisie was allowed to be melodramatic, so was Laurel. Just this once. "He'll take care of you? But I'm your doctor and—"

"Yes, yes. Of course you're my doctor. Always will be." Maisie reached up and grabbed Laurel's hand. "That's sweet of you. Really. But Noah was here when it happened, you see. He was just walking out the door when I slipped on the edge of the Oriental rug in the lobby. He saw me go down, and if it wasn't for him…" Maisie looked away, and Laurel found herself clutching her grandmother's hand a little tighter, trying to make Maisie feel just a little bit better.

"It was nothing. Really." Noah shrugged away the suggestion that he'd been heroic. "I got her up. That's all. I carried her in here. It's only a sprain, and I knew a little ice and a little rest would take care of everything.''

''Only a sprain?'' In spite of the fact that she'd handled hundreds of emergencies, some of them far more serious, Laurel found it hard to breathe. Once again Noah had barged into what was essentially her territory. He'd not only taken over her life, he was trying to take over the care of her grandmother.

Laurel swallowed hard and told herself to get a grip. As hard as it was to believe, she could live with Noah tending to Maisie's injury. What she couldn't live with was anyone saying it was *only* a sprain. This was her grandmother they were talking about, and as young as she acted, she was nearly eighty. No injury was *only* anything. It was something that needed to be watched and given the best of care. Try as she might to remain calm and professional, she found her emotions getting in the way. ''We'll get film. Just to be sure. We've got an X-ray machine at the clinic,'' she told Noah. She turned and headed for the door. ''I'll bring my car around and—''

''Oh, I don't think that's necessary.''

The suggestion was so unexpected and so ridiculous, it stopped Laurel in her tracks. She turned to Noah. ''What do you mean, not necessary? This is my grandmother we're talking about here, Noah. And in case you've been too busy being in touch with play medicine to be in touch with real medicine, she's a geriatric patient. You just don't mess with the care of a geriatric patient because you want to—''

''Play medicine?'' Noah's eyes went wide, and whether he realized it or not, he curled his hands into fists at his sides. ''Is that what you think? That what I do isn't real medicine? That what I do is—''

"What you do is take a bunch of kids and try to teach them to become doctors. No one's arguing with you that that isn't important. Heck, neither one of us would be here now if it wasn't for other doctors like you. But standing in front of a blackboard lecturing about sprained ankles is hardly the same as—"

"No, you're wrong. It's exactly the same as—"

"Give me a break!" Laurel threw her hands in the air. "You can't possibly compare what you do to what happens in the real world. All right, all right, I admit it. You're the object of worship for your students. You're the great and glorious Noah Cunningham. But that doesn't mean what you see from behind your desk is anything more than theory. This isn't theory, Noah. This is real-life medicine. And real-life medicine says that we need to get film. Just to be sure. What if there's a hairline fracture? What if there's been trauma to the hip? Or her head? Or—"

"Now, now. You two are making a great big mountain out of a silly little molehill." Maisie's voice, as calm and as cheery as ever, cut through their argument like a knife through butter. "It's a sprain." Maisie patted Laurel's hand. "Nothing but a sprain. It doesn't even hurt that much." When she looked to Noah to support her position, he didn't back her up.

Obviously, he was as upset as Laurel. His cheeks were as dusky as hers felt. His breathing was as fast. Maisie dismissed the whole thing with a lift of her shoulders. "A couple days off my feet, and I'll be as good as new," she assured Laurel, and when Noah still didn't jump in, she cleared her throat and gave him a pointed look.

"That's right," Noah said. "A couple days off her feet. That's all she needs."

"Okay. Fine." Laurel pulled in a breath. She couldn't fight them both. They wanted to overrule her when it came to medicine? Fine. But they weren't going to completely shut her out of her grandmother's care.

"You've got guests, and I don't have much of a workload for a couple days," she told Maisie. "I can run back to the clinic when I need to. In the meantime…" She gave Maisie a look that told her she wasn't about to tolerate any objection. "You're off your feet, and I'm on duty. You've got guests in Love Me Tender and Noah in Almost Paradise. I'll go home and get my things and move into Smooth Operator. Don't even say a word," she warned when Maisie opened her mouth to speak. "I'm staying here." She spun toward Noah. "And don't you think you can railroad my grandmother into some sort of half-baked medical care just because you happened to be around to play superhero when she needed you. I won't interfere. I can't. Not if Maisie doesn't want it. But that doesn't mean I have to stand by and let you do anything you want. I'm going to be watching you, Noah. Watching you like a hawk."

And with that promise, she turned on her heels and headed toward home to pack her bags.

"Well…" When Laurel's car was gone from the front of the inn, Maisie sat up and tossed aside the ice pack. "That wasn't exactly the reaction we hoped for, was it?"

"No. Not exactly." Noah massaged his temples with his fingertips. "Guess I should have realized she wouldn't move aside and let anyone take care of you. Not without a fight."

"Oh, you realized it, all right." Maisie got up and reached for a couple of throw pillows from a nearby chair. She fluffed them and tossed them onto the couch before she sat down, waiting for Laurel's return so the ruse could continue. "You just don't want to admit it. See? See what happens when you don't listen to your heart?"

Chapter Thirteen

The guests in Love Me Tender were Marty and Darlene Sylvester, an older-than-middle-aged couple from Dayton who wore matching leather jackets, Graceland T-shirts and so-glad-to-be-away-from-home smiles. Nice enough people, but they kept Laurel hopping. They needed extra champagne for the tabletop fountain in their room. They needed plenty of extra scented candles to use around the heart-shaped bathtub in their room. They brought their own collection of Elvis tapes and CDs, but they wondered if the Hideaway might have even more. They made not two, but three trips to the Love Shack the night they checked in and apparently they really enjoyed the Love Nibbles, edible underwear and adults-only board game they picked up there. There was a whole lot of shakin' going on in Love Me Tender that night.

Laurel didn't really mind. Taking care of the Sylvesters almost kept her mind off the fact that Maisie's sprained ankle was being taken care of by a doctor who wasn't Laurel. Almost. She thought about Noah's subversive activities only when she saw him. And she saw him only a dozen or so times every day.

On the second morning after Maisie's fall, Laurel was

carrying another supply of candles to Love Me Tender when she heard her grandmother laughing in the parlor. She paused outside the doorway and peeked inside. With Noah's help, Maisie had installed herself on the brocade fainting couch surrounded by two piles of paperwork she swore she was going to plow through since she couldn't do anything else, two dozen roses that had been sent by Doc—one dozen for each day of her convalescence—a stack of magazines that were mostly fluff and a box of expensive chocolates Noah had had flown in from Cleveland the day before.

She watched Maisie select a chocolate and eat it with relish.

All in all, Laurel thought, her grandmother had taken the pain and inconvenience of her sprained ankle in remarkable stride. She was as cheerful as ever. Her appetite was good. After a couple glasses of wine the night before, she sang along while Noah played a few pop favorites—flawlessly, of course—on the old upright piano that sat in one corner of the parlor.

As much as Laurel hated to admit it—and she hated to admit it a lot—she knew most of the credit for her grandmother's care went to Noah. Laurel had been too busy with the Sylvesters to do anything more than look in on Maisie once in a while. Meg had been occupied making hundreds of dainty appetizers for a wedding scheduled at the Hideaway the next weekend. That left Noah, and he had taken up the responsibility with a vengeance, deciding to stay on an extra couple days until Maisie could be up and around again.

He'd been with Maisie almost constantly since her fall, helping her to and from the parlor each day, checking and adjusting the air cast he'd put on her ankle, fetching and carrying ice packs from the kitchen. He kept her smiling when Laurel suspected she didn't feel much like smiling, and he kept her entertained, which, for a woman as active as Maisie who had been forced to sit still, was a major accomplishment in itself.

All of which made Laurel grateful to have him there. All of which made her feel terrible about the things she'd said to him on the day of Maisie's fall.

As if the scene had been designed to rub salt into the wounds of her guilt, Noah wrapped a fresh ice pack in a towel just as Laurel looked into the room. He tested the temperature against one hand and gently laid the pack on Maisie's ankle.

"You comfortable?" he asked her grandmother.

"Comfortable?" Maisie laughed. "I haven't had this much fun in years. It's a forced vacation. Even if Laurel does want me to get this paperwork taken care of." She pooh-poohed the stack of bills and unanswered mail with a little wave of one hand. "My only complaint is that you've been spending way too much time with this old lady," she told Noah. "Shouldn't you be doing something else?"

"Should be." Even from across the room and with Noah's back to her, Laurel saw him shiver. "I'm getting a pretty icy reception," he said, and Laurel knew exactly what he was talking about. Ever since he announced he was going to be Maisie's attending physician, Laurel had acted like Noah was invisible. At first, it was something of a crusade. Just to prove her point. But the more she saw her grandmother and Noah together, the more she realized her attitude was thoughtless and ungracious. It was time to swallow her pride and let him know how much she appreciated all he'd done.

"Noah?"

When Laurel said his name, Noah looked over his shoulder. He couldn't have been surprised to see Laurel. He'd seen her more than once already that morning. The last time he saw her was in Maisie's office, and she'd headed out one door as soon as he came in the other. This time, she was speaking to him, and at the realization, a smile sparkled over his expression and lit a fire in his eyes. Right before another expression dashed across his face. One that looked suspiciously like guilt.

It didn't make any sense. The way Laurel figured it, she was the only one who had anything to feel guilty about. Holding tight to the thought—and reminding herself that the last things she needed were Noah's sparkle and his fire—she ignored the response that rippled through her. Not a good idea to mix apologies with sex. At least she didn't think so.

"Noah, can I talk to you for a minute? Out here?"

She backed away from the doorway, inviting him into the lobby.

Noah bent to say something to Maisie and walked out of the room.

"How's it going?" he asked, and Laurel couldn't help but notice that he didn't look at her. Funny, she thought she was the only one whose insides were tied in enough tangles to keep the *Jade Moon* in knots for years. He glanced at the box of votive candles she carried in one hand. "The Sylvesters still driving you crazy?"

"Not crazy. They're just keeping me busy. It's okay, though. I ran over to the clinic this morning and took care of a couple patients. My schedule is clear for the rest of the day."

There didn't seem to be much else to say. At least not to the man she had vilified only a couple days before as a medical dabbler, a meddler and an all-around pain in the neck.

All the more reason she needed to talk to him.

"Look…" Laurel pulled in a deep breath and let it out again slowly. "This might not be a good time, but—"

"It's a great time."

She looked up to find Noah looking at her. "I know what you want to talk about," he said. "And that's good, because I want to talk about it, too. You want to talk about Maisie."

Laurel shook her head. "I want to talk about us."

For one heartbeat, she thought he was going to tell her there was nothing to talk about. For two, she figured he was going to suggest another topic of conversation. But in the next heartbeat, Noah's breathing stopped just for a second, and when it started up again, so did the beginnings of a smile. Luckily, he didn't move any closer. They were close enough. Too close. Even with two feet of Oriental rug and a world of hurt between them, she could feel the magnetic pull. Not something she wanted to think about. Not when she was worried about what color sackcloth to order with her ashes.

"You want to go outside?" she asked Noah, and even before he answered, she set down the candles and headed across the lobby and onto the wraparound porch. The weather had turned chilly since the night of the dinner dance, and the wind off the lake was biting. Laurel tucked her hands into the sleeves of her oatmeal-colored fisherman's knit sweater.

"I owe you an apology," she said before Noah sat on the white railing that edged the entire porch. "I've been acting like a spoiled brat. I haven't been talking to you. I haven't been helping out as much as I should. I just wanted to say I'm sorry."

She expected him to jump all over her apology. After all, for once she was admitting that she was the one at fault. Then again, as far as she could remember, this was the first and only time she ever had been the one at fault.

Laurel brushed aside the thought and waited for Noah's reaction. Instead of gloating, he gave her a skeptical look. "You mean you're not mad?" he asked. "About me taking over? About me caring for Maisie's sprained ankle?"

"Oh, I'm mad, all right." There was no use lying. Not about something this basic. Laurel went to stand next to where Noah sat on the railing. "She's my grandmother, and I'm the one who should be taking care of her. On a personal level, I don't just feel obligated, I want to do it. On a professional level...well, I am her physician. I know her medical history and I'll be following up on treatment once you leave. You may be the all-knowing, all-seeing, all-powerful—"

She stopped herself, not eager to go back to a place she'd been trying for two days to get out of.

"I'm just as capable as you are," she said instead, taking comfort in the fact that it was the absolute truth. "I'm just as good a doctor."

"Of course you are!" Noah jumped in with both feet, and Laurel had to give him credit. At least for trying. She wasn't convinced he believed what he said. She wasn't convinced he thought a doctor in a small clinic on a small island could ever be as skilled or as competent as an instructor from a powerhouse medical school. Especially when that instructor at that powerhouse medical school was the great Noah Cunningham.

Another place she told herself not to go. Especially when she was trying to practice a little humility.

"Look…" She glanced over and found Noah watching her, waiting. He looked delicious this afternoon in jeans that were faded in all the right spots and a bright red Cupid's Hideaway sweatshirt. The dinner-plate-size cupid on his chest grinned at her, looking as mischievous and as satisfied as the Sylvesters had when she saw them at breakfast that morning.

"I said a lot of things, and not all of them were nice."

Noah chuckled. The sound was warmer than the blast of nippy air that flowed in off the lake from Canada. "None of them were nice."

He didn't need to remind her. "None of them were nice," she conceded. "But I was worried. And I was upset. And you…you came in and took over and—"

"And it doesn't really matter. Not anymore. There's something you should know, anyway." He sucked in a breath. "I—"

"No. There's something you should know." Leave it to Noah to try to take over. Even when what he was taking over was her apology. "I need to finish," she said. "I was upset and I was worried about Maisie. All I wanted was for her to have the best medical care possible. It took me a couple days, but now I realize that she does."

NOAH WANTED to think that he was too stunned to say anything. Great excuse. Might even have worked if it was true. Deep down inside, he knew what he was feeling had less to do with being surprised than it did with feeling guilty. Laurel was grateful for all he'd done for Maisie? How grateful would she be if she knew the whole sprained ankle story was nothing but a figment of two imaginations warped beyond thinking straight? A story designed to buy him some time on the island and maybe—just maybe—give him the opportunity to show Laurel they just might have a chance together?

Which, now that he thought about it, seemed to be working.

A smile welled up inside Noah, and he let it out at the same time he reached for Laurel. Call him a glutton for punishment. He just couldn't stand being this close to her and not touching her. He couldn't be in the same room with her and not want to touch her. Heck, if the past few days proved anything, it was that he couldn't be on the same island with her and not want to touch her.

"Thanks." It seemed like an inadequate thing to say, especially in light of the fact that she'd paid him the ultimate compliment. "I'm nuts about Maisie and I want nothing but the best for her, too. Which is why—"

"Which is why you're going to stay and keep doing whatever it is you're doing for her. She's doing well, and I'm glad. I'm grateful, Noah. Really. I don't know how to thank you."

"You're kidding me, right?" He couldn't help himself. The opening was just too good to pass up. At the same time, he reached for Laurel's other arm and pulled her close so she was nestled against him with his legs on either side of hers. "I can think of one way in particular," he said, and he was relieved to see that when he offered her a smile, she smiled back. "Truce?"

"Truce." Laurel kissed him on the cheek. "And thanks."

Noah's guilt disappeared beneath the rush of awareness that tightened his body. "Maisie's resting comfortably," he said, "and the last I saw of them, the Sylvesters were headed into their room with a bottle of wine and a pair of fuzzy handcuffs. I don't suppose you'd like to..."

"I'd like to do a lot of things." She linked her arms around his neck. "Only I've got a bed-and-breakfast to run."

"And one guest who needs some special attention."

She looked down to where his hands were propped against her hips. "And this isn't special attention? I've got news for you, this is more special than any of the attention I've ever paid to any other guest."

It wasn't what he wanted. Not nearly what he wanted. But Noah decided to settle for a little friendly bantering. At least for now. After all, the whole reason he'd decided to stay a few days longer was to give Laurel time. To give their relationship the time and the opportunity to grow. Now he had the opportunity. It was up to him not to blow it.

"I'm glad I stayed," he said, grateful they were back on solid ground, grateful to be telling the truth for once. "Maybe we can have dinner tonight? Just the two of us? I'll bet Meg would whip up something special. We could eat out here under the stars."

"And freeze to death!" Laurel shivered, and Noah pulled her closer to keep her warm. She laid her head on his shoulder.

"I'm glad you stayed, too." She glanced at him quickly before she settled against him again. "As much as I hate to admit it, I'm glad you stayed. I'd forgotten how good you were with patients. I always thought you were the king of bedside manner."

"You think my bedside manner is good with my patients, you ought to see me in action with healthy people!''

''I have seen you in action.'' The laughter in Laurel's eyes deepened into something warmer and turned up the heat inside Noah. ''I thought I'd never see you in action again. Then you show up out of nowhere. It's amazing, Noah. Really amazing.''

As quickly as she laid her head on his shoulder, she stood up. She cocked her head and gave him a searching look. ''What are you doing here, anyway?'' she asked. ''And don't tell me you're taking care of Maisie. I know you're taking care of Maisie. And before that, I know you were attending the Chamber of Commerce dinner dance. And sailing with me. But you've never explained why.''

''Why?'' The word tasted like dust in Noah's mouth. He stood and turned to face the lake. Now was not the time to discuss his reason for coming to the island. Not when Laurel was finally starting to warm up to him. Now was not the time to dredge up old wounds, and if she knew why he was here…

Noah drew in a long breath and let it out slowly, steeling himself.

As much as he didn't want to ruin the mood or the promise of that quiet dinner for two they'd talked about, he knew Maisie was right. He had to start listening to his heart. Right now, his head was telling him to kiss Laurel so hard she'd forget she ever asked why he'd come to the island. His body was telling him it was a better than pretty good plan. But his heart was telling him something else. It was telling him it was time for the truth.

He wrapped one arm around Laurel's shoulders. ''I was in Cleveland,'' he said. ''Lecturing at the Case

Western Reserve University medical school. There was an article in the newspaper about me, and Maisie saw it. She called.''

Laurel shook her head, but she didn't try to move away or duck out of his reach, and Noah took that as a good sign. "I know she called. I've known that all along. But what did she—''

"She said she found something that belonged to me. Something that got mixed up with your things when…'' He shrugged, searching for a delicate way to say, *When we fought like cats and dogs and ended up tearing each other to shreds and walking away from a relationship that for one brief shining moment had looked like the real thing.*

There was no easy way to say it, and besides, he didn't have to. Something told him Laurel remembered every ugly detail. Just like he did. Instead, he waded into his explanation again, hoping she'd see where he was headed and fill in all the blanks. "She said that when you packed, you must have just grabbed it, and she told me that before you bought your house in town, you lived here for a while. That's apparently when it got left behind here at the Hideaway. She thought since I was so close, I'd want to come over and get it.''

"It?" Laurel turned to him, her nose crinkled. "What are we talking about, Noah? What did I do, grab that shampoo you liked? The one that smelled like limes? Did I make off with a pair of your running shorts? Or the His towel from the bathroom?''

"How about the Golden Apple?''

Laurel tried to take the news with some sort of composure but the sudden tension in her muscles was a telltale sign. So was the tiny spark of fire in her eyes. Nothing he couldn't handle, Noah told himself. After all, he was listening to his heart, getting things out in the open, speaking the truth because she hadn't given him the opportunity to come clean about the scheme he and Maisie had cooked up. He was listening to his heart, and his heart couldn't possibly be steering him wrong. Could it?

"The Golden Apple?" Laurel's voice was even tighter than her muscles. "You just can't let it go, can you?"

Her words were as sharp as a slap, but Noah refused to let her know it. That didn't keep him from loosening his hold on Laurel and backing off. Not exactly a retreat. Not the way he saw it, anyway. More like an advance to the rear. A chance to regroup. To formulate a logical response.

"I don't think we have anything to argue about," he told her, congratulating himself for keeping his head when she was so obviously about to lose hers. "The award is mine. It was presented to me by our medical school classmates. You remember. Most respected student. Most admired student. Most accomplished student."

"You forgot most egotistical."

"Come on, Laurel." Noah rolled his eyes. A bad choice of gestures if the scowl he got from her meant anything. "Facts are facts. And the fact is, I won the award, and you came in second. It was four years ago. Get over it."

"Over? I'm about as far over it as I'll ever be." Laurel headed for the door and stomped into the lobby. "You're obviously not," she added when she realized Noah was right on her heels. "Not if you'd come all the way here just to pick up the stupid thing."

In and of itself the Golden Apple wasn't worth more

than its marble base and the eighteen-carat-washed apple that sat atop it. But it wasn't the monetary value that made the apple the coveted prize it was. It was the status.

And if there was one thing a doctor with a shining future knew that one who was willing to lose herself on a backwater island didn't, it was that status was important. In the medical world. In the real world.

"Be reasonable, Laurel. There's really no question of ownership."

"Who said there was?" Laurel put on the brakes and turned to him so fast, Noah nearly ran right into her. She settled her weight on one foot. "I'm just surprised that you'd bother to come all the way over here for an award that isn't worth the powder to blow it up."

"Which didn't keep you from packing it up with your things."

"Which was obviously something I wouldn't have done on purpose."

"You think?" Okay, so it wasn't exactly a classical rhetorical question. So it didn't come out exactly as dispassionately as Noah intended. What did she expect? Laurel was being irrational, temperamental and downright touchy. In short, she was acting just the way she'd acted four years earlier when Noah won the award.

It was something they'd fought about—just one of the things they'd fought about—and it looked like at least in this case, time had nothing to do with healing old wounds.

Which didn't mean Noah couldn't try to be the grown-up.

"Look…" When he reached for Laurel's arm, she yanked it out of his grasp. "There's really nothing for us to be fighting about. You scooped up the award when you moved out of the apartment. I can understand why. It was something you wanted very much. Something you worked very hard to earn. It just didn't work out for you, and so you took it. A kind of Freudian slip.''

"Freudian?'' Laurel pulled herself up to her full height. Not very intimidating, in the great scheme of things, but what was the old phrase? Hell hath no fury... A woman scorned was nothing compared to a woman who had been caught red-handed. And after all these years, Laurel had been caught. "You think I took that stupid award on purpose?''

"You think it's a stupid award?''

"I've always thought it was a stupid award.''

"You didn't think it was a stupid award when I won it and you didn't.''

His comment hit the mark, and Laurel stomped away. Not that he was about to let a little thing like that stop him. He'd come all the way to South Bass Island for the Golden Apple award. He'd endured days of rain-forest accommodations, nights of dreaming about Laurel and an assault of memories he'd thought he'd put to rest forever. He wasn't about to leave without at least some compensation.

He followed Laurel down the hallway, and when she punched open the swinging door that led into the kitchen, he was inside with her before the door swung closed.

THERE WAS NO SIGN of Meg in the kitchen, and Laurel figured it was just as well. They didn't need an audience. Not for a rerun of a four-year-old fight. But though Meg was nowhere to be seen, she couldn't have gone far. There was a host of tiny hors d'oeuvres cooling on racks that had been set on the countertops.

Eager for something to do, something that might help hide the fact that her hands were shaking and her self-control wasn't in any better shape, Laurel tested the temperature of one little pastry cup with her fingers and, satisfied, she slipped canapé after canapé onto the aluminum pans Meg used to store them in the freezer.

She thought she heard Noah come into the kitchen behind her. Kind of hard to tell when her blood was pumping so hard. Which wasn't nearly as noisy as the voice inside her head that mocked her. The one that reminded her what a fool she'd been. She'd allowed herself to believe he'd come to South Bass to see her.

"The least you can do is get the Golden Apple for me," Noah said, confirming everything the little voice said. "Maisie said you left it here with some other things when you moved into your house. I've come all this way and—"

"Maisie's wrong." Laurel dumped another canapé on the plate before she turned and leaned against the countertop, her arms crossed over her chest. All Noah wanted was the Golden Apple, huh? Well, that wasn't all he was going to get. He was going to get a big dose of the truth, too. Even if it cost Laurel every shred of dignity she had left. "I didn't leave the award here when I moved, Noah. I took it with me."

"You—" Noah's surprise melted into a blur of righteous indignation. "You wanted the award. You always wanted the award. That proves it, doesn't it?"

"Maybe." She couldn't stand there and face the condemnation she saw shining from his eyes. It wasn't fair. It wasn't right. And besides, it hurt too much.

Laurel pushed off from the countertop, grabbing a cotton kitchen towel as she did. She scraped the towel over her hands and headed for the door. She wasn't sure where she was going, she only knew she had to get there. Fast. Before he could see the tears that were shining in her eyes.

"Maybe it was an accident that I took the award in the first place. Or maybe it was some kind of message from my subconscious. I didn't even realize I had it until I bought my house and started unpacking some of the boxes I'd brought with me from Baltimore. Maybe it was an accident that I kept it all these years. Maybe I should have tracked you down, sent it back. Maybe the whole thing was just a stupid mix-up, or maybe it proves that I just never got over playing second fiddle to the one and only Noah Cunningham. Maybe all that is true. But I'll tell you what else is true. It was no accident that you came all the way here to get the Golden Apple back, and that tells us something, too, doesn't it? The Golden Apple was the only thing you ever cared for." Finished with the towel, she rolled it into a ball and hurled it onto the counter. "It still is."

STANDING THERE watching Laurel leave, Noah felt as if he'd had a fist slammed into his solar plexus. She was out the door before he could even think of what to say. Good thing, too. For once, he'd listened to his heart and laid his emotions on the line. And where had it gotten him? Nowhere fast.

Which only proved he'd been right four years earlier. His heart couldn't be trusted.

Chapter Fourteen

Noah didn't say he was leaving.

He didn't have to.

Like the raw wind that whistled through the oak tree on the front lawn of Cupid's Hideaway, Laurel could feel his decision vibrating through the air. Cutting her to the bone.

She didn't have to look at the ferry schedule, either. She knew he'd choose the four o'clock. By the time he got his things packed and made arrangements to get to the ferry dock, she figured it would be the earliest ferry he could catch. And after the way they'd ripped each other apart about the Golden Apple, the mess they'd made of each other's lives and the angst it seemed neither of them was strong enough to beat, she had no doubt he'd want to get off the island as fast as he could.

Which was just fine with her.

Her heart still stammering, her knees still trembling, her temper still so near the breaking point she couldn't think about all the things they'd said to each other, Laurel stood behind the front desk doing her best to look as if she had something to keep her busy. Which would have been easier if her hands weren't shaking. And more believable if she could do anything other than keep looking at the stairway, hoping she'd catch sight of Noah before he started down so she could skedaddle out of there before she had to face him again.

It also would have been easier if she didn't feel Maisie's eyes on her. Just like she had ever since she and Noah had traded parting shots and stomped off in opposite directions to lick their wounds.

Laurel sorted the stack of mail she'd already sorted six times. "Give it up, Grandma," she said without bothering to look across the lobby to the parlor. She knew that from where she was ensconced on the big Victorian fainting couch, Maisie had a perfect view of the front desk. "Those big, sad eyes of yours aren't going to change a thing."

"They got your attention, didn't they?" She heard Maisie scuffle against the fainting couch, trying to get comfortable. "You're not actually going to let him leave, are you?" her grandmother asked.

Laurel sighed and set down the mail. "Of course I'm going to let him leave." This time, she was sure. Which didn't make it any easier to admit. Or to accept. It didn't make it any easier to picture Noah with his suitcase in his hand, leaving the island and her life. Forever.

In the second it took her to imagine the scene, her anger faded just a little and she sucked in a breath against a jolt of realization. With the anger gone, all that was left was heartache. Better to stay angry, Laurel reminded herself. Better for her peace of mind and what was left of her heart.

"You heard everything he said." She wasn't sure if she was trying to explain what she was feeling to Maisie. Or to herself. "He practically accused me of—"

"Practically." If Laurel wasn't so busy feeling miserable, she might have been able to interpret the sound Maisie made. It was either a cough or a chuckle. "You two are so hung up on the past, you're going to let it ruin your present. And your future."

"Maybe." Laurel knew a losing cause when she saw one. And trying to ignore Maisie Templeton when Maisie didn't want to be ignored was the Waterloo of losing causes. She walked across the lobby and into the parlor, and when she dropped into the chintz-covered chair across from the couch, she reached for Maisie's hand.

"I know what you think," she said. "You think every romance has to have a happily-ever-after ending. Like your romance with Grandpa before he died. Or Mom and Pop. It's a nice fairy tale, but let's face it, it just isn't true. Case in point. You lured Noah here by telling him you had the Golden Apple, right?"

Maisie didn't have to confess her guilt. The blush that stained her cheeks was enough evidence.

"And you did it because you figured once he was here and we saw each other again…"

She didn't need to finish the sentence. She didn't want to. She knew exactly what Maisie hoped was going to happen because, for a while, she hoped it would, too.

"You tried to jump-start a romance and you didn't bother to check and see that the battery was already dead. A long time ago. And I suppose I should be angry at you for it, Grandma, but honestly…" The smile Laurel gave Maisie was a little wilted around the edges but it was sincere. It told her grandmother that while she might take her meddling seriously, she didn't hold it against her.

"You actually did us both a favor. You tried to show

us that we were meant for each other. And instead, all you proved was that we were right. Four years ago. Both of us were right to call things off. We were never meant to be together. Thanks.'' She gave Maisie's hand a squeeze before she let it go. ''I can stop dreaming about him now.''

''So that's that.'' Maisie smiled, too. A smile that was no cheerier than Laurel's. ''He'll leave and—''

''And I'll get back to leading my life. Just like I was doing before he got here.''

''I suppose there's nothing wrong with that.'' This time, Maisie was the one who reached for Laurel's hand. She held it between both her own. ''I'm sorry. I thought I knew what was best.''

''And sometimes, you do,'' Laurel conceded.

''And sometimes I don't. I promise...'' She held up one hand, Boy Scout style. ''My meddling days are over. This just goes to show you that sometimes meddling causes more problems than it solves. You're old enough and wise enough to make your own decisions. Especially when it comes to men. I tried. Honestly, I tried to do what I thought was best for you. I guess all it proves is that sometimes my heart takes off without listening to my head.''

''Nope. You're wrong. It also proves you love me.'' Laurel leaned over and kissed Maisie's cheek. Right before she gave her a look that rivaled the one she'd tried to use on the Wild Wilsons a time or two. She only hoped it had better results. ''Don't ever do it again.''

Maisie crossed a finger over her heart.

So that was the end of that. Satisfied, Laurel got to her feet. ''Can I get you a fresh ice pack or anything?'' she asked.

"Well…" Maisie glanced at her a little uncertainly. "There is something you could do for me, but…"

"But?" Laurel laughed. "You think there's anything I wouldn't do for you? What is it? More expensive chocolates? Another stack of trashy gossip magazines? Come on, give me something to do. It will help take my mind off…" She shook the thought away. "Give me something to do," she said again. "I need to keep busy."

"All right, dear. But only if you insist." Maisie reached beneath a pile of tapestry-covered throw pillows and came up with a bright pink envelope. "I wrote a little note. Just to thank him. For all he's done." She looked to where her foot and ankle were elevated on another stack of pillows at the same time she held the envelope out to Laurel. "You could take it to him."

Automatically, Laurel put her hands behind her back. "You can give it to him when he comes down to leave."

"I could." Maisie was wearing a white angora sweater. She smoothed a hand over it while with her other hand she waved the pink envelope back and forth. "But I think when he's leaving, he'll be too busy to pay any attention."

"Then he can read it when he gets home."

"By the time he gets home, he'll think less of us."

"Let him."

"Yes, yes. Of course you're right. I just wanted to let him know how much I appreciate all his help. I'd do it myself, of course, but…" Maisie shifted her position, and a wave of pain crossed her face.

"Oh, all right." With a groan, Laurel gave in. There was no use fighting Maisie. About anything. She might as well get it over with. "I'll take the note upstairs."

She motioned for the envelope, and when Maisie put it in her hand, Laurel turned and hurried across the lobby and up the stairs. Before she changed her mind.

"Just because I said I'd take it up doesn't mean I have to deliver it in person," she told herself. At the top of the stairs, she stopped and listened, and when she didn't hear any sounds at all coming from Almost Paradise, she knelt, ready to slip the envelope under the door.

A task that would have been a whole bunch easier to accomplish if the door hadn't popped open.

"You don't have to get down on your knees to apologize."

Laurel looked up from sneakers to faded jeans and from faded jeans to a red sweatshirt and a grinning cherub. From there she glanced to Noah's face. He was looking about as smug as the cupid on his shirt.

Suddenly the anger was back. Full force and red hot. "I am not here to apologize," she snapped. "I don't have anything to apologize for." She made a move to get to her feet, and automatically, Noah stuck his hand out to help. Automatically, she accepted it. It wasn't until she was standing with her breasts pressed to his chest and her mouth dangerously close to his that she realized she'd made a mistake.

She got herself out of it as fast as she got herself into it. By pulling her hand out of his and stepping back. By reminding herself that she wasn't there for a long goodbye or even a quick hello. She was there strictly as a favor to Maisie.

"Here." Laurel held out the envelope. "This is for you."

Noah eyed the bright pink envelope as uncertainly as he was eyeing Laurel. "And you were slipping it under my door because…'' He snatched the envelope out of her hand and held it to one ear. "It's not ticking."

"Only wish I would have thought of that." She propped her fists on her hips.

"I'll bet." He did the same thing.

End of story.

Laurel turned to walk away.

"Actually…"

Like it or not, Laurel's heart leaped at the realization that he was trying to keep her there. She slapped it down and cautioned herself. Even if he was going to apologize, she wasn't going to listen. There were no apologies that could make up for all the things he'd said, all the things he'd done. There were no words sweet enough or flowery enough or poetic enough to sugarcoat all the bitterness between them.

Noah moved back a step. "There's something wrong with the hot water faucet in the bathroom sink," he said.

In spite of every word of warning she'd spoken to herself, the realization that he wanted to talk plumbing rather than poetry came as sharp as a slap. Laurel felt herself stiffen and swore it was the first and last time he'd see that he had any power over her. "I'll have it taken care of later," she told him. "After you check out."

He hesitated, but though he was obviously as anxious to get their conversation over and done with as she was, he glanced toward the bathroom. "By that time," he said, "the place is going to be underwater."

"Really?" Concern chased away caution, and Laurel stepped into the room. Even above the trickle of the waterfall, she could hear water running in the bathroom. She pictured Maisie's money going down the drain along with it. Her grandmother had spent her entire retirement savings designing and building Cupid's Hideaway. It hadn't been easy and it hadn't been cheap. Wasting hot water might be the least of Maisie's problems. If it kept up, the sink could overflow, and running water could cause major damage to walls and ceilings.

"I guess I should take a look," she said. She headed into the bathroom, more aware than she wanted to be that Noah was right behind her. What she saw did nothing to lift her spirits. The water was running, all right. Full speed. As much as she hated to admit it, she knew Noah was right. If she waited until he checked out, if she waited until evening when Jake, the guy who took care of their plumbing, was home from his regular job on the mainland, it would be too late.

"I might be able to do something with it," she mumbled, watching the water run. "At least for now." She knelt and opened the vanity that surrounded the sink. There was a water shutoff down there, and Laurel turned it. It didn't stop the water completely, but it slowed it down. "There." With a grunt, she gave it another turn. "That will hold for a while. But I'll need to go downstairs and get a wrench." She got to her feet and turned toward the door. "I'll just head downstairs and—"

She knew Noah was behind her. She didn't know how close. When she turned, she ran right into him. Instinctively, his arms went around her to keep her from falling. Instinctively, Laurel closed her eyes, tempted to give in to the warmth and the closeness.

Right before her survival instincts took over.

She pushed out of Noah's grasp. "I thought you asked me in here to look at the faucet."

"I did ask you in here to look at the faucet."

"Which is why you're grabbing me?"

"Grabbing?" He barked out a laugh. "That wasn't grabbing. That was keeping you from falling on your face. I believe the proper response is thank you."

Laurel snorted her opinion of the suggestion. "I believe the proper response is get out of my way so I can get to the door."

"Fine."

"Good."

When Noah stepped back, she marched around him and made her way down a path lined with head-high philodendrons and trailing grape ivy. She could have sworn she left the door open.

She stopped and eyed it. The door was definitely closed. She gave Noah a twisted smile. "You looking for a little privacy?"

"Me?" He pointed one finger to his chest. It poked the cupid on his sweatshirt in the nose. "I didn't close the door. I thought you—"

"Right." All Laurel could do was shake her head. He'd never let it go. Not the sly teasing or the slick double entendres. Even though they'd proved to each other that the only future they had together was no future at all, he insisted on pushing the envelope. As baffled by his behavior as she was eager to get away from him, Laurel grabbed the doorknob.

It wasn't until she did that she realized the door was locked.

"Oh, come on, Noah!" She backed away from the door, one hand on her hip. "You think this is funny?"

He looked at her as if she'd started speaking some other language. "I think what's funny? That you have to get some tools to fix the faucet? Not exactly my idea of ha-ha."

She pinned him with a look. "How about the fact that the door is locked?"

"Locked?" He brushed past her, as eager as ever to prove that the only one who could be right was Noah. "How can it possibly be locked? It's—" He tried the handle and got as far as she had. Which was nowhere at all. "It's locked."

Laurel checked the dead bolt on the door. It wasn't thrown. "Locked—"

"From the outside."

Her back to the door, she turned to him. "If this is your idea of some kind of joke…"

"Who's laughing?" Noah backed away, glancing around at the plants that surrounded him and the pool and waterfall that hemmed him in on one side and the skylight above his head. "Yeah, like I'd really like to get locked in here. With you."

"Oh, thank you very much." Laurel pushed off from the door. She headed toward the bed and the phone on the table next to it. "I'll call down to the kitchen and get Meg up here and—" She picked up the phone, and it took every ounce of self-control she had not to slam it down. "The phone's not working."

"Well, it was working a couple of hours ago when I called my office." Noah scraped a hand through his hair.

"Well, it's not working now." Was that Laurel yelling? It couldn't be. She never yelled. Yet she could have sworn she heard her own voice, edged with annoyance and something very much like panic, bouncing back at her from the glass-block walls.

Noah didn't sound any calmer. He spun around, clearly as confused as Laurel was. "I'm not sure if I'm supposed to laugh or cry," he said. "What's this all about?"

"About?" She didn't like the tone of his voice or all it implied. "What's this supposed to be about? It's not about anything. The wind probably—"

"Blew the door closed?" Noah rolled his eyes. "Please! That only happens in Gothic novels. And the phone? It's dead because of what? Ice storm? Power failure?"

"Don't be ridiculous." The truth dawned with enough impact to cause Laurel's mouth to fall open. "You don't think—"

"That you arranged this whole thing? Absolutely. Why else did you just happen to be here when the door got locked? Come on, Laurel. Admit it. This is some kind of last-ditch effort, isn't it? Some kind of last-resort ploy to get me to—"

"Stay?" Laurel's heartbeat was racing so fast, she could barely breathe. "You think I arranged this? You think I arranged this so I could spend more time with you?" The theory was flat-out ridiculous. To prove her point, she picked up a pillow from the bed and chucked it across the room. "That's insane. I don't want to spend more time with you, Noah. I don't want to spend another minute with you. I wouldn't have even walked in here except for—"

Another thought occurred to her, and Laurel sucked in a breath. "You lured me in here." She pointed an accusing finger toward Noah and the grinning cupid on his shirt. "You did something to that faucet to make it run like that, and I'll bet anything that if you didn't hear me at the door, you would have called downstairs and told me to come up and—"

"Only I couldn't, could I? Because the phone isn't

working." He paced up and back along the path next to the waterfall. "Which proves that I had nothing to do with—"

"What a sick joke!" Laurel nearly shrieked. She controlled the response, but only by pacing. Up and back along the path on the other side of the waterfall. "You tell me something's wrong with the plumbing so you can get me into your room. And once I start toward the bathroom, you close the door."

"And lock it...how?"

"How?" As if she might find some answers there, Laurel looked at the door. "I don't know how. My mind isn't devious. Not like yours. But it's obvious what you wanted. You wanted to get me alone. To—"

"You think that's what I wanted? And you think my mind is devious?" At the point where the path he was on intersected another that led along the far side of the room and the sitting area that was arranged near the wall of glass, Noah pivoted. He came back the other way, his cheeks nearly the same color as his sweatshirt. "Proof, proof, proof," he said, pulling to a stop where his path met Laurel's. He waited until she swung around and headed his way.

"Proof," he said. "You can't get over the past." He propped his fists on his hips and glared at her. "You thought once you had me locked in here—"

"Proof that you—" to emphasize her point, she poked one finger into the cupid's forehead "—think you're the greatest thing since sliced bread. You thought once you had me locked in here—"

"You'd what—"

"Convince me that things could change between us?"

"Which they never will. You'll always be—"

"The most aggravating and conceited—"

"Stuck in the past and jealous of my success and—"

"Nothing's going to change that, Noah. You always thought you were hotter than hot and you still do. Otherwise you wouldn't think you could—"

"I thought I was hot?" His voice washed over her. Just as loud as hers. Just as close to the edge. "The way I remember it, you thought I was pretty hot, too. Otherwise you never would have—"

"You don't think I meant it, do you? All right, I'll admit it. You fooled me for a while. You schmoozed me with that great Noah Cunningham persona of yours. But once I knew what you were really like—"

"Once you knew what I was really like, you couldn't wait to get into bed with me."

"Oh, yeah?" There was a comeback if she ever heard one. Laurel cringed. But she wasn't about to give up the fight. "The way I remember it, it was you who couldn't wait to get into bed with me. Apparently, you still can't wait. Otherwise, you wouldn't have locked us in here and—"

"And I didn't lock us in anywhere. You're the one who arranged this. Maybe because you can't wait to get into bed with me."

"Ha!" Another retort for the record books. "I wouldn't want to hop in bed with you," she snarled, "if you were standing here naked in front of me."

"Which is just fine with me," he snapped, "because the same goes for me. Double. Not even if you were standing here naked in front of me."

"Oh, yeah?" This time, Laurel didn't even stop to think that she must have sounded like the biggest airhead in the universe. She was too busy. Determined to prove once and for all that she was right and Noah was wrong, she pulled her sweater over her head and tossed it onto the bed. "You want to put money on that?"

"WHAT?" Noah might have been able to come up with something that sounded a little more intelligent if he didn't feel like there was a hand around his neck. Squeezing hard. He watched Laurel tug off her sweater. He watched her unbutton the plaid shirt she was wearing underneath it. He watched her unzip her jeans.

And he was pretty sure he was going to die from wanting her. Right then and there.

Not that he was about to let her know that.

She untied her sneakers, and he stood and watched. She kicked them off, and he moved out of the way as one of them zinged past his head. She peeled off her jeans to reveal a pair of silky pink panties, and his breath caught in his throat.

Right before his conscience raised its ugly head.

It took more self-control than he ever knew he had to try to stop her. "Laurel…" Noah took a step forward as she rolled her shirt into a ball and hurled it at him. And what little self-control he had dissolved in the rush of awareness that pounded through him.

She was wearing a white bra edged with lace, and looking at it—looking at her—caused something to snap. Breathing heavily, he took a step toward her.

"See?" Laurel took one look at the hand he held out to her and crowed with triumph. "Told you so!"

"Told me so, what?" On the defensive, Noah pulled his hand to his side. "You said naked and you aren't naked. Doesn't count."

"Does count." She folded her arms over her chest. Maybe it was just to keep him from enjoying the view so much. Maybe it was because she knew when she did, her breasts would swell over that little lace edge. And his insides would turn to mush.

"You can't resist me, Noah Cunningham. Naked or not, you can't wait to get your hands on me."

"Not true." He wasn't sure why he was trying to fight it. There was no way on earth he could hide the fact that he was aroused. No way on earth he could pretend he didn't care. But old habits died hard, and this old habit was four long years in the making. "But obviously you can't wait to get your hands on me. Otherwise—"

"Otherwise, what?" She glared at him. And it was a wonder he noticed. A wonder he noticed anything except the way that little slip of pink silky fabric hugged her hips. And the way each sharp breath she took caused her breasts to move to the same crazy beat that was suddenly pounding its way through every inch of him.

"I win," Laurel said, the statement so far from everything Noah was thinking, it caught him by surprise. "You want me, Noah. Really bad. And I..." She stepped back and looked him up and down. "I'm standing here not caring a whole bunch."

Whether she knew it or not, it was exactly the dare he needed. Before he could stop himself, Noah stripped off his sweatshirt, kicked off his shoes and removed his jeans.

"So?" He watched Laurel watching him. Watched the way her breath caught and her pupils widened. Watched the way she ran her tongue over her lips.

And he was completely undone.

All the anger he'd been feeling dissolved in one flash of emotion so sweet and so overpowering, he thought it would blast him to kingdom come. He moved a step nearer, his voice dropping at the same time he reached for Laurel.

"Maybe we should call this a draw?"

"Maybe." Laurel's voice didn't sound any steadier than his. Any less breathy. Any more levelheaded. When his arms went around her waist, hers went around his neck. "Maybe we should admit we've both been wrong. About a lot of things."

"Maybe." Noah kissed her neck. He kissed her collarbone. His mouth found hers at the same time his fingers found the hook at the back of her bra. He fumbled with it. Tried again. He told himself it should have been a simple task and easily accomplished, and he knew it was true. If he was thinking straight—if he was thinking about anything except the taste of her tongue and the heat of her body and the promise in each touch she skimmed along his body—he might have been able to do it.

He settled for pushing her bra straps over her arms and dipped his head to take her into his mouth.

Laurel gasped when Noah's tongue found her nipple. He worked it back and forth, tasting and sucking, and she tipped her head back. Her head was spinning. Her knees were weak. If he didn't catch her in the circle of his arms, she was sure she would have collapsed onto the path beside the waterfall.

Which, now that she thought about it, might not be such a bad idea.

"Noah!" She tugged him down with her until they were kneeling together beneath a canopy of tropical plants. At least on the carpeted path, she didn't have to worry about losing her balance as the world spun out of control all around her. At least she could yank

Noah's sleeveless T-shirt over his head and his boxers over his hips.

"Now," she said, pulling back enough to look him over. "Now we can see who was right and who was wrong. Now you're naked."

"But you're not." The smile he gave her was as steamy as the atmosphere in Almost Paradise. He waited while she unhooked her bra and tossed it into a nearby hanging plant before he inched her panties down. He glanced at the bed, but Laurel shook her head.

"Oh, no," she said. She pulled him closer. "I've waited all this time, I'm not waiting any longer. Right here, Noah. Right now."

Instead of arguing, he reached over to where he'd stowed the little pink shopping bag he got at the Love Shack. Goofy or not, there was a time and a place for everything, even glow-in-the-dark condoms. He slipped one on while he kissed her again, and Laurel leaned back. There was only one more thing they needed to settle between them, and she cupped his face in her hands and looked him in the eye.

"You know this doesn't change anything." It wasn't a question, and she didn't really expect an answer.

"I know." The emotion that flashed in his eyes was a mixture of regret and desire.

"You're still too wrapped up in your career..." She gasped when he nudged her legs apart. "You're still conceited and egotistical and annoying and—"

He laughed and kissed her. "And you," he said, smiling at her, "are still holding on to the past."

"You're still leaving."

"I'm still leaving." He nodded, affirming the solemn promise.

"We could never be happy."

"Never."

"I guess that doesn't mean I can't have this to remember you by." Laurel smiled, too. For the good times. And the bad. For what they had before and what they had right then and there. And when she took him inside her, she smiled again.

At the same time, she wondered how she could be so filled with emotion. And desire. So filled with Noah.

And still feel so empty.

Chapter Fifteen

Nothing had changed.

Noah watched the dreamy look on Laurel's face settle into one of pure contentment. He knew just how she felt. He was feeling pretty content himself. Pretty satisfied. Pretty darned jazzed to confirm that what he remembered as terrific sex was just that.

What he wasn't feeling was happy.

The thought caught him unaware—kind of like the emotion itself—and he shifted his position, sliding away from Laurel before she could see the look in his eyes that he knew would give him away.

He snuggled against her, pulling her to his chest, holding her tight. "I guess we both lose the bet," he said.

"I guess." Laurel didn't sound any happier about the whole thing than he did. She pulled away and sat, her knees up and her chin resting on them. "So what did that just prove? That we're both idiots?"

"Something like that." When she reached for her panties, Noah tossed them to her and watched as she slipped them on.

Her bra was dangling from the branch of a nearby plant, and she snatched it and turned away from Noah while she put it on. "You know it doesn't make any difference." She kept her back to him while she shrugged into her plaid shirt, pulled on her jeans, slipped on her sweater. When she was done, she glanced at him over her shoulder.

It wasn't until she did that Noah realized he was still as naked as a jaybird. Odd to be embarrassed by something that only minutes before had seemed the most natural thing in the world. When Laurel turned away to allow him at least a little bit of privacy, he put in his boxers and his jeans.

"Look…" He reached for her, and when she turned to him, he chucked her under the chin with one finger. "I know how you feel. I feel…" He stopped, searching for the words to explain an emotion he didn't understand. When he couldn't find them, he gave her a half smile. "I know how you feel."

"I know you do."

It wasn't much, but it was at least a meeting point. More of a meeting point than they'd been able to find for four years. They both seemed to sense as much, and Noah felt some of the tension go out of Laurel. She returned his smile with one that was just as anemic.

"I'm glad," she said, and cleared her throat. "I'm glad you showed up. Here at the Hideaway, I mean. Looks like we needed to get some things clear between us, and now that we have…" He glanced at the skylight and the sky, where fat, gray clouds were being bounced around by a wind that seemed to have gotten stronger since last Noah had taken notice of it.

"We both lost the bet," Laurel said while she grabbed her sneakers and socks. Holding them in one hand, she raised herself on her toes and gave Noah a kiss on the cheek. "For once, we're even. Thanks."

Noah thought he could never feel worse than he had in those days four years before when Laurel walked out of his life. He was wrong. For a while back then, he'd questioned whether he even had a heart. That question was answered once and for all because when she gave him a smile, it broke in two.

"Thanks for giving me something to remember you by," she told him. She headed for the door then stopped. "I forgot," she said. "The door's locked and—"

"Laurel! Laurel!"

As they got to the door, they heard Meg calling from the hall. She pounded on the door while she called her sister's name. "Laurel, you're in there, aren't you?"

Laurel and Noah exchanged concerned looks, but neither of them hesitated. They were at the door in an instant.

"I'm here," Laurel yelled. "I'm here, Meg, but the door's—"

The handle turned, and the door opened.

"Locked." Laurel finished the sentence at the same time she gave her sister a questioning look. "What's wrong?"

As if she'd run up the stairs, Meg struggled to catch her breath.

"Grandma?" Laurel made a move toward the door. "Is it—"

Meg shook her head at the same time she grabbed Laurel's arm. "There was a senior citizens' tour bus," she said. "Down by the Lime Kiln Dock. There's been an accident, Laurel. Lots of people hurt. They called the guys from the volunteer fire department but—"

Laurel dropped to the floor and pulled on her shoes

and socks. "We'll have to stop at the clinic first for supplies," she told Noah.

He was putting on his sweatshirt and looking for his socks.

"And Doc?" he asked Meg.

"I called." Meg had started down the stairs. "No answer. I'll keep trying while you—"

"Come on." Laurel grabbed Noah's hand, and together they left to see what they could do.

"GLAD YOU'RE HERE, Doc." Dylan O'Connell, the island's police chief, was talking to Laurel even before she was out of the car. Like all cops, he was a man of few words. A trait she found particularly helpful at a time like this. She wanted information, and she wanted it fast. "Thirty-two passengers, as near as we can tell. One driver. We've got just about everybody out. The guys from fire are working on the last couple."

It was nearly dark, but in the pulsing blue-and-red lights of three police cars, Laurel could see a tour bus on its side in the middle of the road.

"Tried to take a curve too sharp, too fast." Dylan was a tall man with wide shoulders and the most no-nonsense attitude Laurel had ever encountered. He supplied the information she needed to put the pieces of the accident together.

"How many serious?" Noah was looking over the scene, too, sizing things up with a quick, practiced eye.

"Hard to tell." When Laurel popped open her trunk and lifted out her medical bag, Dylan grabbed a boxful of the supplies Laurel and Noah had loaded at the clinic. The three of them headed to where a cluster of people was standing around watching the action.

"You called the mainland?" Laurel asked the cop.

"Called 'em." Dylan stepped back to allow Noah to walk alongside Laurel. "But with this wind…" He made a face into the sharp wind blowing off the lake. "They don't know if they can send anybody. Not right now. Said that if the weatherman knows what he's talking about, they might be able to get a helicopter in here by morning if we need it."

"Morning." Laurel looked over the scene. When Meg told them there had been an accident, she and Noah figured they could handle things pretty easily. What Meg hadn't mentioned was that the place looked like a war zone.

Just as Dylan had promised, most of the passengers were already off the bus. Some of them were sitting along the road being comforted by the neighbors who had gathered. Others were huddled in the blankets those same neighbors had brought with them. Those who weren't able to sit had been carried to the side of the road. Some of them were crying, other were clearly in shock. More than one was more worried about a spouse's injuries than about their own.

"Try to get Doc Ross, will you?" she asked Dylan. "And give Carole a call. She'll be a big help."

"Our biggest problem is the weather." Laurel turned to find Noah looking at the clouds scuttling by, and she knew he was right. It was getting nastier by the minute, and they couldn't risk adding exposure to their patients' problems.

"What do you think?"

Something told her Noah knew exactly what she was talking about. He nodded. "I can triage here," he said. "We'll send the worst cases to you at the clinic. The rest—"

"Can go right to the Hideaway." Laurel knew it was

what he was going to suggest. She also knew Maisie wouldn't mind.

She waited only long enough to watch Noah head over to where a frail-looking white-haired woman was crying softly at the side of the road. Laurel got into her car and raced to the clinic. She didn't have to see any more.

She knew she'd left her patients in good hands.

FORTUNATELY, none of the injuries to the bus passengers were life threatening. Unfortunately, it was hard to convince some people—especially people who were scared and hurting—that they weren't in nearly as bad shape as they feared. While most of the accident victims were as cooperative and as manageable as any doctor could hope, others were whiny, insensitive to the needs of their fellow passengers and just downright difficult.

In the hours between when he arrived at the accident scene to assess the victims and when he joined Laurel at the clinic to take care of those most in need, Noah had been browbeaten, scolded, harassed and threatened with everything from malpractice to having his medical license revoked. He'd had his best sneakers ruined by bloodstains, his shoulder cried on and his sweatshirt—which he'd since flung into the nearest trash can—thrown up all over.

He couldn't remember a time when he'd felt more exhilarated or more needed.

The sensation buzzed through his blood, keeping him going through hours of nonstop bedlam. Side by side, he and Laurel had sutured lacerations, swabbed abrasions, wrapped sprains and handled—successfully, thank goodness—one diabetic whose blood sugars had spiked dangerously because of the excitement. They'd calmed an elderly woman who was in the middle of a full-fledged panic attack, administered nitroglycerine to any number of people who were having angina and handed out paper bags so the people who were hyper-ventilating could blow into them.

Now everything was winding down, and the clinic was as quiet as it had been chaotic only a short time before. Now he had the luxury of thinking he'd never worked with a doctor—anywhere—who was as cool-headed, steady-handed and in control of the situation as Laurel.

As if she could feel his gaze on her, Laurel looked up and smiled at Noah from where she was bandaging the arm of an old guy with thick glasses and an Italian accent that was nearly impenetrable. "Doc done in exam room number one?" she asked.

Noah nodded. Doc Ross had finished the last of his patients a half hour earlier and was headed to the Hide-away to see how Maisie was getting on with the pas-sengers who had been sent there.

"Carole's done, too," he said, glancing to where Laurel's receptionist was washing up after cleaning the exam rooms. "She says she wants overtime pay."

"Double time," Carole called.

"You got it." Laurel finished with the bandage and sat back, but not before she gave the old man she was working on a smile and a gentle pat on his good arm. "Police Chief O'Connell is going to take you where you can get some rest," she explained to her patient, and when she gave Dylan the high sign, he helped the old man up and walked him to the waiting patrol car.

She pulled herself to her feet and zipped past Noah, as full of energy as she had been when they got to the scene of the bus accident. When she held up her left hand, he slapped her a high five with his right and hardly even winced.

"You done in here, Carole?" he heard Laurel ask and when Carole apparently answered in the affirmative, Laurel led her to the waiting room by one arm. "Home," she said, giving the receptionist a gentle push toward the door. "And we're officially closed tomorrow." She took a look at the clock and amended the statement. "Today."

"Closed is a good thing." Carole dragged over to the door. When she opened it, Noah was surprised to see the first streaks of morning light were seeping through breaks in the clouds. "We need two-by-fours," she told Laurel, "and we'll have to reorder gauze and—"

Laurel cut her short. "Goodbye, Carole. Get home and get some sleep. And thanks."

When Carole was gone, Laurel turned to Noah. The smile she gave him wasn't nearly as bright as the one she'd given Carole, but it was warmer. "And thank you. I couldn't have done it without you, Noah. You were—"

"Terrific?" He gave her a grin that told her he was teasing.

"I was going to say—"

"Fabulous?"

"I was going to tell you that you were—"

"Supercalifragilistic—"

"Indispensable."

"Really?" The word struck Noah as being better than terrific, fabulous or supercalifragil—whatever. He massaged the back of his neck with one hand while he looked around the empty waiting room. "We did it."

Laurel glanced around, too, looking as satisfied as Noah felt. Her lab coat was stained with blood and iodine. Her hair was a mess. She had a scratch across her cheek thanks to the woman with the panic attack, and her thick knit sweater looked as if it had seen better days. "We did do it." She grinned. "And we did it well. Notice how we didn't even have to tell each other—"

"What we needed or what to do because we always knew. It was like—"

"We were reading each other's minds."

It was true, and they both laughed. At the relief of knowing they'd used their knowledge and their skills to handle a crisis and handle it well. At the thought that even now, with the crisis over, they were still clicking on all cylinders.

Laurel stretched her arms over her head and worked a kink out of her neck while she flicked off the waiting room lights one by one. "I can't believe it's morning." She glanced at the window and headed to the exam rooms to turn off lights. "I can't believe you stayed all night and—"

Noah reached for her arm, holding her in place. "I never considered doing anything else."

"I know." She slid her arm out of his grasp and put her hand in his. She gave his hand a squeeze. "Thank you. Your technique is textbook perfect."

"Surprised? I thought I proved that in Almost Paradise."

It was the first either of them had the time or the nerve to mention what had happened at the Hideaway, and the second the words were out of his mouth, Noah wondered if he'd said the wrong thing. The smile Laurel gave him told him he hadn't.

"I was talking about your medical technique." She shuffled closer.

"Yeah. I know." Noah took a step nearer to her. "I wasn't."

"I never had any doubt about that technique."

"And you doubted my medical knowledge?"

"Never your knowledge. Just how rusty your skills might be. But you…" She moved away from him, pulling her hand out of his, and if the light had been better, Noah would have been able to tell if the color in her cheeks was the remnant of an adrenaline rush or if she was blushing.

"You did great," Laurel said. "I'm sorry, Noah. I'm sorry I ever doubted you. I've spent all these years being jealous of you and what you know and how you use your knowledge and I've got to tell you, you're not a good doctor, Noah Cunningham. You're a great doctor. It was an honor working with you."

"And you…" He knew better than to reach for her again. She'd pulled away, and his head told him that was the right thing to do. Anything else—anything closer—would only put them both back in the place they'd been before he came to the Hideaway. They'd come a long way since then. They'd come a long way tonight, and he was glad. There was no way on earth he wanted to jeopardize all they'd accomplished. If he listened to his heart, if he took her in his arms, he knew he was taking a chance.

He listened to his heart anyway.

Noah grabbed for Laurel's hand and pulled her closer. "You were terrific. The best I've ever worked with. We're a good team, Laurel."

"Wrong." The single word clutched at Noah's heart. Until he saw her smile. "We're a great team."

The words sounded right. They felt right, too. They settled inside Noah, warm and fuzzy at first. But the heat built instantly, and before he knew what he was doing, he had one arm around Laurel's waist. "You tired?" he asked.

"No." Her voice was breathy. Her heart was beating hard and fast. "After all these hours, I guess I should be, but I'm not. I'm feeling energized and—"

"And delicious." Noah slipped one hand inside her lab coat and glided it over her breasts. "You feel delicious and I feel…" He looked at her, searching for the truth in her eyes, and when she smiled at him, his heart squeezed at the same time his gut tightened. "We did a great thing here tonight. We proved we can make our professional relationship work. I think that proves we can make our personal relationship work, too."

"Can we?" Her smile faded, but she didn't object when Noah glided his hand from her breasts to her waist. She didn't object when he slid down the zipper on her jeans and slipped his hand inside.

LAUREL CAUGHT her breath and tipped her head back, dazzled by the wave of sensations that coursed through her. "Noah." She breathed his name when he stroked his fingers into her, clutching his shoulders, sure that if she didn't hang on, she'd collapse right then and there. "Noah, we could—" She wanted to tell him they could go into one of the exam rooms. She couldn't. She couldn't do anything but give herself to the pounding need he aroused in her.

"Do you think we could—"

He didn't let her finish. He brought his mouth down on hers at the same time he caressed her, his touch reaching deeper, taking her to the edge of abandon, and Laurel felt herself peak, then spiral into wave after wave of pure ecstasy. He held her closer, tighter, supporting her as he had all during the long night, and she found herself feeling grateful and overwhelmed and wanting him more than ever.

"Exam room." She whispered the words into his ear, her voice barely audible over his rough breathing, her legs barely steady enough to carry her. They somehow got her there anyway, and Laurel peeled off her clothes and helped Noah out of his. She stroked one hand over his chest, to his groin and back again.

"What was that you were saying about technique?" she asked.

"I was saying…" He shivered when she touched him again, and Laurel smiled, pleased that she could give him the kind of pleasure he was giving her. "I was saying a lot of things, but I think I'm done talking now."

"That's good." Laurel went to the exam table and sat down, spreading her legs so he could get close, and he dipped his head to take her breast into his mouth.

"That's very good," she moaned, reaching for him and guiding him inside her. "That's very, very good."

Chapter Sixteen

"I've been thinking…" Noah was supposed to be zipping the dress Laurel had slipped into when they got to her house. Instead, he was nuzzling his lips against her neck. How could he help himself? It wasn't his fault her hair was still damp from the shower they'd taken together. Or that her skin was still warm. It wasn't his fault the scent that rose off her was a combination of the raspberry bath gel they'd used to lather each other down and the subtle musky aroma of the sex that had brought them both to their knees.

Which explained why he was more than willing to start all over again.

"I know exactly what you've been thinking." Playfully, Laurel slapped his hands away and handled the zipper herself. She shrugged on a navy-blue cardigan and slipped her feet into a pair of backless clogs. "And what you've been thinking is nothing we have time for right now. We've got to get over to the Hideaway and check on our patients." When she walked by, she gave Noah a peck on the cheek. "Later, lover boy. After we make sure everyone is safely on their way to the mainland."

"That's not what I was thinking." It was, but the

way Noah figured it, he didn't have to admit it. She'd find that out soon enough. As soon as they had some time alone together again. As soon as he could start—again—to make up for all those years they'd wasted. "What I was thinking is that there might be a way for me to stay here. You know, permanently."

In the middle of scooping up a cupful of kibble for Felix, Laurel stopped and stared at him. Her expression was so hopeful, it made Noah's heart soar. It was so cautious, he knew she was walking the edge between wanting to believe and reminding herself that she'd believed once, and that believing had resulted in nothing but heartache.

"You're only really busy in the summer," he told her.

Laurel turned away and poured the food into Felix's bowl. "*Only summer* doesn't sound permanent to me. Is that what you want, Noah?" Finished with the dog food, she dropped the measuring scoop into the bag, rolled the bag closed and turned to him, her hazel eyes sparking with the same conviction that rang through her voice. "Because I want more than *only summer*. I want forever. All the time. Every day and every night."

"And so do I." He pulled her into his arms and held on tight. "You don't doubt that, do you?"

"Sorry." She twined her arms around his waist and gave him a squeeze. "Force of habit. And then when you talk about only summer, I—"

"I said you're only busy at the clinic in the summer. I didn't say I wanted to be with you only in the summer." He drew in a long breath, wondering what she'd think of the plan he'd come up with sometime between when they'd arrived at Laurel's home to get cleaned up and when they last made love. "I've got a reputation," he said.

"No kidding." Laughing, she pushed away from him and went to fill two coffee cups. She fixed Noah's just the way he liked it and handed it to him, and he fitted his hands around the cup. Though the laceration on his right hand was nearly healed, the heat still felt good against it.

"What I mean is that I have a reputation in the medical community. I think I could make some demands."

She was intrigued. He could tell by the way she looked at him, her head cocked, her coffee forgotten. "Demands?"

"Demands. You know. Summers off." As excited by the idea now as when he'd thought of it, Noah set down his cup and took Laurel's hand. "That way, we could work the clinic together in tourist season. In the off-season, I could fly out of here for my lecturing engagements."

Laurel's expression was skeptical. "You mean it? Live here? In this backwater, back of beyond, no-where—"

"Point taken!" Noah chuckled and scooped her close against him. "Confession time. I like it here. I want to live here. With you. And when I'm not here, I want you to come with me. We'll travel the country, and you might consider doing some lecturing, too. You're a hell of a doctor, Laurel. You've got knowledge to spare. And besides, I don't want to be away from you. Not ever again."

"Point taken." She breathed the words on the end of a sigh and leaned her head against his shoulder. After what didn't seem nearly long enough, she stepped away and looked at him. "Happily ever after?"

"I think we could be." He leaned in quickly before she could move away and gave her a kiss. "You willing to give it a try?"

She smiled at him, and something told Noah the light he saw in her eyes had less to do with the early afternoon sunlight streaming through her kitchen windows than it did with the emotions that bubbled up in her. The same ones that made him feel as if, finally, he had everything in life he'd ever wanted.

She glided a finger down Noah's cheek and to his lips, and when he gave it a featherlight kiss, she smiled. "Yeah," she said. "I'm willing. But not to give it a try. I'm only willing if this time we're going to make it work."

So was Noah. After all, it was all he ever wanted. Which explained why, when he put his arm around Laurel's shoulders and they walked together to the door, his steps were light.

Which didn't explain the little nagging voice inside him. The one that reminded him no matter how much you wanted something, sometimes it just didn't work.

BY THE TIME they got to the Hideaway, Laurel's mind was spinning. In all the time she and Noah had been apart, she'd never dared to dream that there might be hope for their relationship. Now she was on the brink of her own happily-ever-after, and she could barely breathe because of the sheer joy that filled her.

She'd known how much a broken heart could hurt. Known it too intimately. For far too long. She'd never realized that as bad as that could feel, this could feel so good.

The road to Cupid's Hideaway was crowded with cars, a van from a Toledo television station and more islanders than Laurel usually saw in the middle of the week. The danger was over, but the excitement obviously wasn't. She and Noah got out of her car, and she slipped her hand in his. They passed Dylan O'Connell getting interviewed by a blond TV reporter—and looking mighty nervous about it—a host of neighbors carrying trays of food and dishes of pastries toward the Hideaway and Doc Ross standing under the huge oak tree on the front lawn, raking the leaves that had fallen during the windstorm at the same time he regaled anyone within earshot about his exploits of the night before.

"Poor Maisie!" Watching it all, Laurel shook her head. "It must be killing her to sit with her feet propped up while all this is happening. Knowing her, she's just itching to get into the middle of things and—"

Even as she spoke, the front door of the Hideaway swung open and Maisie hurried out on the front porch carrying a tray filled with a thermal coffee carafe and enough cups to serve the small army of folks waiting outside. She wasn't wearing the air cast Noah had insisted she use, and that in itself was enough to make Laurel stop and stare at her in wonder. The fact that she wasn't favoring her sprained ankle was another.

"Grandma?" Untangling her hand from Noah's, Laurel moved through the crowd and called to Maisie, taking the front porch steps two at a time. "Grandma, what are you doing up? You should be off your feet. Somebody else can help these folks and—"

It wasn't the fact that Maisie turned to Laurel that made the rest of the words catch in her throat. It was the look on Maisie's face. Like a kid caught with one hand in the cookie jar. Like a chocoholic found with a stash of Hershey bars.

Like an old lady who had sworn her meddling days

were over. One who took one look at Noah over Laurel's shoulders and blushed from the ribbed neck of her pink mohair sweater to the roots of her white hair.

"What's going on?" Laurel didn't bother to ask Maisie. She knew she wouldn't get an answer. At least not one she wanted to hear. Instead, she turned to Noah. "What is this all about?"

"About?" Maisie set the tray she was carrying on a table and waved Meg over, instructing her to pour coffee for anyone who wanted it. "This isn't about anything," she said, adding a giggle that was apparently designed to convince Laurel she was telling the truth. "I'm feeling much better. That's all. And there's so much to do that I—"

"I don't think it's working, Maisie." Noah followed Laurel up the steps. "She's a doctor, remember. Something tells me she can tell by the way you're walking that—"

"Her ankle was never sprained." The words sounded hollow in Laurel's ears. As hollow as she felt inside. She swung around and gave Noah a look that wasn't as astonished as it was dazed. "You made it up. You made up the whole thing. Her ankle was never sprained and you—"

"We had to do something, dear." Maisie patted her arm, and Laurel jumped as if she'd been hit by lightning. She'd been so focused on Noah, she'd nearly forgotten her grandmother was there. "Yes…well…" Sensing her reaction even if she didn't understand it, Maisie gave her a quick smile. "I'll leave you two alone," she said, and she hightailed it across the porch as quickly as she could to help Meg with the coffee.

Which was probably a good thing. Something told

Laurel her grandmother shouldn't be part of the ugly scene she felt brewing.

She crossed her arms over her chest. "You want to tell me what's going on?"

"Going on?" Noah laughed. Bad move. He knew it as soon as he did it. He tried to hide his laugh behind a cough and only ended up sounding, and looking, more guilty than ever. He glanced at the crowds of people and the senior citizens they'd treated the night before who were filing out of the Hideaway and heading toward the bus that had been brought to take them to the ferry and home.

"Let's go someplace a little more private, huh?"

It was a good idea. The hand Noah put on Laurel's arm was not.

She jerked out of his grasp and headed inside.

Not exactly private there, either. There were people all over the lobby, people gathering the suitcases that had been brought to them from the demolished bus, people helping each other toward the door and munching Meg's special cookies, the ones Marty and Darlene Sylvester were handing around on huge platters. There were people saying their goodbyes to their fellow passengers, exchanging phone numbers and e-mail addresses and advice about the best way to treat their cuts and sprains and the arthritis that had flared thanks to the accident.

Laurel shook her head, deciding immediately that though it was definitely the time, this wasn't the place. Without a word, she grabbed Noah's hand and yanked him into the Love Shack.

With the door closed, it was blessedly quiet inside the gift shop. Laurel moved behind the counter, putting something solid—something real—between herself and the feeling of betrayal Noah had awakened.

"All right," she said. "Explain."

"Explain?" Noah shrugged. Like it was no big deal. Which it was. Even if he didn't want to admit it. "There's nothing to explain."

"Except that I've been watching you play Marcus Welby to that sweet, hurting old lady. You remember, the one who was never hurt in the first place."

"Laurel…" He made to take her hand, but Laurel slid it out of the way and tucked it behind her back. "Look…" Noah sighed and looked at the ceiling, obviously searching for the right words to explain everything that had happened. As if there were any.

"After the dinner dance…after the fight we had about the Golden Apple and how ridiculous it was that you ended up with it after all these years—"

"Ridiculous? Is it?"

Too late, Noah realized his mistake. He scrambled to save himself. "Okay, not ridiculous. Bad choice of words. After the fight we had about how you couldn't let go of the past—"

"Is that what we were fighting about?" Laurel almost laughed. She would have if her insides didn't suddenly feel as if they'd been twisted into a million tiny knots. "Funny, the way I remember it, we were fighting about something completely different. Let's see…" She tapped one finger against her chin, thinking. "Yeah, that's it. We were fighting because you admitted that all you ever wanted was that stupid award. Status. Accolades. Honors. The only part of being a doctor you ever really cared about was the part that would put your picture on the cover of the medical journals."

"Not true, and you know it." Noah pulled back his

shoulders. "And besides, what difference does it make what we were fighting about, anyway? We were fighting, and I was going to leave and…" He pulled in a breath and let it out again in a huff. "I didn't want to leave. That's why Maisie and I came up with the sprained ankle idea. I needed a reason to stay."

Laurel's temper went from white-hot to ice-cold in record time. So did her insides. She wrapped her arms around herself, trying to hold back the chill. It didn't help.

"Reason to stay?" She tried to swallow around the ball of emotion that blocked her throat and found she couldn't. "Wasn't I reason enough?"

"Of course you were." He gave her a look that should have melted the ice. It was the same look he gave her when they were making love. The same one he gave her as they worked side by side in the clinic. The one that told her he thought the world of her.

But maybe the world wasn't enough.

The thought settled inside her, making her ache. Laurel reached under the counter and pulled out a brown paper shopping bag. "Here." She handed him the bag and prayed he'd take it and leave. Before he could see there were tears on her cheeks. "It's the Golden Apple," she said when he didn't look in the bag. "I brought it over here to give it to you. I guess it's all you've ever wanted."

He took the bag and shifted it from hand to hand. "You're wrong, Laurel."

"Am I? Then I guess I've been wrong about a lot of things. Why didn't you just tell me the truth?" She shook her head, trying to put some order to the emotions that racketed through her with each painful heartbeat. "Why did you have to lie?"

"Lie?" Noah's expression was grim. "I guess I had to lie because I don't trust my heart."

Laurel walked around the counter and went to stand in front of him. It was the toughest thing she'd ever done. The toughest words she'd ever had to speak. She made herself say them. Not because of what had happened four years earlier, but because of what had happened in the last few days. What they did. What they almost had.

"I'm sorry, Noah," she said, and she headed for the door. "If you can't trust your heart, I can't, either."

THE WIND blowing off the lake was calmer than it had been the night before. Not that it made any difference. Noah felt as if it was slicing him in half, all the way through to what was left of his heart.

He watched the whitecaps the wind kicked up on the lake, waiting along with the passengers from the ill-fated bus trip for the next ferry to the mainland.

"About time, too," he grumbled to himself. He'd been on the verge of taking the ferry and heading back to putting his life in order more times than he cared to admit. On the verge. And never did it.

Never, until now.

He leaned against the wooden railing that separated passengers from the cars that were loaded onto the ferry first. At this time of year and in the middle of the week, there usually weren't many of them. But with the extra traffic brought onto the island by the accident, things were plenty hectic. Good thing, too. Something told Noah too much quiet wouldn't be good for him. Not now. Not for a long time.

When another group of senior citizens headed under the wooden roof of the waiting area, Noah scooted into the corner. The last thing he felt like doing was making small talk.

"Hey, Doc!"

At the sound of a man's voice, Noah's spirits plummeted. Hard to get lower than low. Hard, but apparently not impossible.

He turned and found himself looking at a right cheek he recognized. It was one he'd bandaged the night before.

"Good to see you, Doc!" Before Noah could acknowledge the man he remembered as Chester Bligh, Chester was pumping his hand. "Glad to have a chance to thank you. Personally, I mean. You did a hell of a job last night."

"All in a day's work." Noah cringed. He wasn't usually given to clichés. Then again, he wasn't usually dealing with a heart that had been kicked out of him, either. He figured he had a good excuse. "Remember to see your family doctor once you get home," he told Mr. Bligh. "You'll want to have him take a look at that cut, make sure everything's healing just right."

"Oh, this?" Chester waved away Noah's concern. "This is nothing more than a scratch. Hey, you're talking to a guy who was on Iwo Jima." He pulled back his shoulders, every inch a Marine. "You think this little thing is going to stop me?"

Noah didn't, but there didn't seem to be any point in mentioning it.

Together, they watched the ferry pull into the dock. Slowly, vehicles were loaded on, and after a few minutes, the crowd surged forward.

"No, what I want to talk to you about is the missus." Chester glanced over his shoulder to where a frail-looking lady with dark eyes and black hair streaked with

silver sat on a bench. Noah recognized her as the diabetic bus passenger whose blood sugars had skyrock-
eted after the accident.

Chester's expression softened, and he wasn't an old
soldier any longer, just a husband who adored his wife.
"You did a good job with her, Doc. A real good job.
You and that lady doctor you were working with, you
two must really love your work. I've never seen two
people work so well together. Like you were reading
each other's minds."

"Yeah." Noah tried for a smile. From the confused
look on Chester's face, it was apparent it didn't work.
"She's a good doctor."

"And you're a good doctor." Chester thumped him
on the shoulder. He went over and helped his wife out
of her seat, and Noah watched them head onto the ferry.

He waited until all the passengers had gotten on before he lifted his suitcase in one hand and the brown
bag that contained the Golden Apple in the other. He
didn't bother to look back.

Once he was on the ferry, he didn't walk upstairs to
the long benches where passengers could sit on the
eighteen-minute trip to the mainland. He stayed on the
deck where the vehicles were parked and stared at the
water.

"You like what you do?"

It was Chester again. Looked like the guy couldn't
take a hint.

Noah turned to him and found the old man and his
wife smiling at him. "What I do—"

The words stuck in Noah's throat. What he did was
travel around the country living on an obscene expense
account and acting like the god of the medical world.
What he did was hold court, issue orders, impart knowl-

edge with the kind of arrogance that didn't teach medical students anything but that doctors were better than everyone else.

What he'd found out the night before was that what he really enjoyed was working side by side with Laurel, administering the kind of hands-on medical care that healed bodies and touched spirits. The kind of medicine he'd forgotten existed.

The realization came like a thunderclap and left Noah shaken. A fact that didn't escape Chester's notice.

While Chester clapped a hand on Noah's shoulder, Mrs. Bligh gave him a searching look. "You all right, Doctor?" she asked.

Noah wasn't sure. Maybe he was all right. Maybe he wasn't. Maybe he'd never know until he did what his heart was telling him to do.

"I'm…" He looked to where the workers were drawing up the ramp between the boat and the island. "I don't know," he said at the same time he ran toward the ramp. "Tell them…" He hopped onto the island and waved at the Blighs. "Tell them to hold on to my suitcases on the other side. I'll come and get them. One of these days."

The brown bag with the Golden Apple inside it clutched in one hand, Noah took off from the ferry dock.

He might not know if he was okay. He might not know if he was rational. But he knew where he was headed.

And he knew exactly what he had to do.

Chapter Seventeen

Laurel was just about to cast off when she heard footsteps pounding along the dock. She didn't look up. Why bother? Chances were, whoever it was, the person was running to somewhere else. To someone else. Chances were, the light steps and the smooth, even running stride had nothing whatsoever to do with her.

Besides, even if they did, she was pretty sure she didn't much care. If someone was looking for her, she'd bet a dime to a doughnut they wanted something. And after eighteen hours of giving her medical skills and her knowledge to her patients, and her body, heart and soul to Noah, she had nothing left.

"Laurel!"

She didn't look up when she heard her name called. It was just a trick of her imagination and the wind that, though not nearly as fierce as it had been the night before, was still potent enough to kick up a three-foot chop on the lake and send the *Jade Moon* rocking from side to side.

"Laurel!" Noah screeched to a halt on the dock beside her boat.

Pretty hard to ignore a man who was breathing as

hard as if he'd run the entire length of the island. And clutching a brown paper shopping bag.

Pretty hard to ignore the stumbling rhythm of her heart, either.

Laurel grabbed one of the shrouds and looked at Noah over the strip of water between the dock and the sailboat. "What..." Her voice wasn't nearly as confident. It faltered over the words. "I thought...I thought you were on the ferry."

"I was on the ferry." Noah hauled in breath after breath. "But I had to tell you...I had to let you know that I finally figured it out. I..." He set down the bag and put his hands on his knees, drawing in a few more ragged breaths. When he stood, he grabbed on to the same shroud Laurel was holding. His hand only inches from hers, he looked into her eyes.

"It took the accident," he said. "It took the accident and working with you to make me realize that all the knowledge and power in the world doesn't do a doctor any good, not if he isn't really practicing medicine."

A tiny thread of warmth unwound inside Laurel. She knew better. If nothing else, the past should have taught her that. It should have taught her to beat down the hope. To shut it out. To block it from her head and her heart.

Call her a slow learner. She told the past to shut up and looked into the promise of the future that shone in Noah's eyes.

"It took you to show me." He reached across the space that separated them and ran a finger along her cheek. "It took you to teach me," he said. "His heart is the only part of him a doctor can trust. The only part of him any man can trust."

When Noah leaned closer, Laurel did, too, and when

he kissed her, she let the warmth of his lips seep through her, melting the cold and filling the places that had felt so empty such a short time before.

"I love you, Laurel." Noah's voice was a whisper against her lips. "My heart tells me that. And my head tells me that. And, hey…" He smiled. "My body knows it, too."

"Which means…"

"Which means it's time for that happily-ever-after. Marry me?"

"We tried that before."

"That was an engagement. This is marriage. The real thing. Soon. Today. Right after we…" He looked at the paper bag next to him on the dock, and he didn't need to explain what he had in mind.

When he tossed her the bag, Laurel caught it and stepped back to allow Noah to hop on board.

THEY WAITED until they were out far enough that they couldn't see the island.

"New horizons," was the way Noah explained it. "Not my life or yours. Ours now."

At just the right moment, they walked to the bow, the paper bag held between them.

"You're not going to fall in again, are you?" Laurel asked.

"Only in love. Now and forever." He kissed her at the same time he opened the bag.

They reached inside, and together they lifted the Golden Apple award into the afternoon sunlight.

"Doesn't look like much now, does it?" Laurel shook her head. "All these years, I've been jealous of you about this thing? It looks like the kind of hokey decoration Maisie would love to add to the Hideaway."

"Careful! This is a big-time award." Noah grinned at her over the sparkling apple. "It's a big-time nothing. It doesn't mean a thing. None of it does. Not if we don't have each other." He lifted one eyebrow. "Ready?" he asked.

"Ready," Laurel said.

And together, they heaved the Golden Apple award overboard.

BY THE TIME all the excitement died down that night, Maisie should have been exhausted. She wasn't. The bubble bath and catnap she took before their guests arrived had energized her. The extra glass of sherry she'd had after they were gone helped, too.

Of course, it didn't hurt to know things had worked out exactly as she'd planned.

Humming softly, she crossed the lobby and closed the door of the Love Shack. Funny, she hadn't realized anyone had been in the gift shop that evening. Unless...

Maisie glanced up the stairs toward Almost Paradise and grinned.

"Of course." She purred the words. She was tempted to peek into the Love Shack and see what was missing but decided against it. The least she could do was give the newlyweds a little privacy along with the use of Almost Paradise for their wedding night.

Which didn't mean she couldn't go upstairs. Just to make sure everything was all right.

At the top of the stairs, Maisie paused and bent her head, listening. She heard the rumble of Noah's voice, and though she couldn't hear what he said, she could imagine it well enough. She'd never seen a man look happier than he had when the mayor said those magic words, "I pronounce you husband and wife."

She'd never seen a bride look as pretty as Laurel had, either, and when Maisie heard her giggle in answer to whatever it was Noah suggested, Maisie decided her work was done. Content, she turned to head to her room.

It wasn't until she did that she noticed something was different. She stepped back and looked at the carved wooden sign hanging next to the door. The snake looked the same as ever, smug and satisfied. But a yellow and red Italian silk tie had been added to the sign.

Maisie's contented smile turned into a full-fledged grin.

Looked like the new Mr. and Mrs. Noah Cunningham had made their first decision together as husband and wife. And something told her the decision was unanimous.

The tie wound in and out of the wooden branches, over the snake and under the apple. It completely covered the word *Almost*.